## SHANE WAS FROZEN THERE IN THE DOORWAY OF THE SHELTER. THE ROAR OF THE TORNADO DROWNED OUT EVERYTHING ELSE.

If he closed the door now, he might live, but he would be leaving Iris to die.

Ames and Iris slid a few inches away from the shelter, the power of the tornado dragging them. Something snapped in Shane's head then, and all his hesitation disappeared. Knowing that at any second he could be hauled off his feet, he dove across the floor at Tarker Ames. He reached up and grabbed the man's assault rifle and turned it around so that its muzzle was only inches from Ames's side.

Shane felt the wind tug at him inexorably, and all three of them slid several inches along the floor.

The tornado ripped up the corridor twenty feet from where they lay.

He pulled the trigger.

# FORCE
## MAJEURE

also by Christopher Golden:

Body of Evidence thrillers:
*Body Bags*
*Thief of Hearts*
*Soul Survivor*
*Meets the Eye*
*Head Games*
*Skin Deep*

with Rick Hautala:
*Burning Bones*
*Brain Trust*

Prowlers series:
*Prowlers*
*Laws of Nature*
*Predator and Prey*
*Wild Things*

# FORCE MAJEURE

## CHRISTOPHER GOLDEN

### AND

## THOMAS E. SNIEGOSKI

**SIMON PULSE**
New York  London  Toronto  Sydney  Singapore

First Simon Pulse edition August 2002
Text copyright © 2002 by Christopher Golden and Thomas E. Sniegoski
Chapter heads taken from *The Inventions, Researches and Writings of Nikola Tesla* (Barnes & Noble Books)

SIMON PULSE
An imprint of Simon & Schuster
Children's Publishing Division
1230 Avenue of the Americas
New York, NY 10020

The text of this book was set in Trump Mediaeval.
Printed in the United States of America

2  4  6  8  10  9  7  5  3  1

Library of Congress Control Number 2002103258
ISBN 0-7434-2670-3

For Dave Kraus,
a truly unstoppable force of nature

# ACKNOWLEDGEMENTS

The authors would like to thank the termineditors—Lisa Clancy, Micol Ostow, and Liz Shiflett (bon voyage, Liz!)—for all their tireless work and support.
And . . .

As always, this is for LeeAnne and Mulder, without them my life would be pretty boring, and also for Chris Golden who makes me look good.

Special thanks are also due to:

Mom and Dad, Mom and Dad Fogg, Tim Cole and the crew, David Carroll, Jon and Flo (sorry about the wood chipper), Bob and Pat, Eric Powell, Don Kramer, Greg Skopis, Meloney Crawford Chadwick, Ken Curtis, and Dan Ouellette, the computer man supreme. Thank you one and all.

—T. E. S.

My love and gratitude to Connie and our boys, Nicholas and Daniel, and eternal thanks to Tom for everything. He bore the brunt of the storm. (Makes a pretty good umbrella, that Sniegoski.)

A debt is also owed to Peter Donaldson, Supergirl Allie Costa, John G. (Mr. PhD) for the science, and of course to the late Nikola Tesla (super-genius).

Finally, my thanks go out to Mom and Peter, my brother and sister and their families, the Russo clan, and to the usual suspects: Jose, Bob, Stefan, Rick, and Meg.

—C. G.

# FORCE
# MAJEURE

# PROLOGUE

Mason Beal shuddered as he stared out through the rented room's single window. The frost coating the inside of the glass was just another reminder of how cold and uncomfortable the hotel room actually was.

With another shudder he rubbed his hands together, then cupped them and brought them to his mouth, blowing hot air into them for warmth. He looked away from the filthy window and gazed about the room that had been provided by his mysterious benefactors. There was a bed in the corner covered by a faded, lime-green spread. On one side of it were a nightstand and lamp, on the other, a small dresser. A dingy kitchenette completed the package. *All the comforts of home*, he mused.

A car horn blared outside on St. Mark's Place. Nerves jangling, Mason glanced at his watch for what seemed like the hundredth time since he had arrived in Manhattan's East Village. And why shouldn't they be? He was here for a meeting that would change his life forever.

Convinced that time was somehow slowed

by the cold inside, he trudged despondently to the circular metal table in the kitchenette and sat down to await the arrival of his appointment. His heart beat too fast, but he knew that it would not slow until he had unburdened himself of the disk in the pocket of his heavy winter jacket.

A disk he had stolen from his employers at the Cassandra Group.

With a hitching sigh, Mason pushed his black-framed glasses further up the bridge of his nose, then reached nervously shaking fingers into the front pocket of his flannel shirt to retrieve his half-empty box of Marlboro Lights cigarettes and a book of matches.

Mason had been approached by an agency known as the Cassandra Group. They told him they were doing intensive study for the Pentagon on battlefield psychology. As one of the preeminent researchers in the field of brain chemistry, he had believed they wanted to find out if there was an effective treatment for post-traumatic stress disorder, a way to relieve the guilt and horror that often lingered in the minds of soldiers, sometimes causing them to be completely debilitated by their experiences.

A valiant pursuit.

They had made him an offer he'd have been an idiot to turn down and then moved him to the Cassandra Group's central headquarters in Nevada.

*How did things turn from good to bad so*

*quickly!* he wondered now as he tugged the final match from the book and lit the cigarette dangling from his mouth. Mason blew the smoke from his lungs up toward the water-stained ceiling and remembered how perfect everything had been. The group had given him a condo, a company car, amazing benefits, and all he had to do was the job he had wanted to do in the first place.

It had been a sweet gig until his superiors had decided he was enough of a team player to get high security clearance, until he learned what it was he had actually been doing for them all that time. The research he had been doing had not been intended to relieve the guilt and horror of soldiers who had been psychologically scarred by war.

The Cassandra Group had no interest in helping veterans.

Their intent was to chemically relieve soldiers of their guilt and horror—and any other moral baggage that would keep them from being effective killing machines—before they ever reached the battlefield.

When he found that out, Mason had been filled with revulsion, but he had no idea how to react. He was not naive enough to think that he could simply walk away.

And then the E-mails had begun to arrive.

Mason again glanced at his watch, his impatience growing. If he had to wait much longer he was afraid he would lose his nerve.

He took another drag from the cigarette.

*What if you succeed?* That was all the e-mail had said. At first he thought it was some kind of joke, but every night when he checked his computer, the same cryptic message would be waiting. Mason had never replied, nor had he reported it to his superiors. The question haunted him, but he was too frightened to respond, not believing that he could fight the group's plans without it costing him his life.

He stood up suddenly from the table, anxious with the memories that eventually led him to this squalid place. Mason began to pace, the warped wooden floor of the rented room creaking beneath him. He puffed nervously on his cigarette, remembering the day when he had finally replied to that e-mail.

*What if I don't want to succeed?* he had written.

Mason jumped as the single radiator beneath the window popped and hissed. He placed his hand on the gradually warming metal and noticed a disgusting collection of cigarette butts, dirt, and who knew what else on the floor behind it. *Convenient*, Mason thought as he finished up the last of his smoke and made a contribution to the graveyard of filth left by the room's previous inhabitants.

Those responsible for the e-mails had finally revealed their identity. They called themselves the Truth Seekers—silly as *that* sounded—and they believed it was their duty to expose injustices in the world, especially those perpetrated by secret factions of the United States government in the name of justice and national security.

They offered him a deal, a way to wash the blood from his hands. In return for incriminating information about the Cassandra Group, they would help him to escape, give him a new identity and relocate him to someplace where the recriminations of his actions would not affect him. The Truth Seekers did not sugarcoat their concern for his safety. The Cassandra Group and their government connections would no doubt order him killed for what he was about to expose.

Mason reached into his jacket, removed a computer disk from the pocket, and stared at it. This was what they wanted, information about the Cassandra Group, their subsidiaries around the world, and their employees. Deep down he knew what he was doing was wrong. The files he had copied were highly classified—but if this was the cost, his coin to pay the ferryman to take him to freedom, then he would pay it gladly.

He placed the disk inside his shirt pocket—keeping it even closer now—behind the cigarette pack and looked at his watch yet again. The Truth Seekers were now officially late. The last e-mail message he had received before disabling his computer and fleeing Nevada had given him specific instructions on how to travel to New York and the address where he would make the exchange. It had taken him more than four days to reach the city according to their directions, and the fact that the person or persons he was supposed to be meeting were late filled him with unease.

At first he thought the rapid knock was coming from the radiator, but realized it was somebody at the door.

He went to the door and had his hand on the knob when he recalled something the final message from the Truth Seekers specified. As clichéd as it sounded, the person on the other side of the door was supposed to give a password.

"Yes?" Mason asked as he leaned into the door, holding his breath as he waited for the appropriate response.

The silence from the other side seemed to last for hours. Then came a man's voice, speaking the phrase he had been waiting for.

"Shell shock."

Mason finally exhaled and turned the knob. He pulled the door open and looked at those who would be his saviors.

There were two of them, a man and a woman. His eyes fell upon the woman first. She was attractive in a plain kind of way. She stood beside the man, her cheeks a bright pink from the frigid temperatures outside.

There were flecks of melting snow in her stylishly short red hair. She was wearing a waist-length, black-leather jacket and jeans. At first glance the man appeared to be young but as Mason studied his eyes he realized he was probably older than he appeared. The man smiled and Mason shivered. There was something cruel in that smile.

"So, are we going to conduct our business out here in this drafty hallway," the man asked, gazing at his partner and then back to Mason, "or are you going to ask us inside?"

Mason pulled the door wider and made a sweeping motion with his arm for them to enter. "Sorry, I'm a little nervous. I was beginning to worry that you might not be coming." He shut the door behind them.

The woman shook the water droplets from her hair as she undid the belt of her jacket.

"It started to snow. Slowed us down a little, but here we are."

Mason walked away from the door wringing his hands nervously. "I'm . . . I'm not sure how this is supposed to go, but I'm Mason. Mason Beal."

The woman looked at her partner, who had been casually checking out the room.

"We're supposed to keep this as impersonal as possible," the man said as he unzipped his ski jacket, "but I can't see any harm."

He stepped toward Mason, reaching out to shake his hand. This close, he seemed somehow larger than he had been in the hall, more imposing.

"Hello, Mason. My name is Tarker Ames."

Tarker Ames hated Mason Beal the minute he saw him. He loathed his round, pale features, his chubby body, and the beady eyes behind his dark-framed glasses.

Mason held out his hand and Tarker shook it and let it drop. Then his partner stepped forward to shake Beal's hand.

"Iris Green."

While the two of them shook, Tarker turned slightly and pointed to the bed. "Do you mind if I sit?"

Mason retreated to take a seat himself at the kitchen table. "Not at all. Please."

As he sat, Tarker noticed that his partner moved closer to the room's radiator, the heat at her back. She had taken a kind of official stance, legs slightly spread, hands clasped behind her. He guessed she was about to get down to business. He had only been working with her a short time, but he could see that she was the type of girl who didn't like to monkey around. He liked that in a woman.

"So, Mason," she asked, "you were able to acquire the information we requested?"

Mason patted the front pocket of his shirt.

"Yes, I have it right here. Everything you asked for."

Tarker crossed his legs, adjusting the cuff on his corduroy pants. "Were you careful, Mason?" he asked, not looking at the man.

"C-careful?" Mason stammered. "Yes. Yes, I did everything you told me to. The Cassandra Group should have no idea."

Tarker slid off his coat like a snake sloughing off its skin. "I'm not worried about the Cassandra Group, Mason. I'm worried about who they report to."

"You mean the government?" There was definitely a trace of fear in his voice.

Tarker laughed and glanced at his partner. "What do you think, Iris? A little bit of yes and no in that question?"

Iris didn't look at all pleased. She cleared her throat and addressed her answer to Beal. "What Tarker is trying to say is there are numerous agencies that work outside the system for the benefit of the government, and the Cassandra Group is most likely a subsidiary, shall we say, of one of those larger agencies."

Tarker stood and stretched.

The scientist looked as though he were going to burst a blood vessel. "If it's them you can make sure they don't find me—right? That's why I'm giving you this information, so I can start over?"

Iris stepped away from the radiator and moved toward the man. "We'll do everything in our power, Mason." She held out her hand. "Let me have the disk."

He reached into his shirt pocket and produced the disk, but then hesitated. "Before I give it to you, let me ask you something. This information . . . you're not going to use it to hurt anybody, are you?"

Tarker walked toward the man. "Nothing like that. We'll just be using the information to make certain the American people know the truth. Remember, we are the Truth Seekers."

Tarker held out his hand.

"Let's have it, Mason. I'm sure you want to get this show on the road."

Mason nodded and handed him the disk. Tarker passed it on to his partner. "Here you go, Ms. Green," he said with a smile. "Stick that in your handbag, or whatever you ladies are carrying these days."

She snatched the disk from his grasp, her angry gaze boring into his.

"I can think of a more fitting place to stick it," she said as she placed the disk inside a jacket pocket.

Tarker smiled at his new partner, amused by her feistiness.

"So, what now?" Mason asked, fumbling at his shirt pocket. "Where do we go from here?"

Tarker watched the scientist pluck a cigarette from a crumpled pack and place it inside his mouth.

"I'm a nervous wreck here, mind if I smoke?"

The scientist stood up from the chair and began to pat himself down, searching for something on his person.

"I imagine I'll need some new identification or something, right?" The unlit cigarette bobbed in his mouth as he spoke. "I need a light. Do either of you smoke?"

Tarker produced a lighter. "Didn't you get the talk downstairs, Mason? No smoking in the rooms. It's the law."

"I can't help it. I was going to quit when I ran out of matches, but seeing you have a lighter—I'll quit tomorrow." He held out a hand to Tarker and grinned. "Please?"

Tarker held the silver lighter in his hand at face level and smiled back. "Haven't you heard, Mason?" he asked as he tossed the lighter toward the man.

The scientist reached up to catch it.

"Those things'll kill you."

Tarker hit Mason Beal so hard that his head snapped back violently and he went sprawling to the floor, cigarette dropping from his lips. The lighter slid under the table, and Tarker strode calmly over to retrieve it.

The scientist stared up at him in horror, bruise already rising on his cheek, his lip split and swelling. Mason's mouth struggled to work, and his voice came out as a pathetic squeak. "You aren't from the Truth Seekers at all. You're—"

Tarker kicked him in the side, and the man curled into a ball. He launched another kick at the whimpering scientist's head.

Iris grabbed him by the shoulder, spun him around.

"Ames," she hissed, eyes narrowed with righteous anger. "That's enough. You're way out of line."

His nostrils flared and he fumed, glaring at her. Then Tarker forced the easy grin back onto his face. "Hey, Iris. We're a team, right? Relax."

He raised his hands as if to surrender and backed away from the scientist, who now lay unconscious and bleeding on the floor.

"What the hell is wrong with you?" Iris demanded as she knelt beside Beal on the floor. She felt the man's fleshy neck for a pulse. "You could have killed him."

Tarker produced a folded-up Kleenex and wet it with some saliva. He rubbed the wet tissue where Mason Beal's blood had stained his hand.

"Yes," he replied matter-of-factly. "Yes, I could have."

# CHAPTER ONE

*"The power of the wind has been over-
looked.
Some day it will be forcibly brought to the
position it deserves."*
—Nikola Tesla

Shane Monroe stared in frustration at the
wrench in his hand and muttered something
vaguely threatening at the length of steel, as
though the tool were somehow at fault. He
had already scraped his knuckles up once
when the wrench slipped. Now he put the tool
back to work attempting to tighten the last
stubborn bolt that attached the odd-looking
device to the four-legged platform bolted to
the floor of the circular room. This time he
leaned into it, putting his weight onto the
wrench, and at last the bolt turned.

"Yes!" Shane whispered in triumph.

It was not the sort of precision work he
was used to doing in this laboratory, but
despite his mutterings it felt refreshing.
Complex mathematical theories, fragile

meteorological equipment, and super-magnets were his life these days. Skinning his knuckles while working a wrench was actually a break.

Careful not to disrupt any of the sensitive thermal monitors located beneath the flooring, Shane stepped back and surveyed what he had created. The apparatus was constructed of steel and copper for conductivity. A long rod—well over a foot in length and encircled by thick silver coil with a sphere at its end— protruded from the center of the mechanism. Above it the specially constructed room rose in a long cylindrical shaft that extended farther than his eyes could see, up through the center of the Foundation building and all the way to the roof. A series of large vents had been installed at intervals all around the steel-walled room, along with a powerful system of hidden fans placed at angles in order to manipulate air currents.

*Everything looks in order*, Shane thought as he returned his attention to the machine bolted to the platform in the center of the room. *Now just don't make an ass of me and we'll be in business.*

His eyes burned with exhaustion and he rubbed at them, then gazed at his watch and sighed. It was after eleven P.M. He had been working on the installation of the Tesla super coil for well over four hours. Back on campus his two best friends, Geoff and Spud, would have given up waiting for him by now and long since gotten on with their mini film festival of the evening. But he was close now. He could feel it. Everything else, even his friends, had to take a backseat right now to this project.

"So much for *True Romance* and a couple of beers," he muttered to himself as he put his tools away and turned to the glass window that looked into the environmental chamber's control booth.

Carl Bennett stood by, watching. Bennett was his adviser on campus and his supervisor here at the Foundation, but more importantly than that he was an old friend of the family, an associate of Shane's late father. With his thinning hair and thick glasses, Dr. Bennett looked every inch the kindly uncle he had become to Shane since he had arrived at Hazeltine University.

Dr. Bennett smiled and motioned for Shane to come back into the control center. The airlock door was slightly ajar, and Shane pulled it closed behind him as he stepped out of the chamber, shutting and sealing the door with a twist of its steel handle.

"Hey, Dr. Bennett." Shane placed his toolkit on the shelf in a plastic cabinet and turned to face his supervisor. "I thought you would've been outta here hours ago." He self-consciously shoved his hands into the pockets of his jeans and looked at the floor.

Bennett smiled at him good-naturedly. "Trying to get rid of me so you can test out your new theory, Monroe? Is that it? Get the old man out of your hair so you can work in peace? I think I see what you're up to. Where's June?"

"Left a couple of hours ago. She told me to lock up when I was through." Shane shrugged lightly, as if the absence of June Mendelsohn, his project coordinator, was no big deal.

"Really?" Dr. Bennett asked, one eyebrow arched. "And did she realize at the time that you were going to continue working, or did she think you were going home?"

Shane tried to keep the sly grin from his lips and failed. "Couldn't really say."

Dr. Bennett sighed. "Shane, come on. You've got privileges here that some of your ambitious fellow students would kill for. We take only the best and brightest, sure, but the Foundation provides opportunities that can make a career. Other than typical laboratory controls, there aren't very many things we ask in return. But one of them is—"

"I know," Shane interrupted. "I'm not supposed to run experiments without the project coordinator. But Dr. Bennett, June's almost never around when I'm here. She has five other student projects to oversee. If I have to wait for her every time I want to do a test run, I'll never solve this thing."

The older man frowned as he studied Shane. After a moment's hesitation he stepped closer to the glass window and peered into the environmental control chamber.

"Would you look at that contraption," Dr. Bennett said. "Didn't I see that in a Frankenstein movie?" He turned away from the window and grinned at him. "It sure as hell looks impressive, but to tell you the truth, Shane, I cannot imagine it will work."

Shane sat down at a computer terminal and clicked to open a file. "If you would just look at my notes, I think you'll see why—"

Bennett held up his hand. "Shane, you're brilliant. No argument from me. I respect that intelligence immensely. I see more of your father in you every day. But your theories are just a little too wild for me. And I suspect that's true of June as well. On the other hand, if she has doubts about your research, that does not relieve her of the responsibility to oversee it. I'll have a talk with her tomorrow." He frowned. "No, Monday. It's the weekend, isn't it? Don't you have something else to do on a Friday night?"

Shane frowned. The truth was, he did have something else to do. But if he was really as close as he felt he was, there was nowhere he would rather be right now.

Bennett motioned with his hand to the chamber beyond the window. "I'm not giving excuses for June's neglect, Shane. But the Foundation built this environmental control chamber three years ago, long before you came along. Even before that, we'd been trying to duplicate the various environmental and atmospheric conditions needed to create severe weather. And we weren't the only ones."

It was all Shane could do not to roll his eyes. Nothing Bennett was telling him was news. He knew the whys and wherefores. Scientists had been trying for ages to replicate weather patterns in a closed environment in order to understand the mechanics of meteorology. If they could understand the weather, then they might learn to undermine severe weather conditions created by nature. Blah blah blah. This was the project that had been keeping Shane up at night. It was condescending for Bennett to lecture him about it now. Dr. Bennett was a good man, but he could be a bit of a windbag.

"We've made a lot of progress, Shane. We understand a lot more than we used to, and we're educating ourselves. But we made that progress using solid scientific theory and methods. Not archaic pipe dreams."

Reluctantly, Shane closed the file and turned away from the computer, spinning halfway around in his chair. "All right. Tesla was a nut. Fine. Probably he was. But that's what people said about Copernicus and da Vinci and who knows how many others. Just because he was eccentric doesn't mean that his theories were unsound. If you'd study them instead of just brushing them off—"

He cut himself off. Bennett had one eyebrow raised again and he stared at Shane as though he could not decide whether to be offended or to pat him on the head like a puppy. Either way, Shane wanted to hit him. He owed Carl Bennett a great deal—he would not have been on this project without him—but with as little sleep as he'd had, and as excited as he was, he didn't need his adviser raining on his parade at the moment.

"Look, Dr. Bennett, you're right, okay? The Foundation has made progress. But that progress has been limited. If you can't create a tornado artificially, you'll never be able to defuse one. It's a force of nature. Learning about it isn't enough. You brought me in here and gave me this impossible task as busy work, to show me what it was all about. Give it to the new kid, it'll make his head explode. But you know what? I looked at it as a challenge. I looked at it the same way I looked at the television set I took apart when I was five. I wasn't sure what all the pieces were for, but I was going to learn."

Bennett chuckled. "Your mother still teases you about that."

Shane wouldn't be put off. Not now, after all this time. He had spent months going through the notes on all the experiments the Foundation had done, dissecting every step. He had been driven to discover why their efforts had not borne fruit and what could have been done differently to change the results.

"It's been a long haul, Dr. Bennett, filled with lots of disappointments, but this time, this time I think I'm on to something."

Bennett sighed and shook his head. "But, Shane . . . Tesla?" After a moment, the man shrugged. "All right, tell me. What did you learn from him that we didn't already know?"

For a moment, Shane was at a loss for words. He had not expected Dr. Bennett to listen, even skeptically. After a moment he smiled and walked toward the observation area, where he could see inside the testing chamber. He turned to face Dr. Bennett again.

"I did a paper on Tesla in high school," Shane explained. "I bought the usual spin on him back then. Crackpot genius. But some of that research stuck with me, obviously, 'cause when I started on this project I remembered he had done research into atmospheric instability caused by electrical discharge. When I went back and looked at the publicly available biographies and things, the information was really scarce, so I used the password you gave me to access the Foundation's database. For a group that thinks Tesla was nothing but a crank, you'd be surprised how many files on his work the Foundation has. There are some amazing papers of his in there—stuff I hadn't seen anywhere else."

Bennett frowned slightly, but nodded.

"We have our sources. If it's of any interest to our work here, we probably have a copy. Not certain you should be poking around in there without authorization, though."

Something in his tone made Shane hesitate, but now that Bennett had given him an opening, he was not going to be thrown off-track.

"Near the end of his life, when people really started to think he was out of his mind, Tesla was working on what he called *directed lightning*. It was World War Two, and Tesla wanted to create a more sophisticated version of his Tesla coil. He thought he could channel energy so efficiently, it could be used to shoot down Luftwaffe bombers. In some ways it was a precursor to the orbital missile defense system that's so controversial now. Those papers of Tesla's gave me the seeds of what I was looking for."

Dr. Bennett sighed openly and leaned back against a lab table. He crossed his arms. "I'm well aware of Tesla's so-called death ray theories, Shane. What could it possibly have to do with us?"

Shane held up a finger, hoping to ward off the man's impatience. "Okay, this is where it gets interesting. Bear with me. What are we missing from our efforts here? I mean, we can generate the ground-level moisture and heat necessary for a tornado to form. We can replicate the kind of cold front you'd get in nature and collide it with that warm air. We can easily funnel high velocity winds into the mix at the height necessary, right at the top of the chamber. We can artificially induce a wind shear. You yourself figured out the formula for updraft versus vertical downdraft to imitate some of the climate conditions of a thunderstorm. So what are we missing?"

Bennett walked over to the environmental control chamber and stared inside at the mechanism Shane had constructed. All of the impatience had gone from his demeanor, replaced instead by the scientific curiosity Shane had always admired in him.

"What are we missing?" Dr. Bennett echoed. A tiny smile played at the edges of his lips. "Spin. We can electrify the chamber, charge the air inside, but unless we can find a way for the discharges to be generated from within the storm itself, we'll never be able to really duplicate the conditions necessary."

Shane slid his hands into his pockets and leaned against the glass. "What if I told you I can do that?"

Bennett raised one eyebrow and gave him a dubious sidelong glance. "Explain."

"Tesla's papers were supposed to have been brought back to his homeland after his death. Either not all of them were returned, or some were copied, but in the research I did in the Foundation database, I found his plans for what he called a *super* coil. The Tesla super coil produces significant electric discharges and projects them into the atmosphere. I think they'll heat the surrounding air *and* create a more sustained vertical updraft."

An annoyed look crossed Bennett's face. "What do you mean, produces? This thing is just a theory. It doesn't exist."

Shane grinned. "Well, it didn't. Until I built it." He hooked a thumb over his shoulder and gestured at the mechanism inside the chamber. "That 'contraption,' as you called it? That's a Tesla super coil. The vertical updraft will carry a continuous stream of electrical discharges into the controlled atmosphere."

Behind them, a door suddenly opened and they turned to see a janitor pushing a bucket into the room.

"Not now!" Bennett snapped at him. "Come back later."

Grumbling, the man backed out of the room as Bennett stared back into the chamber, his hands splayed on the glass.

Then he turned to Shane again. "All right. Assuming this super coil works, you'd still have to figure the correct voltage—"

"Done."

"Even so, Shane, how can you be so certain the supercharged air will cling together enough to rotate, rather than merely clash? You've been studying chaos theory enough to know the odds."

"Yes, I know the odds!" Shane said, throwing up his hands. He strode across the lab and gestured to his computer. "I've been running numbers on this thing for months. The first day I came to work with you, you stressed those odds to me."

He turned to face his adviser again, this brilliant and respected man who was also one of his father's closest friends, and he wondered who he was really trying to impress: Carl Bennett or Don Monroe.

Shane paused, but this time Bennett did not interrupt, did not wave his theories away. Instead, the man simply waited for him to continue. Shane nodded.

"A tornado is an attractor over a region of phase space. The fundamental tenet of our research is that as long as the characteristic conditions for a tornado are created, even if imperfectly, there is a noninfinitesimal chance of having a tornado form, having it collapse out of the atmospheric brew we create.

"I've figured out how to provide the electrical charges we need, *where* we need them. But the Tesla super coil does more than that. It also produces an extremely powerful magnetic field within its circuitry that causes a secondary effect—the rotation of ionized gases." Shane started to make a counterclockwise spinning motion with his finger. "If things are correctly designed, with a vertical magnetic field angled properly—"

"You could use the coil's magnetic field to guide and abet atmospheric rotation." Bennett stared at him, understanding lighting up his eyes.

"And you'd have your spin," Shane told him.

Bennett glanced into the chamber again, then walked to Shane's desk and sat down in front of the computer. He cleared the screen saver and began to scan the file Shane had been working on, squinting as he studied the notes.

"You really think it could work?"

Shane nodded once. "Took me a lot of sleepless nights, but I've done the math. No guarantees, but yeah. I really think it could."

Bennett ran his hand across his chin as he studied the complex notes written by his student. He looked up at the young man with serious eyes. "Then what are we waiting for?"

Shane smiled. "Well. June isn't here. So I guess we'll have to wait until Monday. If she can make the time for—"

"You're a funny kid, you know that?" Dr. Bennett teased. "Pipe down and get to work."

With a laugh, Shane dragged a chair over to the sprawling control panel that operated conditions within the environmental control chamber. His fingers went to a keyboard and began to enter in the codes that would establish the environment he needed to produce

the desired effects. Most were prepro-
grammed, but the voltage and angles used on
the super coil were things he had just devised,
and so he entered those from memory.

Bennett hovered over his shoulder, watching. There was a sudden rush of air and a
shudder passed through the room as the
chamber beyond the glass sealed and became
a closed environment.

"Everything looks good so far," Bennett
said, his eyes traveling over the various
instruments and gauges on the control panel
and back to the computer screen.

Shane's fingers again moved over the keyboard and a new screen appeared. On this one
was a temperature gauge that showed a red
indicator slowly rising. "Floor thermals are
rising nicely," he said, just as much to himself
as to Dr. Bennett. "Some nice, moist ground-
level air coming up."

Bennett had signed onto another of the
computers next to Shane. "What do you
think? Time for the fans?"

Shane continued to stare at his screen
watching the temperature gauge continue to
rise. "Give it a little longer to saturate the air.
We have some nice clouds forming."

"It's a bit like leading an orchestra, isn't
it?" Bennett observed.

They waited.

"Okay, hit the fans now," Shane said, his
eyes never leaving the computer screen.

A low, rumbling vibration filled the room as a series of high-powered fans kicked in to produce a southeasterly wind just above the surface of the heated floor. The thick glass partition was dappled with droplets of moisture.

"Looking good so far, Shane. When do we activate the wild card?"

There was a steady rumble of gale force winds from within the environmental chamber. Shane bit at his lower lip as his mind again reviewed the process for which his entire theory was based. *If the super coil does what it's supposed to do . . .*

"Shane?" Dr. Bennett asked. "What do you think?"

He glanced at his adviser and then back to his computer screen. With the mouse, he clicked to open the operating window for the Tesla device. For just a brief moment, Shane hesitated. He'd given Bennett the hard sell. If this didn't work, his adviser might force him to abandon this line of research.

Everything up until this point they had done before, but this was as far as they'd gotten. Shane clicked on the command to activate the super coil.

"Show time."

Both he and Bennett stood and peered through the rain-dappled window. Rainfall from high above cascaded down onto the steel and copper construct that housed the super coil as it suddenly came to life. Powerful bolts of dancing electrical energy radiated from the sphere atop the rod that protruded upward from the center of the machine. The flashes were so bright that both he and Bennett shielded their eyes. The two said nothing as a low, vibrating hum filled the air.

Shane could feel Bennett's eyes suddenly upon him. "We've got our charge, but where's the spin?"

He squinted as the flashes of lightning created by the device continued to shoot up into the stormy atmosphere within the chamber. The roar of the high winds was loud, but the lightning sent the staccato sound of thunder booming through the lab. Something new was happening within the environmental chamber. Shane stood closer to the glass. The water droplets had begun to move in a horizontal fashion, streaming across the glass.

Bennett saw this as well and went to another gauge on the control panel. "Mother of God, we have cyclonic winds of one hundred and seventy miles and climbing. We don't need the fans anymore." He went to his computer and typed in a command. The fans were turned off. Bennett returned to the gauge. "I don't want to jinx this but I think . . ."

Shane was still standing, his eyes darting from his computer screen to the water-soaked window. Visibility was now zero. He could barely make out the lightning flashes from the coil.

"Don't say it," he said. "It could still all fall apart, but what I'm hoping is that the electromagnetic field produced by the coil provides the storm with enough cohesion to—"

A roar like some great, bellowing beast suddenly filled the room. Shane looked about, startled by noise.

"We have winds of over two fifty now," Bennett said above the roar.

The sound was coming from the environmental chamber. Shane had read about the sound but never imagined that he would ever be lucky enough to hear it.

It was the angry voice of a force of nature, a tornado.

Shane looked over at Bennett, a grin practically splitting his face in two. The physicist did not look up from the gauge.

"Three hundred miles an hour, Shane. Can I say something now?"

There was an intensity in the man's voice that he had never heard before. It was an odd mixture of excitement and something else. *Perhaps fear*, Shane thought as he gazed back to the sight beyond the glass.

Shane laughed. "Go right ahead, you can't jinx it now."

"You did it, Monroe!" Dr. Bennett bellowed. "I can hardly believe it, but you did it!"

The sound that followed was louder than before, like a hundred freight trains suddenly blaring their horns at once. And the room shuddered. Alarms started to sound, and Shane immediately began to check on the conditions within the chamber.

"The wind is too strong," he said to Bennett, who watched from over his shoulder. "It's tearing up the instruments. We have to shut it down."

There was a loud cracking sound, and the two looked up with horror to see that the glass partition had splintered.

"Shut it down," Bennett said, stepping back warily.

Shane again went to the screen that controlled the Tesla device.

The man-made tornado within the environmental chamber let out a wail of rage, and the room shuddered again as the force of nature tried to break free of its confines.

The alarms continued to blare their warning.

"Shane?" Bennett prodded, watching the glass and the chaos beyond with something akin to fear in his eyes.

"I've shut down the coil and am injecting cool air into the chamber through the vents," Shane replied, eyes never leaving the myriad windows on his computer screen.

Again there was a roar—but this time it was weaker.

"It's breaking up."

The alarms stopped, and the room was eerily quiet.

Shane watched as Bennett reached a cautious hand to the window and touched the jagged cracks that had appeared there. His fingertips came away wet.

"Another few seconds and it probably would have imploded."

Shane nervously put his hands in his lap. "Sorry about that. I . . . didn't think that it would be so strong and—"

"Sorry?" Dr. Bennett said, interrupting the boy. "You're sorry, Monroe?"

Then he started to laugh.

The laugh was contagious, and Shane joined in. "I'm sorry I messed up the chamber," he said, shrugging his shoulders and smiling.

The door to the control chamber suddenly came open, and the night security guard stormed into the office. He had his weapon drawn.

"Is everything all right here, Dr. Bennett?"

Shane looked wide-eyed from the guard to his adviser.

Bennett smiled and gripped Shane's shoulder and squeezed.

"Believe it or not, Charlie, everything is fine."

# CHAPTER TWO

*"No mechanism could be simpler, and the beauty of it is that almost any amount of power can be obtained from it."*
—Nikola Tesla

Shane pointed out his apartment as Carl Bennett drove slowly down Beacon Street. Gazing out the driver-side window, Bennett double-parked, throwing his hazard lights on. He turned and looked at Shane with a grin.

"Last stop for the designated driver taxi service, home of Shane Monroe—*super* genius!"

Bennett emphasized the word *super* like the Coyote did in the Road Runner cartoons, and they both chuckled. The scientist was a huge fan of the Warner Brothers cartoon characters. Shane had mentioned it once to Spud and Geoff and they had picked up on it, started to call him "Wile E."

Shane let his head fall back against the headrest, still laughing softly. "Okay, maybe I'll give you genius—but not super. There's nothing super here."

Bennett had taken Shane and the few other people still working in the Foundation building out for celebratory drinks. Five of them had crammed into Dr. Bennett's Avalon and had driven until they'd found a small Chinese restaurant on Tremont Street that was open until two A.M. The three beers he'd had at Peking Tommy's had done wonders to unwind him, but Shane knew they weren't the only reason he felt so exhilarated. The beer buzz was nothing compared to the thrill of proving his theory.

"You did some amazing work tonight, Shane. I want you to know how much I, and the Foundation, appreciate it."

Shane gazed out the passenger window as another car slowly passed. He could hear the heavy pounding bass of dance music from within the vehicle. "I did what I was hired to do." He shrugged and looked at Bennett with a satisfied grin. "I'm just psyched that I was right."

"You were *right*, all right," Bennett said with a shake of his head. "Listen, get inside and get some rest. Enjoy the weekend and come in on Monday as late as you want. You deserve a break."

Shane opened the door, and the car's interior filled with light. Both he and Dr. Bennett squinted against the sudden illumination. He climbed out of the car and glanced back in at his adviser.

"Will you be in on Monday?" Shane asked.

"Count on it. Hell, I'll be there this weekend. I want to make a few phone calls and start filing reports on exactly what went on tonight. Never mind getting the chamber fixed. But I'd better not see you. I want you to rest up. This is just the beginning."

"Thanks for everything, Dr. Bennett," Shane said as he began to shut the door. "I'll see you Monday, then."

"Shane?" Bennett called to him.

He leaned back into the car.

"I just want you to know, I think your dad would have been really proud."

Shane smiled sadly. "Thanks, Dr. Bennett. Drive carefully." He slammed the door shut and waved as Bennett's car pulled away with a few beeps of the horn.

The night air was cool, and Shane stood for a moment, just breathing it in. Someone had a wood-burning stove, and the air was thick with the rich smoky scent of it. He fumbled around the inside of his book bag for his keys. When he had retrieved them, he climbed the four steps to the old brownstone and let himself into the foyer.

Shane collected his mail—nothing but advertisements—and went up the two flights of stairs to his apartment. Inside, he locked and bolted the door, a habit since moving to the city, then tossed his book bag on the desk.

The light on the answering machine blinked, indicating that he had one message. He reached down and tapped the play button.

"Hey! It's me!" *Spud.* "Where the hell are you? We're putting the movie on in, like, ten minutes. Better get over here or you'll miss it and the beer'll be gone. I thought you said you wanted to see *True Romance* again. Traitor. Probably still at the lab. All right, look, we'll catch up tomorrow."

Spud made kissing noises and hung up.

Shane considered calling his friends to tell them about what had happened tonight, but then he glanced at the clock and decided that was a bad idea. It was going on three o'clock in the morning, and he figured they'd be less than impressed with his timing. He sighed as he pulled off his sneakers and tossed them in the corner. In the quiet of his apartment, Dr. Bennett's last words reverberated through his mind.

*I think your dad would have been really proud.*

As Shane got ready for bed, his eyes slid to the top drawer of his dresser. He walked over and pulled it open. It was filled with odds and ends, paperwork from school, some tools, a stuffed monkey wearing a graduation gown his mother had given him, and a framed picture. Carefully he moved the items lying atop the picture and pulled it from the drawer. For a long moment he stood staring at it, this photograph of him with his father.

In the picture Shane was three, maybe four years old, and his father held him in his arms. His mother had told him it had been taken at a family cookout for the Fourth of July that year. His father was grinning in the picture, and his hair was a mess, all the stress of his life forgotten in that snapshot moment. Of the many photographs his mother had of his father, this was Shane's favorite, yet he rarely took it out to look at it. Much as he liked it, the photo only exacerbated the sadness and anger that he still felt at the loss of his father.

*Tonight, though* . . . tonight was different.

Shane moved some stuff aside on top of the dresser and propped the picture up. He kept his eyes on it as he backed away and sat down on his bed. He remembered another time, when he was older than in the picture, a time when he had come downstairs late one night to use the bathroom and found the light still on in his father's study. He had pressed his face to the barely open door and peered inside. His father had been working on a special project for over a month and had kept himself pretty much isolated from Shane and his mother. He never knew what his father had been working on but there he was, hunched over paperwork at his desk, scribbling furiously.

Shane got under the covers, eyes still on the old photo, caught up in his memories. He wasn't sure if he had made a noise that night or if his father had just happened to look up. But he remembered how his father had smiled warmly, set down his pencil, and motioned for him to come in. His father had picked him up and put him on his knee, squeezing him in a loving hug. With that memory in his mind, Shane closed his eyes and began to drift off, feeling as though he could almost smell his father's Old Spice aftershave.

He fixed his pillows behind his head and opened his eyes again. There were cracks in the white plaster ceiling, and he traced them with his gaze as he did every night before he finally succumbed to sleep. Tonight the jagged fissures were replaced by the image of the mathematical equations that covered the papers on his father's desk that long-ago night.

"I'm gonna help you with your work an' then you're gonna be proud of me." Shane thought those were the words he had said to his father then. If not those precise words, then something close to them. His dad had hugged him closer, kissed him on the side of the head, and whispered in his ear.

Now, as Shane drifted off to sleep, he heard the words as he heard them that night. "I will always be proud of you," said the voice from the past. Though he might have dreamed them, for Shane was fast asleep.

* * *

The persistent trilling of the cordless phone pulled Shane from somewhere dark and deep. He poked his head out from underneath the covers and looked around the room, trying to gauge the time by the amount of sunlight spilling in from beneath the pulled shade. Failing at that, he resorted to the digital clock beside his bed.

10:57 A.M.

*No way,* he thought.

It felt as though he had just put his head on the pillow. He moaned as he grabbed the phone from the recharger and placed it against his ear as he lay back down on his pillow.

"Hello?" he said, voice raspy with sleep.

"I was just about to hang up," his mother replied. "Don't you have a machine?"

Shane closed his eyes and rubbed them with his free hand. "Kicks in after ten rings or something. How ya doin'?" His mom, Nancy, was a hell of a lady, but he would never understand how she could always sound so cheerful.

"Fine, thank you." He heard the shuffling of papers in the background. "Haven't heard from you in a while, and I thought I'd call to make sure everything's all right." His mother paused. "Is it?"

"Is it what?" Shane asked, his brain not up to the intricacies of conversation quite yet.

Nancy laughed. "Is everything all right?

Have a late night or something? Too many beers, perhaps?"

He had started to yawn, but it was stifled midway through by the sudden burst of memory that flooded into his head. *It worked*! His mind really had been fuzzy, but now all the details of the previous evening's success came flooding back to him. The only black spot on his excitement was the fact that he wasn't supposed to discuss his research with anyone outside the Foundation. Still, it was his *Mom*.

"No beer, Ma. Just . . . well, I made a major breakthrough last night at the lab. I was up really late and—"

"Shane, that's wonderful!" she cut in, obviously just as thrilled as he was. "That's the best news I've had all week. Congratulations!"

"Thanks," he said, though hesitantly. "I'm sorry I can't give you too many details, but—"

"Hey, it's me, remember? I was married to one of you top secret science guys."

Shane laughed. "It's nothing like that. You make it sound all mysterious. I'm sure I'll be able to talk about it—I just want to talk to Dr. Bennett first, make sure I'm not breaking any rules. The cool thing is, nobody believed it, y'know?"

"Good for you, kiddo," his mother said. "Good for you. Maybe now you'll be able to take some time off."

"Not likely," he replied. "This is just the tip of the iceberg, I think. Now we have to perfect it."

"Well, I hope you give yourself a break now and then," she said warily.

"Says the workaholic," Shane replied. His eyes went to the clock again. It was now almost noon. "What are you doing home, anyway?" Again he heard the rustling of papers. His mother was a pediatrician over at the North End Clinic and was seldom at home at this hour, even on a Saturday. "You didn't get canned, did you? I told you what would happen if you kept selling your patients on the black market."

"Nope. They haven't caught me yet. I'm just going in late today. I had a guy come out to take a look at the roof. I've found a few shingles in the yard, and I think it may be time I have a new one put on. There hasn't been work done on that roof since before your father died."

For a long moment, Shane did not respond.

"Are you still there?" his mother asked.

"Yeah. Sorry."

Nancy Monroe sighed. "You have no idea how much you remind me of your dad. I can't tell you how many nights I woke up in an empty bed because he was working on some project. He always said he couldn't sleep until the problem was solved."

"Sounds familiar." Shane smiled sadly to himself. "I still miss him," he said to his mother softly.

"Every day," she responded, and Shane was reminded that he wasn't the only one who still felt the void left by his father's passing.

His thoughts were interrupted by a succession of rapid-fire knocks at the door—Spud's trademark, just in case he was still sleeping. The knocking was punctuated by Geoff's muffled voice calling out his name in a high-pitched falsetto.

Shane sat up and threw his feet over the side of the bed. "Hey, Ma? Sorry, but I should go. Geoff and Spud are here." He padded barefoot across the hardwood floor toward the door.

"All right. I just wanted to check in," his mother replied. "You take care of yourself and try to get some more sleep, okay?"

"Doctor's orders?" he asked, smiling as he undid the chain and slid back the dead bolt on the door.

"No," she responded warmly. "Mother's orders. Love you, Shane."

"I love you, too," he replied as he swung the door open wide to allow his visitors access.

"Love you, too, Ma!" Geoff called loudly.

"Give them hugs for me," his mother added.

"I don't think so," Shane said, ignoring his friends for a moment. "You can deliver them in person next time you're here. Gotta go."

His mother said good-bye and Shane hung up the phone. When he turned around, Spud was shaking his head, an expression of grave disappointment on his face.

"Not even dressed," Spud said in disgust. "What a lazy piece of crap."

Shane shot him the middle finger.

Geoff shut the door. "You know, you tell your mommy you love her with such ease. Maybe it's time you bared your soul to the lovely Nevart?"

Spud started to laugh as he sat himself down on the end of Shane's bed. "That's not what he wants to bare to Nevart." He picked up the Houdini biography Shane had been reading and started to flip through it from the back.

It always amazed Shane that of all the other students on the huge Hazeltine campus, he'd ended up friends with these two goons. Geoff Solomon was an engineer, a large, soft-spoken guy from Detroit who'd grown up in a neighborhood where the only white kids he knew were even worse gangbangers than the crew that worked the corner near his house.

There were only two ways, Geoff had once said, of getting out of his old neighborhood, college or prison. "Might surprise you how many people choose incarceration," he'd said.

They all knew it was a hell of a lot more complicated than that, but Geoff did not really like to talk about it, so Shane and Spud left it alone.

Spud was a chemistry major. His real name was Arthur Wilcox Jr. His mother had called him "Bud" his whole life, but he was from Idaho, so once he arrived at Hazeltine, it was only a matter of time before nobody knew he even had a name other than Spud. He didn't seem to mind, though. Spud was a little guy, maybe five five, and Shane had always thought he liked the nickname because it added character. He was never afraid to be the life of the party, that was for sure.

"Do we have to talk about my love life on an empty stomach?" Shane sighed.

Geoff rolled his eyes and shoved his hands into his pants pockets. "Hello, cranky pants. From your ray of sunshine mood, I'm guessing another night of burnin' the midnight oil."

Shane grinned as he pulled on a pair of sweatpants. "It's still on fire, actually. Had a huge night last night. And I have the week-end off."

"Very cool!" Geoff crowed. "Wile E. Coyote strikes again."

Spud looked up from the Houdini book, genuine amazement on his face. "Can it be? Shane Monroe takes a holiday?"

With a nod, Shane grabbed a towel and his shower kit from atop the bureau. "A weekend. But yep. Let me just take a shower and we can get some lunch. We going to the football game?"

Spud lay back on Shane's bed. "Indubitably."

Geoff nodded. "Soitenly," he said in his best Three Stooges voice. "Just hurry. I'm hungry."

"Hurrying," Shane replied as he headed for the door, towel over his shoulder.

With gleeful abandon, Shane sprayed ketchup across his small basket of crinkle-cut French fries, then shoved a couple into his mouth.

Geoff took a sip from his bottle of Sam Adams and sat back in the booth, finished with his lunch. "Let me get this straight. Your experiment worked 'cause you used technology developed in the eighteen hundreds by a guy everyone thought was some lunatic mad scientist?"

"Mad scientist?" Spud asked through a mouthful. He swallowed and reached for his drink. "Did he look like Vincent Price? That would be so typical if he looked like Vincent Price."

Shane pushed his plate away, ignoring Spud's question. Sometimes it was best just to not respond. One innocent reply could start a thirty-minute dissertation on makeup effects in old horror movies, radio serials of the thirties, or the sale of wartime bonds. Not that Shane wasn't interested—after all, Spud was listening to his own little diatribe—but his head was working on the experiment even as he talked about it, and he didn't want to get sidetracked.

"Tesla's theories may have been a little wacky," Shane admitted, getting them back on track. He had become more and more fascinated with the scientist who had immigrated to the United States in the 1880s, and felt he had to defend Tesla. "But the man invented the alternating current power system we use every time we plug something in. Not to mention fluorescent lighting. So he wasn't completely crazy."

Spud nodded in earnest support. "Fluorescent lights are good."

Their waitress drifted over and asked if they were finished. As she cleared their plates away, Geoff leaned forward and put his elbows on the table.

"Wasn't Tesla the guy who thought he could *direct* lightning to shoot down enemy bombers during World War Two?"

Shane was about to defend Tesla again when Spud interrupted.

"No, man, no. I know that one. It wasn't this Tesla guy, it was Blofeld—definitely Blofeld with the death ray."

As Shane started to laugh again, the waitress dropped the check down in the middle of the table and thanked them. He unzipped his book bag and fished around for his wallet. "Thanks for clearing that up, Spud. I always seem to confuse Croatian inventors with fictional leaders of evil organizations hell-bent on ruling the world."

"*De nada,*" Spud said with a big smile as he tossed his portion of the tab down onto the table. "Always glad to be of service, my friend."

Geoff threw his money down as well, leaning forward to slip his wallet back into his pocket. "Seriously, Wile E. You can't give us any hints about what you're doing over at the Foundation? You dangle all kinds of tasty bits in our faces and you still can't tell us what the hell you're doing?"

Shane put his money down and took some change from the pile on the table. "Nope, can't tell you—sworn to secrecy. But I *can* tell you it's not a death ray. How about that?"

Geoff stood up and stretched as he reached for his coat. "I guess it's something," he said, slipping into his jacket and zipping it up.

"Like even if he did tell us what he was doing we'd have any idea what he's talking about," Spud said to Geoff. "I can barely work the remote on the DVD player."

"How do you wake up each morning?" Geoff asked, feigning horror.

As they left the restaurant, Shane felt better than he had in a long time. It had been weeks since he and the guys had been able to just hang out together, and he planned to make the most of the weekend before diving back into the project on Monday.

It had rained for a little while that morning, but fall in New England was like that. By eleven thirty it was all over, and by one o'clock when the football game the Hazeltine Hawks were playing against Dartmouth was scheduled to begin, the sun was shining, the birds were singing, and all was right with the world.

At least until the Hawks started to lose.

Hazeltine University was one of the most respected academic centers in the world, but their football program had never been more than mediocre. Still, with the cutthroat atmosphere that abounded at the University and the stress it caused among the students, parties and sporting events took on an exaggerated importance for entirely different reasons than might exist at other colleges and universities.

Shane was in the tail end of his second year of an accelerated PhD program that would give him his doctorate in six years. He had been a sort of prodigy all his life and could have skipped ahead a dozen times, probably graduating high school at fourteen—but that was the last thing he had wanted. Instead he had taken classes that had challenged him as much as possible while remaining with students his age. Shane had enjoyed growing up with the same kids, having a group in his hometown he could hang around with. Now, though, he just wanted to get all of the education out of the way and get on to the science as soon as possible.

Of course, that did not mean he was going to forego parties and music and football games and the occasional beer. Without those things, he might as well skip higher education altogether.

So on that Saturday afternoon, Shane sat in the bleachers with Geoff and Spud and watched as the Hawks were painfully humiliated by Dartmouth. Still, the Hazeltine students cheered every gained inch of ground, every successful pass, every bone-crunching block. They did not expect the Hawks to win, just to try hard. And so they cheered.

While they watched the game, Spud polished off a chili dog. As he licked his fingers, he glanced at Shane again.

"So what's up with Nevart?" Spud said. "Seriously. Any potential there? Or is the love unrequited."

"Not exactly love," Shane replied. "Just intrigued by her is all."

Geoff snorted with laughter, though his eyes never left the field. "Intrigued," he said. "Is that the science-geek term for drooling lust and a total mad crush?"

Spud practically choked on his drink. Shane tried to shoot Geoff an angry look, but failed. Instead, he offered a self-deprecating smile and just shook his head.

As he turned his attention back to the field, Shane held his breath for a second. One of the Hawks' defensive linemen snagged an interception. A roar went up from the crowd. Bag of peanuts clutched in his hand, Shane stood up with the rest of them to watch as number twenty-seven ran the ball back twenty-two yards before he took a bulldozer of a hit and went down hard. A second later he was up, looking around to see if there were any flags on the field.

There weren't. The play was good. Now the Hawks were on Dartmouth's thirty-five yard line and it was a first down. They were back by ten, but if they could convert that interception into a touchdown drive, they would still be in the game.

Shane smiled. It was nice to think about something besides physics for a while.

# CHAPTER THREE

*"The first gratifying result was obtained in the spring of 1894 when I reached tensions of about 1,000,000 volts with my conical coil."*

—Nikola Tesla

On Monday morning Shane slouched in his seat in Reston Hall, long legs crossed at the ankles. The auditorium was well-ventilated, but with more than seventy students in his Quantum Theory and Atomic Physics class, it could still get a little stuffy thanks to Professor Malenkov's insistence that everyone sit at the front. Despite the open windows and the early fall breeze that washed the room in warm, earthy smells—or perhaps because of them—Shane had trouble keeping his eyes open.

Throughout the class, his head bobbed, chin dropping toward his chest before some instinct snapped him awake again. He had a lot of respect for Sergei Malenkov, and the last thing he wanted to do was have the man catch him napping. Still, it was a beautiful fall morning. He was itching to get back to the lab at the Foundation, but if he couldn't do that, there were loads of other places he would rather have been than in Reston Hall. Stretched out on the Central Lawn with his jacket bunched up under his head, taking a little nap for one. Or, better yet, he could go back to his apartment and play his acoustic guitar for a while.

*No*, he thought quickly. *Get it out of your head. Just this class and lunch, then you can go bask in the glory.*

The truth was he was less interested in basking in whatever little glory there might be at the Foundation than in continuing his work, trying to perfect his control over the process. But for the moment, he was stuck here. Reluctantly, Shane forced himself to sit up a bit straighter. He was relieved to see that Professor Malenkov was not looking at him, so he hoped the man had not noticed.

As Shane sat up, he jostled Noah Shapiro's elbow.

Noah leaned over to whisper to him. "You really repulse me, Monroe."

Shane shot him a look intended to silence him. He didn't want to get caught talking in class any more than he wanted to be seen sleeping.

"Seriously," Noah whispered. "I mean, I can barely make what Malenkov is saying into English, and you're just z-ing away. It's grotesque. I'm guessing your parents lived in some radiation zone when you were in the womb, cuz your brain? It's not natural, Shane. It just isn't natural."

"Would you shut up," Shane muttered out of the corner of his mouth.

For a second, Noah did shut up. He glanced up at Professor Malenkov, made sure no one was paying attention to them, then leaned in toward Shane again.

"Seriously? You're a lovable freak, but you're still a freak. No wonder Junstrom hates you so much. Poor bastard has to work his ass off just to be second best."

Shane dipped his head toward Noah, bangs falling across his eyes. The guy's words rankled him.

"I work my ass off, too," he hissed.

Noah gave him a dubious grin. "Shane, you're sleeping in Quantum Theory."

Anxious, Shane glanced up at the front of the room. Malenkov still didn't seem to have noticed them, but he saw Nevart Arora, one of the graduate students who was a teaching assistant for the class, glance back with a frown.

Shane forgot all about Noah. Nevart had grown up in London, but her father was from Sri Lanka, or at least that was what Shane had been able to find out about her by asking around as subtly as he could. Wherever her parents were from, the combination of their genes had produced not only the most beautiful girl he had ever seen, but a brilliant physicist as well. Much to Geoff's and Spud's amusement, he had been fascinated with her since the very first class of the semester, but he didn't have the guts to say anything to her. He had been foolish enough to admit it to his friends, and they ribbed him about her constantly.

It was twenty past three when class let out, and Shane stretched in his seat, joints popping. He and the guys had gone to an off-campus party on Saturday night, then wandered around Harvard Square in Cambridge on Sunday. A very cool, relaxing weekend. But now it was time to get back to work.

He stood up, scratched at the blond stubble on his chin, and filed out of the row of seats right behind Noah. As they hit the aisle, though, someone tapped him on the shoulder. Shane turned to find himself face-to-face with Nevart. Her skin was like burnished copper, but her eyes were blue. The two were so incongruous that he found it almost impossible to look away from her.

"Hey, Shane. We boring you?" she asked, a conspiratorial grin on her face.

"No," he said quickly, alarmed. He was afraid she knew who was talking after all, or worse, had seen him drifting off. "Professor Malenkov's lectures are always interesting. He puts a great spin on things."

Nevart gazed up at heaven for a moment. "'A great spin,'" she repeated. "We're boring you."

The T.A. glanced at a girl next to her. It was the first time Shane had noticed anyone else was part of the conversation. The girl had black hair tied back in a severe ponytail and funky black-framed glasses that gave her a smart but edgy look. From what he could tell the only makeup she had on was dark red lipstick and eyeliner, but it worked for her.

"Shane Monroe, this is Josie Elliott. Have you two met?"

Josie held her books tightly in front of her, but she kept her eyes firmly on Shane as she shook her head.

"I don't think so," Shane said. "Nice to meet you."

He held out his hand, and she clutched her books a little tighter so she could give him a quick shake.

Nevart smiled at him, and for just a moment he thought he smelled like cinnamon. The woman amazed him, but he knew he was going a little overboard, especially since the chances that she would ever be interested in him were about a million to one. Not that he felt there was necessarily anything wrong with him, but Nevart was probably three or four years older and miles ahead of him in her life.

"I was hoping you could do me a favor." Nevart said.

"Anything," Shane said, before he could catch himself.

Nevart smiled. "I was hoping you'd be willing to tutor Josie once a week. I think she'll have no problem with the class if she has someone to help her through some of the more labyrinthine theories."

*Damn*, Shane thought. Nothing against Josie—whom he didn't even know—but with classes and his work at the Foundation, the last thing he needed was to spend time tutoring someone. On the other hand, he'd just told Nevart he'd do anything for her. How could he not be willing to make sacrifices for a woman who could smile like that and still use the word *labyrinthine* in casual conversation?

Then he glanced at Josie again and saw the girl shift uncomfortably. Nevart had probably figured he'd be less likely to say no if Josie was standing right there—and she was right—but it couldn't be any more fun for Josie to be put on the spot than it was for him.

Shane nodded. "I'd be happy to."

Josie's serious-girl face slipped a second, and she actually smiled.

Nevart clapped a hand on Shane's shoulder, thanked him warmly, and then backed up. "I'll leave you two to work things out," she said.

Then she was gone. Shane scratched the back of his head and glanced at Josie sheepishly.

"So the only time I can really do this is Monday afternoons. Like, right now, I mean?"

"Today?" Josie asked, gazing at him from behind those interesting black frames.

"No," Shane said quickly. "I mean, yes today, Monday. But not today, today. We can start next week, if that's okay. In the meantime, I can give you my number and if you have anything you really need help with before then, you can call me."

Josie nodded, the deal done. "Great. I really appreciate the help."

"No big deal," Shane said as he pulled out his notebook and started to jot down his number.

"Actually, it is," Josie replied. "Nevart says you should probably be teaching this class instead of Malenkov."

Alarmed, Shane widened his eyes and looked around nervously. "Jeez, don't say stuff like that. I get enough crap as it is. I don't want anybody thinking that *I* think that."

One corner of her mouth turned up. "Don't worry, mastermind. Your secret's safe with me."

Iris Green sat on the leather couch in the dark paneled office and picked lint from her dark brown pants. She had been waiting well over forty minutes for her scheduled audience with the assistant director of the Department, and her patience was wearing a little thin.

She stood abruptly, adjusted her suit jacket, and began to pace. From time to time she ran her fingers through her short red hair. The receptionist gave her the eye and then resumed typing something into the computer before her. Iris walked over to a framed print on the wall. She thought it might be something from Monet—stacks of hay in a farmer's field. She tried to concentrate on the piece, on the soft colors, in an attempt to calm herself.

The secretary's intercom buzzed, and Iris jumped. She turned to glance at the woman, who spoke quietly into the phone at her desk. The secretary looked at her and smiled coldly as she replaced the receiver. "The assistant director will see you now, Agent Green."

"Thank you," she said as she walked toward the closed door beyond the secretary's desk. As she reached for the knob, she took note of the fact that there was no name on the door, the silver brackets used to hold the occupant's identity and title empty, as if whatever lay beyond that door could change at any moment.

*This is how it is with the BBD*, she thought as she turned the doorknob. *Nothing is permanent in an organization that doesn't officially exist. Nothing to tie you down or to*

*be tied to you; any rented space in any part of
the world can be your office.*

As she stepped into the poorly lit office,
she wrinkled her nose at an unexpected
smell. Dog. And a poorly housebroken one at
that, given the odor coming from the carpet.
A large man sat behind a desk covered with
manila files, an overweight German shepherd
panting on the rug by his side. Iris closed the
door behind her, and the man looked up
slowly from an open file, then directed her
attention to an older man with a pale com-
plexion and thinning white hair who was
seated in a chair against the wall.

"Agent Green, I'm Assistant Director
Remington," said the dog owner from behind
his desk. "This is Director Larch. We were in
the middle of a discussion when you arrived. I
apologize for the delay."

"I'm at your service, sir," Iris said
begrudgingly. "If you'd prefer, I could come
back later."

Remington interrupted her with a wave of
his hand—the dog perked up its ears and
watched that hand as though it might hold a
treat. "That won't be necessary, Agent Green.
Your business with me shouldn't take long.
I'm sure Director Larch won't mind waiting
while we address your request for a transfer
out of field division."

The way he said those words made Iris
hesitate. They were too studied, too much

information. She looked at Larch, who sat impassively in the chair at the back of the office, unremarkable and yet unnerving in a dark suit, white shirt, and scarlet red tie. He adjusted his glasses and returned his hands to his lap—the first time she'd seen him move since she'd entered the office. She doubted very much that his presence was coincidental.

"Agent Green, I'm going to be blunt," Remington said as he held up the transfer request she had sent two days earlier. "What the hell are you thinking?"

Jaw set, Iris placed her hands behind her back and stood as if at attention. She felt Director Larch's cold gaze upon her and did her best to ignore it. "After completing some recent fieldwork with my partner, Agent Tarker Ames, I came to the conclusion that it would be in my best interest, and that of the department, for me to be transferred somewhere else—possibly intelligence, where the skills I honed with the FBI could be—"

Remington set the sheet down and leaned back in his chair as he interrupted. "What did Ames do to piss you off, Iris?"

Still feeling Larch's stare, Iris kept her gaze locked on Remington. "If I can be frank with you, sir, I have issues with Agent Ames's . . . let's say *overzealous* use of violence in the field. I find it . . . disturbing to say the least."

Remington let his hand hang down beside him and stared at Iris thoughtfully as he ruffled the fur on the back of the shepherd's neck. The dog did not respond at all. In fact, Iris thought it looked rather bored.

"Agent Green," Remington said at length, a chill creeping into his tone, "you're not a fool. The Department exists in the shadow of the intelligence community. Most Americans wouldn't believe we existed if you told them. There's a reason we keep such a low profile."

"Sir, I know that—"

"Let me finish, Agent," Remington said as he scratched behind the dog's ears. Idly, the animal began to wag its tail. "As much as people would like to think otherwise, we live in very dark times. There are things going on every minute of every day that would make most people sick to their stomachs. There are forces at work out there that would do everything in their power to see our way of life, what our country's forefathers worked so hard to build, destroyed. We will not allow that to happen, Agent Green—the Department will not allow that to happen."

The assistant director looked back at her written request. "You came to us with the highest recommendations. We believed that your skills would compliment those of Agent Ames's—and we still do." He placed the transfer request into the folder and closed it. "Your request has been denied. Take a few days, adjust your attitude to the way things are going to be."

Iris gaped at him, stunned. How could he expect her to continue working with her Neanderthal of a partner, especially now? Ames would no doubt hear about her request for a transfer. "Sir, please, I mean no disrespect, but I don't feel I can maintain an effective partnership with a man I feel could very well be mentally unstable."

Director Larch crossed his legs and slowly turned his gaze to the assistant director, awaiting his response. His eyebrows rose with curiosity. Remington sighed loudly, as if he were some horrific, fire-breathing beast. When he spoke, his voice was no louder, but there was an edge present and something that was mere millimeters away from threatening.

"Tarker Ames is one of the finest agents in our employ, Agent Green, as I am sure you will also be someday. Learn from him. That will be all."

Iris was numb. She wanted to say more, but knew it would fall on deaf ears and probably result in some form of disciplinary action. Remington had returned to the paperwork on his crowded desk as if she had already left his office. She turned to leave but not before catching a clearer glimpse of Director Larch. His eyes were dead, like those of a cold-blooded predator. If a forked tongue had snaked from between his pursed lips, it wouldn't have surprised her in the least.

Without another word she strode from the room, her superior's decision leaving a bitter taste in her mouth. She gently closed the door and walked across the reception area.

"Have a nice day, Agent Green," the assistant director's secretary chirped.

Iris bit the inside of her cheek to prevent herself from telling the woman behind the desk what she could do with her nice day.

The room was silent except for the pop and groan of the heating system as it blew hot air into the office from a series of baseboard grates that ran along the walls. Remington gazed at the file in his hands and waited for his superior to comment. He moved a stack of papers from one side of his desk to another. Finally he couldn't wait anymore and broached the subject himself. "Agent Green has enormous potential. She just has to adapt to a new way of thinking. In a few months I'm sure she'll be fine."

Larch grunted. "I see a potential liability," the director said softly, his dry voice almost a whisper. "You may want to consider cutting her loose, General."

Remington turned at last to meet his superior's gaze. "I don't think that'll be necessary. I've studied her file—career as well personal—and I can't think of a better fit for our group. Someone needs to play Jiminy Cricket to Ames. You'll have to trust me on this one, sir. Agent Green just needs to be acclimated to a new reality. Don't you remember your own early days, Director? When you discovered the world wasn't quite as normal as you thought it was?"

In silence, Larch casually adjusted the sleeves of his suit jacket. After a moment he looked up again. "I've been at this so long, I don't even remember what normal is," he said, voice little more than a snarl. Then he rose and strode toward an unobtrusive door at the back of the office.

# CHAPTER FOUR

*"If I truly have a gift for invention, I will not squander it on small things."*
—Nikola Tesla

The Cambridge Research Foundation was on Mount Auburn Street, half a mile from Harvard University. Most people had never heard of Cambridge Research, but those who had figured it was very likely better endowed than that well-known Ivy League school down the street. Each year they picked the best and brightest students from science programs at the most prominent local universities and brought them on board various research projects, some of which were expected to yield groundbreaking results, and others that were considered mostly brain-teasers for the most brilliant among them.

It was an honor to be chosen, or so Carl Bennett had told Shane time and again. And in his heart, Shane knew that was true. But it had bothered him that he had been assigned what had been considered nothing more than busywork, a puzzle for him to work on but that he was never intended to solve.

Yet solve it he had.

The bus's engine rumbled low and deep, and he felt it in his chest like the bass drum thumping out of the speakers at the U2 concert he'd seen at the Fleet Center the month before.

Shane blinked as he realized it was his stop. The bus driver was about to shut the door when he stood abruptly. He clung to the metal rails along the ceiling and hurried to the front. Several passengers scowled at him, but the driver was too jaded to even give it that much effort. He just stared out through the windshield until Shane had stepped off. With a hydraulic hiss, the doors closed behind him. The bus roared as it pulled away.

Several minutes later he entered the lobby of the Cambridge Research building, remembering the first time Dr. Bennett had taken him here. He had been surprised that the administration at Hazeltine would give one of their professors so much leeway to pursue outside interests. He had tenure, even though he was probably not around enough to have earned it. But soon enough Shane realized that Carl Bennett's stature in the scientific community was such that he was worth his weight in media coverage. Part of that came from the fact that he headed up an entire department for the Cambridge Research Foundation.

Shane recalled the conversation he'd had with Dr. Bennett that first day.

"The insurance companies and lawyers call it *force majeure*," the professor had said. "Earthquakes, hurricanes, tornadoes, all kinds of natural disasters . . . forces majeure cause so much death, destruction, and misery in the world that the scientific community has been trying forever to understand them. If we could figure out what causes such horrible events in nature, we might be able to predict them, even someday actually prevent them."

Shane grinned as he walked across the foyer of the building, thinking about all the amazing things that could come of what he had accomplished.

The clock on the wall just inside the lobby read one o'clock. Dr. Bennett had given him permission to come in later, but what was the sense, really. Shane fished through his book bag for the always-elusive identification. He looked toward the front desk for the security guard who always waved him onto the elevators, and was surprised to see that he wasn't there.

Instead, a pair of grim-faced, official-looking men in dark suits stood by the wooden desk. One of them, clipboard in hand, looked up.

"Can I help you?" the man said sharply, coming out from behind the desk.

"I work here. Can't seem to find my I.D. and—"

"Name?" the man asked, his eyes going to the sheaf of papers attached to the board.

"Uh, Shane Monroe," he said hesitantly. There was an air about this man that made him extremely nervous.

"Ah, yes. Mr. Monroe." The guy made a mark next to Shane's name on the sheet. "You're supposed to see General Remington as soon as you come in."

"General who? What's going on?"

The man with the clipboard turned to the other. "Daniel will take you right up."

Daniel, who was equally unsettling, made a gesture for Shane to approach the elevators. "This way, Mr. Monroe."

Shane stood before the elevator and watched as the man removed a security key from his pocket and slid it into the slot.

"What's this all about?" he asked.

The doors slid open, and the man motioned for Shane to enter. "The general will explain."

When they were inside, Daniel hit the button for the ninth floor. As the elevator rose, Shane's mind raced. Had something happened to Dr. Bennett? A picture formed in his mind of the slight damage done to the weather chamber the night before, and he wondered if he had gotten Dr. Bennett in trouble. Or, even worse, himself. *And why are we going to the ninth floor? That's just the cafeteria and the lounge.*

Shane looked up as the elevator shuddered to a stop, and Daniel directed him onto the cafeteria floor. The place was bustling with activity, as it always was at this time of the morning, but it was activity of a different kind. No trays. No food. All the action seemed focused around one table, and as he looked closer, Shane realized he didn't recognize a single person. They were all like Daniel and the guy in the lobby with the clipboard. Men and women in dark suits, all hustling around with grave expressions on their faces.

A cluster of strangers parted, and Shane caught a glimpse of an intense-looking man sitting at one of the tables. He was the center of all the excitement, the eye of the storm. It didn't take a genius to figure out that this was General Remington.

As he and Daniel stood waiting to be noticed, Shane studied the large man at the table. He was working on a laptop computer and shuffling large piles of paperwork, which he extracted from an open briefcase on the seat beside him. A growing cloud of smoke hovered above his head from a cigarette that dangled from the corner of his mouth. Shane's eyes went to a sign on the yellow cafeteria wall that labeled this room a smoke-free zone. He guessed this General Remington was just too busy to read.

The general abruptly looked up from his

papers and glowered at Daniel. He pulled the cigarette from his mouth. "What?" he snarled.

"Shane Monroe, General."

Remington stared. "Thank you, Daniel," the large man said. Without another word, Daniel turned and walked toward the elevators. Calmly, Remington balanced his cigarette on the edge of the cafeteria table, picked up a pile of papers, and placed them inside his briefcase. Then the general stood up. "You're Monroe?"

Shane nodded.

"General Maxwell Remington." He held out a beefy hand.

Tentatively, Shane approached the table and took the man's hand. His handshake was firm, powerful, the hand rough and callused.

"Sit down," Remington said as he broke off the handshake. "Let's talk."

Shane pulled out one of the yellow plastic chairs and sat. "Excuse me, but what's this all about?"

Remington retrieved what was left of his smoke from the edge of the table where it had left an ugly brown burn. He took a long drag from the cigarette. "It's about you, Shane," he said, exhaling a noxious cloud before dropping the butt to the floor. "All about you, and what you accomplished here the other night."

Shane glanced around the cafeteria at the

strangers who had invaded it. "This is about the Force Majeure project?" His head started to pound and his mouth felt dry.

The general nodded slowly. "That's exactly what this is all about, son."

Shane bristled at the use of the word *son*. The air was still fetid with the acrid odor of cigarette smoke, and he wondered if the man's clothes always smelled that way, if he carried it around with him like a cancerous halo.

"You've done amazing work for the Foundation."

"It wasn't just me. June Mendelsohn—"

"Yes. Your project coordinator. She didn't pay enough attention to what you were doing, as far as I'm concerned. She's been assigned to other projects. Transferred out of state," the general said matter-of-factly. "Dr. Mendelsohn did nothing. Neither did the four or five other teams who have worked on the project over the years. No one else has had the success that you had on Friday night. Take credit where credit is due. You've earned it."

The general gave him an awful grin with yellow teeth. Shane imagined it was meant to make him feel comfortable, but it had the opposite effect. The way June had been dismissed unsettled him as well. She hadn't taken the Force Majeure project seriously, but then nobody else had either. That was no reason for her to be transferred. He shifted in his chair and pulled up the sleeve of his coat to look at the time.

"Not to be rude, sir, but why did you want to talk to me? I'm sure it wasn't just to tell me how good a job I've done." He heard the edge in his own voice and regretted it instantly. Nervously, he cleared his throat and again made eye contact with the large man across from him. "Something tells me you people aren't exactly scientists."

Remington laughed, a wet rumble of a sound. "True, Shane. We are not scientists, but there are an awful lot of them on our payroll, if you catch my meaning."

*Of course there are,* Shane thought. *You're the government.* Shane said nothing, but his heart began to race. He knew where this conversation was going. And now he began to understand why they had transferred June. Not because she had failed to recognize the potential in the project, but so that she would not be aware that it had succeeded.

"What you did Friday night, Shane. Could you do it again?"

Shane writhed uncomfortably in his chair. "Yeah," he said. "Yes, I could do it again."

Remington nodded slowly, pleased with the response. "So it wasn't a fluke?"

A tinge of annoyance rippled through him. "Well, I didn't go in there and just start pushing buttons, if that's what you mean. I spent months working on my theory and—"

"Could you make it bigger?"

The question stopped Shane mid-sentence. He looked at the general, unsure if he heard him right. "I'm sorry? Bigger?"

General Remington nodded his head again.

"How . . . how big?" Shane asked in a whisper.

Remington leaned in closer to the table, closer to Shane. "Big enough to drop it down on an enemy target and blame it on God."

Shane felt as if he'd been kicked in the stomach. "Are . . . are you serious?" he asked, though he knew full well what the answer was. Suddenly he felt horribly, ridiculously naive.

The general fished another cigarette from the pack near his hand. His steel gray gaze never left Shane. "Very. So . . . could you do it? Hypothetically?"

As the man produced his lighter and ignited the cigarette's tip, Shane abruptly stood. *I'm done.* "Y'know what? I've gotta go. There's some work I have to do before my class tomorrow."

Remington motioned toward the chair. "Shane, please. Sit. I didn't mean to upset you. It's just that the people who finance the Foundation's studies like to look at all possible applications for the research they are helping to fund. It's my job to ask the questions."

Shane's heart raced. He took a deep breath. "I really have to go."

He turned and began to move toward the elevators.

"Sit," the general snapped.

Shane stiffened but pressed on. He felt the general's eyes burning into his back like laser beams, but he did not turn around. As he approached the elevator, the doors slid open to permit yet another ultraserious man with a clipboard onto the floor. He moved around the man and into the elevator, then turned to push the lobby button and caught sight of General Remington, who stood at the table watching him go. For a minute, Shane thought the man was going to come after him, but Remington simply stared, puffing on his cigarette. Slower than seemed possible, the doors closed and the elevator began its descent.

*I've gotta do something*, he thought. *Gotta talk to someone.* His mind raced as he watched the red numbers above him tick down. There was only one person he could talk to, only one person who could understand the severity of what just happened.

He had to speak to Dr. Bennett.

"I'm sorry," said the pretty work-study student behind the front desk in the Physics Department. "Dr. Bennett isn't in today." She smiled up at Shane. "Do you want to leave him a message? I think he'll be in tomorrow."

Shane lowered his head and sighed. Dr. Bennett had told him he would be at the Foundation on Monday, but he had not been there. And now this. His legs were trembling, and he felt light-headed. He didn't have the patience to deal with something like this now. "If he isn't in, why has his private line been busy for the last twenty minutes?"

The girl became flustered and cast a nervous glance down the hall that led to the offices of the university's physics professors. "He told me he didn't want to be disturbed and . . ."

Shane stormed by her desk and down the hall toward Bennett's office. The other student called after him once but offered no chase. Shane had to talk to Dr. Bennett, to warn him about Remington. His door was shut, and Shane knocked three times before entering. Bennett was behind his desk talking on the phone. He glared up at Shane.

"I'm sorry, Dr. Bennett, but this can't wait," he said as he closed the door behind him.

The professor turned the back of his chair to Shane and faced the window. "I wouldn't concern yourself," Bennett said to the person on the other end of the line. "I'll handle it. . . . No. That won't be necessary. I'll handle it. . . . Yes . . .yes, that'll be fine. Good-bye."

Bennett spun around and scowled at Shane

as he hung up the phone. "What's the problem, Shane?" he asked as he picked up his glasses from the desk. He slid them on and opened a file in front of him. "As you can see, and were probably told by Emily out front, I'm very busy today. If this can wait until tomorrow, I—"

Anxious, Shane moved away from the door to lean on the desk. "Have you gone to the Foundation today? Do you have any idea what's going on over there?"

With a frown, Bennett looked up from the file and removed his glasses. "Calm down, Shane. Sit. What are you talking about?"

Shane sat on the edge of the chair and gripped the front of the professor's desk. "I went in early today, just to check some things out, and there were all these government guys there. They said June's been transferred out of state. Some military guy, General Remington— a *general*, Dr. Bennett—was asking me all kinds of questions about my work on Force Majeure and whether it could be duplicated on a larger scale. I think they want to use it as some kind of . . . weapon."

He watched Dr. Bennett closely as he spoke and was surprised to see that there wasn't much of a reaction at all. Bennett leaned back in his chair and put his hands behind his head. "First of all, yes, they are from the government, and second, I think you need to settle down."

"You . . . you know about this?" Shane asked, stunned.

Bennett leaned forward in his chair. "Wake up, my friend. The Foundation receives much of its funding from various science organizations with strong ties to the United States government. The Force Majeure project is going to get a lot of attention now. We've achieved a level of success with the project that was unheard of until your innovations. I have standing instructions from my superiors to report any success with that project, and that's what I did."

"I can't believe I'm hearing this." Shane buried his face in his hands. "*You* called them? When, Friday night? Was that before or after we went out to celebrate?"

Bennett picked up a paper clip and began to twist it out of shape. "Shane, my responsibilities at the Foundation include keeping those who fund our projects informed. Why would I do otherwise? That's my job. I'm afraid I don't understand what your problem is."

Shane pushed himself forward in the chair again, the anger he had felt with Remington beginning to return. "You don't understand what my problem is? I've put a lot of time and energy into something that some bloodthirsty asshole wants to use to kill people. Jesus, Carl, if they do that, have you even thought about what kind of civilian casualties you're talking about? It isn't a gun, for God's sake. It's a force of nature."

"I can see General Remington used his charm on you." The scientist shook his head with a sigh and tossed the twisted paper clip on top of a stack of manila file folders. "Look, he is a former military man. Marines, I think. He examines *all* potential applications for any of the projects we have going at the Foundation. Of course he's going to ask about military uses."

There was a sick churning in Shane's stomach. His heart was heavy, and he felt the heat of anger rising again in his cheeks. "That's what he said too." He stared at his adviser with new eyes. He felt dirty and repulsed, something he never believed he would feel about his work, or about Dr. Bennett, for that matter. "I thought I was doing something that would help people, not hurt them."

"Oh, come on, Shane," Dr. Bennett replied, obviously frustrated. He stood up. "It's really not a big deal. This is how it is everywhere. I guarantee that the Force Majeure project will be used exactly as expected. It's just that the government has to examine all the angles to make sure they're getting the most bang for their buck."

Shane nodded, letting the words wash over him. As much as it pained him, he knew what he had to do. "I'm leaving the department," he said, glancing up from the floor to Dr. Bennett.

The professor's face twisted with confusion. "You can't be serious."

"Very." He snatched up his book bag from beside the chair. "I'm going to the registrar's office now to change my major."

Bennett started to come around his desk. "Think about what you're saying, Shane. Don't you think this is a little drastic? You've got one of the best scientific minds I've ever seen, and the future payoff from that is going to be like nothing you've even dreamed about. You can write your own ticket. Look, let's go to lunch and discuss this—my treat."

He reached for his jacket, which hung on the coat rack by the window, but Shane's words stopped him.

"I've made up my mind, Dr. Bennett. I'm sorry but I can't be part of this." He turned toward the door.

"Think about it, Shane. This decision will affect the rest of your life. Please, don't do anything rash." Bennett smiled at him. "Besides, what would you change your major to? It's not like us physics geeks fit in many places."

Shane shrugged as he opened the door. "I don't know, maybe biology, premed, or something. Suddenly the idea of saving lives seems very cool to me."

He shut the door behind him, cutting off any further protest from his former adviser.

Slinging his book bag over his shoulder, he walked up the hallway and out of the physical science building, headed for the Registrar's office.

The sky seemed grayer now than when he had gone in, and the air had grown quite chilly. It was autumn still, but the cold snap to the wind made Shane think it was going to be a very long winter.

# CHAPTER FIVE

*"So energetic are these actions and so strangely do such powerful discharges behave that I have often experienced a fear that the atmosphere might be ignited, a terrible possibility . . ."*

—Nikola Tesla

The first official day of spring had come and gone, and Shane was having doubts about whether the sun was ever going to shine on Boston again. A damp wind kicked up from nowhere and threatened to yank his Red Sox cap from his head. He tilted his chin down and grabbed the bill of the hat, holding it in place. *Spring's just around the corner*, he reminded himself as he crossed the street onto the Hazeltine campus, buffeted by the chilling wind. *Just a little late this year.*

Shane felt uneasy as he passed the Cole Science building, where the physics department was housed. He pulled his cap down tighter against the wind and quickened his pace. He didn't want to take a chance of

possibly running into Dr. Bennett and being
put in a really awkward situation. Ever since
the debacle in the fall he had done his best to
avoid contact with his former adviser, though
considering how busy switching over to
premed had kept him, that had not been very
difficult.

At first he had found the differences
between the two courses of study jarring.
Physics dealt with the properties and interac-
tions of matter and energy; it was easy to
keep an intellectual distance. But medicine
was something else entirely. A doctor's life
was the treatment and prevention of disease
and injury. Shane had no idea how they could
do what they did—how his mother could do
her job—and not take their patients' well-
being extremely personal. Sometimes he
wondered if that was the truth of it—that one
couldn't be a good doctor and not be
*involved*. He still wasn't sure if he had that
in him, if he could put himself on the line
like that.

Still, after three months, he found medicine more fascinating with every passing day.

As he glanced at his watch to check the
time—he was meeting Spud and Geoff for
lunch—someone called his name. A feeling of
dread spread through him as he tried to figure
out what he would say if it was Dr. Bennett.
Again the person called out to him. Shane
could hear footsteps coming up fast behind

him and reluctantly he stopped and turned around.

Ray Junstrom strode quickly toward him, the smile on his face not quite friendly but not quite smug either. "I thought that was you going by. How's things in the world of premed? Bored yet?"

Ray bumped Shane's shoulder as he came up beside him, as though they were childhood friends instead of rivals. Or, at least, Ray thought they were rivals. Shane couldn't be bothered with that kind of petty competitive stuff.

"Far from it," Shane replied.

"Heading for class?" Ray asked.

"Not until later. Just meeting some friends for lunch at the student center."

When Shane changed majors, Ray had begun to be noticeably more friendly toward him. Apparently, now that they were no longer in the same major, there wasn't any reason to keep up the nastiness, and it was safe for Ray to be at least civil toward him.

Ray fished a pack of cigarettes from inside the pocket of his navy blue windbreaker and placed one in his mouth. Shane frowned, trying to figure out how a guy supposedly as smart as Junstrom had started smoking in the first place.

"I'm heading over there myself," Ray said, turning around to walk backward so the wind would not blow out the match he was using to light his smoke. "I'm supposed to meet Nevart. You remember her, don't you? Real cute T.A.?"

Butterflies immediately fluttered in Shane's stomach. Of course he remembered her. "Yeah, I think so. She's the one that T.A.'d Malenkov's quantum theory course, right?"

Ray took a drag on his smoke and nodded. "That's her. We're supposed to have a meeting or something about tutoring some of the more challenged members of her classes. I haven't decided yet if I'm going to do it or not. If it pays, I might."

Shane felt a sudden flash of guilt as he remembered that Nevart had asked him to tutor as well. After what happened with the Foundation and switching majors, he had never even bothered to tell Nevart he wouldn't be able to help, or why.

"Plus, I'm still doing work at the Foundation," Ray continued. "I don't know if I'm even going to have the time."

Shane had heard through the grapevine that Ray had been invited to join the Foundation team not long after his own resignation. He was curious about what project the other guy was assigned to, but didn't want to broach the subject.

"You were smart to change when you did, Monroe." Ray flicked the filter from his cigarette beneath a bush as they approached the student center. "Just look at all the free time you'd be missing out on if you hadn't."

Nevart Arora was waiting by the front entrance to the student center cafeteria. Shane knew it was her by the way she leaned against the wall. He hated to admit it but he had studied her from afar so often that he could pick her out of a crowd on body language alone. She noticed them as they came closer and broke out in a wonderful smile that probably had little to do with him, but a lot to do with Ray.

"Hey, Ray," she said, pushing off the wall and strolling toward them.

Her beautiful blue eyes then fell upon Shane, and the butterflies in his stomach exploded in fluttering flight.

"Long time no see, traitor," Nevart teased, her smile becoming mischievous. "What have you been up to since defecting to the other side?"

Shane couldn't help but stare at her. The last time he had seen Nevart had been at the Prudential Center Christmas Tree lighting, but he thought about her often.

"Ah, you know," he replied, trying to sound casual. "I've mostly been discovering cures for diseases that haven't even been thought of yet."

Nevart laughed softly, and Shane relaxed.

"Had lunch yet?" Ray asked Nevart, taking her focus away from him. Shane scowled.

Maybe the rivalry still existed after all.

"No, actually, I haven't. I was thinking we could talk over a bite?"

Ray leaned to the side and grabbed hold of the door handle. He pulled it wide and held it open for her. "Sounds good, let's do it."

Nevart went into the dining hall and turned to look at Shane again. "Want to join us?"

For a brief moment he thought about blowing off his friends but decided against it. "I'm meeting some friends. Maybe another time?"

She nodded. "I'd like that."

Her eyes lingered on his for one last moment before she turned to accompany Ray further into the dining hall. Shane watched them go, damning himself for not having the guts to just ask Nevart on a date. It ought to have been the simplest thing in the world. He had certainly done it before with girls in high school and in college. Some had said yes and some had said no, but those were the risks. The thing is, with Nevart, he thought maybe it was a risk he wasn't willing to take.

Still . . . *I'd like that*. Those words had to mean something, didn't they? Or was she just being polite? Shane sighed. He had never met a girl who could make him feel so insecure.

Downstairs in the main hall, Shane spotted Spud and Geoff at their usual table in the far corner. Both of them already had their

lunch trays and were in the midst of eating.
He strode over, pulled out a seat, and tossed
his book bag onto it. "Hey, gentlemen. How's
it hangin'?"

"Didn't think you were gonna join us,"
Spud said through a mouthful of sandwich.
He started to chew again as Geoff made a
grotesque sound that could have been a laugh
through a wad of food.

Shane sat down. "What's that supposed to
mean?"

Spud swallowed and held up a finger. He
took a swig from a can of Dr Pepper, belched,
and continued. "We saw you come in with
the lovely lady Nevart and the dastardly
Junstrom."

Paying them little attention, Shane
unzipped his bag and got out his wallet.
"And?"

"And doesn't it just rot your socks to
know that they're doin' the wild thang?"
Geoff prodded. He cast a devious glance at
Spud.

Shane took his meal card out and then
put his wallet back into his bag. "You know
what? Remind me to never share anything
personal with you two clowns. I like her,
yes. Have either of you ever even kissed a
girl?"

The two of them grinned like children.

"And, anyway, it's just lunch," Shane said
as he dropped his bag back on the chair beside

him. "Nevart wants Ray to tutor some of her students, that's all."

Geoff moved some of the lettuce around on his plate. "Shane, y'know, we're friends and everything, but if you don't grow some balls soon, I don't think we can be seen in public with you anymore. You like her so much, but this is the first time you've seen her in months. Why don't you just ask her out, for God's sake?"

Spud pointed half a sandwich at him, emphasizing the point. "Our dear Geoffrey has asked an excellent question. Shane, she's a grad student, so you almost never cross paths with her. But every time you've got a golden opportunity, you let it fly right by. So why didn't you ask her?"

Shane sighed, exasperated by the relentless attack. "You know exactly why. Don't make me repeat myself."

His two friends looked at each other and shrugged their shoulders in unison, then gave him a theatrical glance and shrugged again. "We don't know what you're talking about," Spud said.

Shane made a mental note to never again meet the two jackasses that he used to call friends for lunch. He buried his face in his hands for a moment and then looked up at them again. "She's at least three years older than me. What does she want with an undergraduate?"

"Never know until you ask, baby cakes," Spud said.

"Maybe she's a cradle robber," Geoff suggested supportively.

Shane was suddenly angry with his friends but didn't understand why. They were like this constantly. He should have been immune to their antics. But there was something about what they were saying that irked him to no end. Maybe it was how right he knew they were.

He got up from the table. "I'm going to get my lunch."

As he waited in line with a tray, his eyes scanned the crowd for signs of Ray and Nevart. He found them at the far end of the room near the floor-to-ceiling windows that looked out onto a nicely landscaped section of campus often used for graduation photos.

The line shuffled slowly forward, and Shane couldn't help but think about what Spud and Geoff had said. He tried to concentrate on what he was going to have for lunch but caught himself looking back to the table where Nevart sat with Ray. A little voice that sounded an awful lot like Spud whispered in his ear. *Never know until you ask,* said the voice. And instead of getting mad and pushing it aside, he listened to the voice and agreed.

Shane stepped from the line and headed toward Nevart's table. "What the hell are you doing, Monroe?" he muttered to himself, but he did not slow down. The worst she could say was no. *Actually*, he thought, *the worst she could say is a lot crueler and more humiliating than just plain no.* But he doubted Nevart would be cruel. And even if she turned him down, at least he would get Geoff and Spud off his back.

As he approached the table, Shane recognized a couple of the other students from his old physics class at the table with Nevart and Ray. Noah Shapiro was among them and he glanced up and gave a little wave. They all seemed to be having a pretty good time together, and Shane wondered if he should hold off, ask her another time.

But then he was at the table, and Nevart had noticed Noah's wave and looked up to see him standing there.

"Hello again," she said amiably.

"Hey. Do you have a second?"

A puzzled expression crossed her face, and he felt like running away, but then she rose from the table. Ray Junstrom was giving him the evil eye, but Shane ignored him.

"So, what can I do for you, Mr. Monroe?" Nevart asked as they moved a short way away from the table together.

Shane felt all of her lunch companions staring at him and willed himself not to look over at them. He wanted to run screaming. Instead, he focused on those amazing blue eyes. "I just wanted to apologize for never getting back to you about that student you asked me to tutor. It was a weird time for me, and . . ."

*Coward*, screamed the Spud-like voice in his head.

"That's okay, Shane. No big deal. I found someone else pretty quickly and she's doing just fine. Don't worry about it."

Shane pretended to wipe sweat from his brow and he smiled. "Whew. That's a relief, 'cause I figured if you were mad at me there was no chance in hell you'd let me take you to dinner some night." He felt a little nauseated but didn't let it show.

Nevart's eyes widened with surprise, then she smiled and looked down at her feet, as if she was embarrassed. "Did you just ask me out on a date, Shane?"

"If that's a bad thing, no I didn't. It was just an uncontrollable slip of the tongue, like a more sociable form of Tourette's syndrome or something." Shane looked around the lunch area and noticed the lines were shorter.

She chewed her lower lip a moment, regarding him carefully, that same mischievous smile on her face. "What if it isn't a bad thing?"

He was stunned. "Well," he began, "if so, I guess I'll try skydiving and bungee-jumping next, 'cause after this? Not going to be so hard."

Nevart started to laugh, shaking her head. "Am I that terrifying?"

"You have no idea," Shane assured her.

"So when were you thinking?"

"How about Friday? We could have dinner at this Thai place I know, then maybe walk around Newbury Street or something. If the weather's not too bad." He sighed. "I am so bad at this kind of thing."

"I don't know. You seem to be doing all right. And Friday sounds great," she said, pulling a pen from her pocket. "Let me give you my number."

Shane patted himself down in search of scrap paper. He didn't have anything to write on and his bag was back at the table. "Wait a minute, I'll get something to—"

She stepped closer to him and grabbed his hand. Pulling it to her, she began to write. "Don't wash your hands until you write this down in a safe place, all right?"

He stared at the number, then back at her. "Got it. Thanks."

She slipped her hands into her back pockets and just looked at him for a second, then glanced at the people at her table. "I really should get back."

"Oh, right. Of course. Sorry to keep you," Shane said, closing the hand that she had written her number on into a fist. "I'll give you a call sometime this week and we'll talk about Friday."

Nevart turned to go back to her table. "Talk to you later in the week, then," she said, almost shyly. She waved good-bye and went to sit down.

He headed back to the lunch line and stood there gazing at the number on his hand. A jolt of excitement passed through him. He could hear sounds of clapping and cheering coming from somewhere in the cafeteria and turned to see what was happening.

It was Spud and Geoff. Spud had climbed up onto a chair and was applauding him. Geoff was clapping as well. They must have watched the whole thing. Shane laughed and placed his order for lunch. The clapping and cheering continued in the background.

*Now that they were right,* he thought, *they're gonna be absolutely unbearable.*

Nancy Monroe sipped a cocktail and perused her menu while she waited for her son at the Legal Seafoods restaurant in the Prudential Center. She had left work a little earlier than expected because of a late cancellation and, despite rush hour traffic, managed to make it to the restaurant with plenty of time to spare. Her watch said five past six, which meant it was nearly six o'clock. She liked to set it fast so she always had a couple of minutes to spare.

Out the window beside her, rush hour continued. The cars were bumper-to-bumper going up Boylston Street, people hurrying every which way as they began their commute home. It was times such as this that she missed the city. She and her late husband had lived in Boston proper for five years before she'd become pregnant with Shane. It was then that they had bought their first house on the South Shore and moved away.

A shame, really; they very seldom had bothered to come into town after that. Yes, she'd commuted to work in Boston's North End five days a week, but it hadn't been the same. Her husband had always wanted to spend more time there, but they never could find enough hours in the day with raising a child, maintaining their careers, and owning a home. Now that her husband was gone, it always made her sad to think about the things they should have done.

She took a dainty sip of her gin and tonic and placed it back on the center of the napkin. Glancing away from the window, she caught a smiling Shane coming across the restaurant toward her with a bouquet of flowers in one hand.

"Sorry I'm late," he said as leaned over to peck her on the cheek and place the bouquet of mixed spring flowers in her lap. "Happy birthday." He removed his dark brown leather jacket and placed it over the back of his chair before sitting down.

She smelled the flowers. "Thank you,

honey. It's a nice little reminder that spring is almost here." She gazed out the window again. "Though you wouldn't know it to look outside."

Nancy placed the flowers under the table by her feet as Shane ordered a Coke from the waiter. "Don't forget to remind me about these when we leave," she said.

He nodded as he took a sip from his water glass.

Shane's mother studied him from across the table. It was a special occasion, her birthday, and he'd actually worn a tie. Her little boy was certainly growing up.

"What's this?" she asked, plucking at her chin and making reference to the beginnings of a goatee Shane was growing. He gave her the look that told her to mind her own business, and she began to laugh. "It looks good. Really. I don't want any trouble."

The waiter returned with Shane's drink and told them he would be back for their order. They each picked up their menus.

It had become tradition that she and her son go out to dinner, just the two of them, on their respective birthdays. They'd been doing it for years, and she hoped it would continue for many more. With her insanely busy schedule at the Health Center and Shane's studies, it was their chance to reconnect, to catch up.

She'd been pretty concerned over the last few months. Shane had been very upset about something but had been vague about what it was. It had eventually led him to change his major, though he seemed to be adjusting just fine. And if he wanted to be a doctor, well, who was she to argue? But, as his mother she needed to be certain he was all right.

"How's everything at school? Still happy you chose premed?"

He looked up at her. "Yeah. It was a little crazy at first, but I've got it under control now." Thoughtfully, he glanced back at the menu, a tiny smirk on his face. "This doctor stuff is turning out to be pretty easy."

His mother laughed. "You're such a creep. Just you wait and see. Don't come crying to me when you need help studying for your midterms."

The waiter returned with a basket of freshly baked rolls and left with their food orders.

"So," Shane said as he spread butter on half of a roll. "What kind of birthday have you had so far?"

"Let's see, I had a case of severe dehydration from that nasty stomach virus that's been going around, a case of conjunctivitis, a few upper respiratory infections, and, oh, let's not forget the head lice."

Her son brushed the crumbs from his hands and turned in his seat to get something from the pocket of his coat. "Well, I don't know if this will come close to head lice, but I got you something."

She was touched. "Shane, you didn't have to do that. Going out to dinner with you is enough. You don't have extra money to be spending on me."

He handed her a small paper bag, folded at the top. "Excuse the fancy wrapping paper. I picked it up on the way over; that's why I was a little late. Happy birthday."

She opened the bag and withdrew a compact disc by Peter Gabriel. Shane knew he was one of her favorites, but she had never seen this particular recording before. "Thank you so much, honey. I didn't even know he had anything new out."

He seemed pleased that she liked what he had bought for her. "It's an import," Shane said. "He did the music for the big millennium celebration in England a few years back. I thought you might like it."

She turned it over to gaze at the titles of the various song tracks. "I love it, thank you."

They talked for a little while about music and her work and his studies and, sooner than they would have expected, their food arrived. The meals were excellent, and each of them cleaned their plates but left room for coffee and dessert. They split a piece of cheesecake with cherries.

"So, seriously, everything is good?" she asked again before taking a sip from her cup of coffee.

"Everything is fine," he promised through a mouthful of cheesecake.

She watched his face for telltale signs of upset. "I know how much you loved your work with physics. Whatever happened must have been pretty awful."

He put his fork down and leaned back in his chair. "I'm over it. I thought about it a lot at first, but I realized I'd drive myself crazy if I didn't let it go."

"Do you want to talk about it?" Nancy asked. "I'm all ears."

Shane shook his head. "No, that's all right. I really can't. Let's just say I did what was best for me and everyone else and call it done."

"And Carl Bennett? Have you seen him since . . ."

He shook his head again. "Not since I told him I was changing majors. He's probably pretty pissed at me, but . . ."

Shane looked at her across the table. There was a seriousness there that she had never quite noticed before. All the other times she had looked into the eyes of her son she had seen the gaze of a child. For the first time she realized she was looking at the eyes of an adult.

"I did what I had to do, Mom."

She reached across the table and touched her son's hand. "That's all that really matters," she said supportively. "As long as you feel what you did was right."

* * *

Shane stood before the medicine cabinet mirror in his cramped bathroom and examined the hair he was cultivating on his chin. He recalled his mother's expression tonight when she asked him about the goatee and tried to determine if she thought it looked stupid or not.

He turned his head, looking at the blond hair sprouting from his chin from a variety of angles. *Not too bad*, he thought. Shane combed the coarse hair with his fingertips and again studied his reflection in the mirror. Maybe he should give his mom a call in the morning and ask her flat out if she thought the goatee was a bad idea.

They had had a nice night together, and Shane was reminded of how cool his mother actually was. They had been through a lot together with the death of his dad, and it had made the two of them incredibly close. Being away at school made it tough for them to see each other as often as they liked, but it made the time they did spend together all the more special.

He leaned forward and examined the hair on his chin even closer. It was supposed to make him look a bit older, more mature, but at the moment the fuzz was growing so slowly that he looked younger instead, like some high school kid hoping to impress the girls. That was not the image he wanted to project Friday night with Nevart. With a sigh, Shane reached for his razor. Maybe he'd make another try at the goatee at some point.

When he had finished shaving, Shane turned the light off in the bathroom and padded barefoot to the center of his studio apartment. The television was on, and something caught his attention. It was one of those late night sensational news shows. At the moment they were running grainy video footage of a powerful tornado as it tore up a village in some third world country. He reached for the remote on the bed and turned up the volume so he could hear.

". . . still coming to terms with their loss in this tiny Colombian farming village, where a storm like this is so unusual, no one in the village can remember the last time a tornado struck here. With the changes in world climate, incidences of freakish weather conditions have become all the more common, but . . ."

Shane stepped closer to the television. It showed the village called Curaca, practically wiped from the face of the planet by the force of the tornado. It was as if the area had been scoured by the anger of some scorned ancient deity, nothing left to show that a village and farmlands had ever been there. Nothing but dark, rutted earth and absolute destruction remained.

He felt the beginnings of something awful

stirring at the back of his mind.

A survivor from the village was on next. The old man was pathetic, his clothes torn and covered in drying mud. Someone draped a red blanket over his shoulders as he spoke in his native tongue of the terror that had befallen his village. A man's voice translated as the old man spoke, tears streaming down the dark, leathery skin of his face.

"It was a fine day. A beautiful day. And then without warning the skies grew dark and a powerful rain began to fall." The man started crying uncontrollably as he threw his hands up to the heavens.

"Why did God do this to us?" the translator droned, lacking any of the old man's emotion. "It was like the fury of heaven. First the lightning shot up from the jungle into the sky. Then the tornado came, like a great black finger coming down out of the sky and erasing everything it touched. What did we do to anger God so? What did we do to make Him take away so many?"

The man completely broke down and the story ended, fading to black for emotional emphasis before returning to the studio. The pretty blond host began to talk about unusual weather conditions that had been springing up with destructive force all over the world and the dangers they posed to everyday life.

Shane felt his legs begin to tremble as the germ of a hideous idea began to form in his

head. He sat down on the bed's corner and
continued to listen with growing dread. A
supposed expert from the National Weather
Service was on next. When posed with the
question of why these strange storms had
been occurring, the man didn't seem to have
any real answers.

*It's not possible,* Shane thought. *They
could never do such a thing.*

"There is no rational explanation for
these freak storms," said the man from the
National Weather Service. "What I think
we're dealing with here, Cindy, is a constantly changing environment that will, of
course, affect our weather patterns. We've
seen the effects of global warming on our
environment, as well as El Niño and La Niña.
I think what we've witnessed over the last
few weeks is just the shape of things to
come."

Shane's mouth grew remarkably dry and
he swallowed, his eyes never leaving the television. Select aspects of the story echoed
through his mind.

*"The lightning shot up from the jungle
into the sky."*

*"There is no rational explanation for
these freak storms."*

And no matter how hard he tried to suppress them, to lock them away, the thoughts
tumbled forth. He grabbed the remote and
pointed it at the television. He didn't want to

hear any more. Maybe he could still convince himself that what he was thinking was absolutely crazy. But he couldn't shut it off. He had to hear more.

The next guest was almost too much for him to bear. It was a short, balding man dressed in a very conservative blue suit and wearing horn-rimmed glasses. He was in a studio somewhere in Alabama and he was explaining his theory of the severe freak weather conditions. With a straight face he explained that these people were facing God's wrath. The sinners were being punished for transgressions against the Lord God. The ugly little man then went on to further explain that all the areas hit so far had been in countries known for exporting illegal drugs, support for his theory of God smiting the guilty.

"God is striking down the enemies of His righteous people!" bellowed the man while shaking a Bible at the television camera.

"Oh, shit." Shane shot to his feet as his conversation with General Remington echoed in his ears.

*"Hypothetically, could you build it bigger?"*

*"How big?"*

*"Big enough to drop on the enemy and blame it on God."*

Shane stumbled toward the television as the program broke for a commercial. He was in shock, his mind racing with the impossible and improbable.

"It's not God or the environment," he whispered to the TV, which was now showing an advertisement for a calorie-free sugar substitute. "It's me. I did this," he said as he raced to the bathroom, barely making it before he threw up.

# CHAPTER SIX

*"I remember that when I later called on
an official in Washington with a view of
offering the invention to the government,
he burst out in laughter upon my telling
him what I had accomplished."*
— Nikola Tesla

For what seemed the thousandth time that
morning, Shane gazed at the photocopied
paper advertising a midnight showing of
*2001: A Space Odyssey* in Kraus Hall that
weekend. It had been hung on a crowded
bulletin board outside the physics department, where he had been waiting since very
early in the morning. None of the staff were
in yet; the lights were still off inside and the
door locked. Shane's eyes burned after his
sleepless night, and he closed them briefly
to squelch the increasing irritation as he
turned from the board and leaned back with
a sigh.

He had to see Bennett as soon as possible
to discuss his suspicions about the Force

Majeure project. He saw the image of the old Colombian man every time he closed his eyes, and it had begun to make him feel sick to his stomach. If his research was contributing to the deaths of innocent people and the destruction of property, there had to be some way that he could voice his protest.

Shane heard the jangling of keys and looked down the hallway to see Carl Bennett casually strolling toward him reading a folded copy of the *Boston Globe*. He was fishing through his pocket for his keys.

"Dr. Bennett," Shane said as he pushed off the wall to confront his mentor.

Bennett looked up and seemed a little stunned at hearing a voice this early in the morning. But recognition blossomed across his face as he realized who was speaking to him.

"Shane," he said happily, sliding his newspaper into a leather satchel that hung from a strap over his right shoulder. "How are you? I was beginning to think you'd transferred out of Hazeltine instead of just this department."

Bennett approached, sticking out his hand for a shake. Shane took it in his and looked into the eyes of his former adviser. "We have to talk, Dr. Bennett." He paused, looking down the hall at two women who were busily chatting as they approached their offices. He stepped in closer to the man and whispered, "They did it."

There was a look of confusion on Bennett's face. "Who did what?"

Shane swallowed, and it made a dry clicking sound. "They did what they asked me to do. They're using it as a weapon."

The professor immediately let go of his hand and moved to the door of the physics department. "Let's talk inside my office." He didn't even bother turning on the lights as he navigated the workstations toward his office. Using another key, Bennett let himself in and left the door open so Shane could follow. He turned on the lights and hung his windbreaker on the wooden rack crammed into the corner. "Would you mind explaining what the hell you're talking about?" he asked, almost petulant.

Shane shut the door behind him and set his book bag down at his feet. "Those government people asked me if I could take my research and do it bigger to use as some kind of weapon, and I think they've done it without me."

With a dry laugh, Bennett ran a hand through his thinning hair. Shane noticed there was more gray there than he had seen before. Bennett took a seat behind his desk. "I wish I had a tape recorder, because I'd like to play back what I just heard and watch your expression as the stupidity of what you said sinks in."

The professor's words cut deep but it

wasn't enough to sway him from his beliefs.
"I know it's crazy—don't you think I *know*
how it sounds?" There was a tension in his
voice that he had been trying to suppress but
now seemed to be getting the better of him.

His former adviser stared across the desk
at him, eyes filled with something Shane had
never expected to see. Disappointment. And
it hurt him as if he had been punched in the
gut with a sledgehammer.

"Is everything all right at home, Shane?"
Bennett asked. "At school?"

Shane closed his eyes in frustration, pulled
his bag up onto his lap, and unzipped the top.
He began to fumble around inside and withdrew a large stack of papers. "Every-thing is
fine. Just hear me out. I was up all night
pulling information off the Internet and I
think I can make a case for what I suspect."

He put the papers in front of Bennett, who
glared at them doubtfully. *It might as well be
a pile of crap*, Shane thought as he stepped
back. Bennett lifted the pages and put them
down on the desk without even looking at
them. His chair squealed as he leaned back.
He gazed up at the ceiling, crossing his hands
on his stomach.

"I really can't believe I'm having this conversation—and with you of all people." He
came forward in his chair again and glared at
Shane. "Please, share what could have given
you such an absolutely insane idea."

"I saw a news show last night," Shane began, carefully examining each word before saying it. "There was a story about a freak tornado that destroyed a village in South America."

Bennett listened, nodding his head slowly.

"They interviewed one of the survivors, an old man, and the things he said about the tornado—how it had suddenly appeared . . . all I could think of was what I had done in the lab."

Bennett put his head down on his desk briefly and then looked up at the boy. He was smiling. "Shane, it was a freak storm. They happen all around the world every day. Have you forgotten this is the reason we *do* the kind of research we do at the Foundation—to be able to predict the probability of an atmospheric anomaly like the one you saw in the story and prevent it? That tornado may have been freakish in its formation, but do you honestly think there was some clandestine sinister force behind its creation? It's quite a leap, after all, from what you did in the lab to doing it out in the world."

"Not so far," Shane replied, knots in his stomach. "It was my research, remember. And it's not so far a leap at all."

"C'mon, Shane. Listen to what you're saying. Life is not a James Bond movie."

Shane kept his growing frustration in check and jabbed a finger at the stack of papers on the desk. "Look at what I've found before you tell me I'm nuts."

Bennett took a pair of glasses from his shirt pocket and put them on. He picked up the printouts and began to read. "What exactly are these?"

"After I watched the story I got online and looked up recent occurrences of tornadoes around the world."

The physics professor continued to skim the pages, placing each on the desk as he finished.

"Then I looked at specific details of each, looking for any clues that may hint at anything . . . unnatural."

Bennett reached the last of the pages and set it down on top of the others. He let out a sigh as he removed his glasses, folded them up, and returned them to his shirt pocket. "Shane, I don't see anything here that suggests what you're saying is anything more than some twisted paranoid delusion."

Furious, Shane grabbed the paperwork on the desktop and flipped it over. "Medellín, Kandahar, Veracruz; can't you see it? It's as plain as the nose on your face."

Again, Bennett shook his head. "No, but what I do sec are examples of severe weather conditions that are most likely the result of extreme atmospheric changes in the present—"

"The locations I've marked, they're all

drug trafficking hot spots," Shane interrupted. He pulled a map from the middle of
the stack and pointed to several X's made
in red marker on specific regions of each
country.

"What?" Bennett asked, again pulling his
glasses from his pocket. "I still don't know
what you're trying to prove here, Shane."

"All the places recently hit by freak,
destructive storms are areas responsible for
the production or distribution of illegal drugs
into this country. Now, you look at my data
and tell me I don't have a reason to be suspicious."

Bennett leafed through the papers again
and looked up into his former student's face.
"I still don't see it. I'm sorry, but I don't.
What I do see is a serious case of paranoia that
has gotten the better of someone whom I
once believed to be extremely levelheaded."

Shane felt as if his world were crashing
down all around him. How could he make the
physicist see that he wasn't jumping to con-
clusions? "The man I spoke to at the
Foundation a few months ago. Remington. He
asked me if I could duplicate my experiments
on a larger scale to be used as a weapon.
Please, Dr. Bennett, look at the printouts
again. There is a pattern. When I refused to
work with them, they must have taken my
data and somehow adapted it to the natural
environment and—"

"Listen to yourself, Shane. Even with your success in the lab, what you're suggesting isn't possible yet, whether some government agency wishes it were or not. And besides, there hasn't been any further research done on the project since you left the Foundation. The entire thing has been put on hold pending review. It's pretty much dead, Shane. You have nothing to worry about."

With a heavy sigh, Shane moved his book bag to the floor and sat down, the lack of sleep beginning to catch up. "It was just so bizarre. The coincidence. And what the old man said about the lightning."

"Coincidence, Shane. That's all it is."

He sat back in the chair with his eyes closed and rested his head against the wall. "I even called the National Weather Service and got them to admit how odd the conditions were. They said that they'd never seen anything quite like it."

There was chilling silence, and Shane opened his eyes to find Dr. Bennett staring at him.

"You called the National Weather Service about this? I can't believe it. Just when I think you've topped yourself, you pull another one out of your hat. Unbelievable."

Shane was beginning to feel more and more like an idiot under the scornful eye of his former adviser. "Dr. Bennett, I really did think I had reason to suspect—"

Bennett held up his hand to silence him, his eyes closed for emphasis.

"It's all right, Shane. But I think it would be best for both of us to forget that this discussion ever happened."

"I just don't want you to think that I've suddenly gone psycho. Screwy or not, I saw a pattern, and it really scared me. I figured you were the best person to speak to."

"I'm glad you came to me first," Bennett said with the smallest of grins. "Do you realize what wild talk like this could do to your academic career?"

Shane stood and slung his book bag over his shoulder. He wanted to get out of Dr. Bennett's office as quickly as possible, before the man had a chance to commit him. Although he did not think the professor was trying to make him feel like a moron, every second that went by had him imagining himself an even bigger fool.

"Sorry. I guess I let my imagination get the better of me. Maybe I'm more stressed about school than I thought, huh?" He headed for the door. "Thanks for setting me straight. I'll see you, Dr. Bennett."

He had the door open and was just about to step out when Bennett called after him. Shane turned.

"Our conversation," Bennett said to him from behind the desk, "it stays inside this office. You have nothing to worry about."

Shane smiled. "I appreciate it," he said, not wanting to be there any longer and closing the door as quickly as he could. As he hurried down the hallway, he thought about where the biggest rock in Boston might be so he could crawl under it.

*How could I have been so stupid!* he thought as he passed the reception desk. The cute student who had been there the last time he was in the physics department was working with headphones on. She didn't even look up as he passed her desk. That was fine with Shane. He wanted nothing more right now than to be invisible.

Once outside the physics department, he shifted his bag from the left to the right shoulder and noticed the zipper was open. Then he remembered his notes—he'd left the evidence of his insanity on Dr. Bennett's desk. Bennett had seemed pretty cool about keeping the incident between them and would probably dispose of the incriminating paperwork accordingly. But what if he didn't? What if someone else who wasn't so cool got a hold of them? Shane decided to go back.

*I'll just ask for the papers,* Shane thought as he again passed the student, who was so engrossed in whatever she was doing, she still did not notice him. He couldn't see any real harm in asking for them back; if anything, it would prove that he really had come to his senses.

The door was ajar, and Shane was just about to rap lightly when he heard the physicist talking on the phone.

"Yes, he was just in my office," Dr. Bennett said.

Shane froze.

"I really don't think he poses any real threat, but . . . yes, yes he does suspect that his theories were used."

*Oh, Jesus*, Shane thought, his mind afire.

"I don't think so. He did mention talking to someone at the National Weather Service, but said I was the only one he'd broached his suspicions to."

There was silence from inside the office, and Shane slowly let out the breath he was holding.

"I don't appreciate your tone, General. I simply thought it would be in your best interest to know that he suspects."

*The general.* In his head, Shane saw an exaggerated cartoon image of the man he had spoken with months ago, cigarette smoke streaming from his nostrils and ears. Then the image shifted to a recent memory, the look on Bennett's face minutes ago when he'd dismissed Shane's claims as paranoia.

*You son of a bitch*, Shane thought. *You absolute son of a bitch.*

But his anger was quickly replaced by trepidation. If Bennett was going to such great lengths to cover up the truth, it was probably a good idea if Shane did not reveal what he had now overheard. There was no telling what would happen then. He turned and practically ran past the front desk and out the door. His heart was racing, and he felt horribly nauseated.

He had to get hold of himself, had to think this through clearly.

He had to tell somebody.

But whom could he trust?

And . . . the biggest question of all . . . now that he had admitted to Bennett that he knew the truth—that some covert agency in the U.S. government had used his research to massacre civilians—what would that agency do about it? How far would they go to protect their secret?

The entire walk back to his apartment, Shane glanced anxiously over his shoulder.

Something was chasing Iris Green.

She didn't know what it was—or where she was, for that matter—but she could hear it shrieking and roaring as it pursued her. Iris whirled around to confront it but came to the disturbing realization that she was in total darkness. *It wasn't this dark before.*

The attacker was closer; its unearthly screams and mournful moans grew steadily louder. *It must be huge,* she thought as the cool ground beneath her bare feet began to vibrate and shake. *It must be really huge.*

The sounds were deafening. She raised the weapon that she discovered in her hand and aimed it in the direction she believed the threat was coming from.

*I'll shoot,* was what she wanted to say, but Iris found herself suddenly speechless, the air stolen from her lungs. She pulled the trigger in rapid succession, but the hammer fell on empty chambers every time.

*No bullets . . . no breath,* she thought as she allowed the gun to fall from her grip. *Totally useless.* Iris watched the gun tumble slowly toward the ground as if through water and wished it were possible to breathe again.

In that moment of distraction, her pursuer snatched her from the ground and twisted her in the air. It shrieked in manic glee as it spun her around faster and faster. She wanted to scream but couldn't. Her hollow lungs burned.

Somehow she could still see her gun, still falling through the inky darkness, and she wondered if it would ever reach the ground. As if on cue, the weapon landed below her, and the darkness exploded into millions of razor-sharp shards.

Daggers of darkness drawn toward her spinning, breathless form. Razor-sharp shadow knives piercing her body with the sound of breaking glass.

The sound of breaking glass echoed in her ears as Iris sat up with a gasp and surveyed her surrounding. For a brief moment she forgot that she wasn't on assignment, that she was back in her Washington one-bedroom apartment.

Her eye went to the alarm clock and she saw it was a little after nine in the morning. She ran a hand through her thicket of bedhair, then froze when she heard the unmistakable sound of glass being swept up somewhere in the apartment.

Silently, Iris removed the Smith & Wesson 3954 from the top drawer of her nightstand and climbed out of bed. The nine-millimeter had a full clip—she had cleaned and loaded it only a few days before—and now she carefully moved toward her bedroom door. Drawn by the ongoing sounds of the cleanup, she pulled the door open. The noise was coming from the direction of the kitchen.

Was there anyone who had a right to be in her home? She didn't have a cleaning service. Her mother lived in Ohio, so there wasn't a chance of her popping by for some maternal tidying, and it certainly wasn't a significant other. She hadn't had a date since becoming involved with the Department.

Weapon pointed toward the ceiling, Iris padded down the hallway, senses alert for potential danger. The entrance to the kitchen was just a few feet away on the left. She took a deep breath and quickened her pace. She positioned herself in the doorway, legs spread apart, and leveled her Smith & Wesson at the intruder squatting by the open refrigerator door. "Move and I'll shoot," she said, voice clipped, cold.

The squatting figure was in the process of sweeping up the glass and juice of a broken pickle jar. He stopped, dustpan and brush in hand, and slowly turned to face her. It was Tarker Ames.

"I'll leave you the money for a new jar a' gherkins, ma'am, but please don't shoot," he said with the faint hint of a southern drawl.

Tarker stood and held out the shattered pieces of glass in the dustpan. "Barrel?"

Iris slowly lowered her weapon, stomach fluttering with unease. A stray thought went through her head. Had the Department sent him to eliminate her? She pushed the idea away, pretending to herself that it had been a joke. But the unease lingered. She pointed to a closed pantry door on the other side of the kitchen. "In there. What are you doing here?"

Her partner strolled to the door and opened it. He swept the pieces of glass, pickles, and juice into the trash can. "Looking for some milk for my coffee. I didn't see the jar." He stepped out of the pantry and shut the door behind him. "Sorry to say but I think I just destroyed the only still edible thing in the refrigerator."

She leaned against the door frame. "That

still doesn't tell me why you're here. Not to mention how you got in. I'm positive I didn't leave the door unlocked."

Tarker smiled again as he went to the kitchen sink and ran a blue rag beneath the water. Ringing the excess from it, he walked back to where the pickle jar had broken. "Wetwork isn't the only thing I'm good at, Green. You might want to invest in some new locks. The ones on there now are pathetic. As to why I'm here, well, we have an assignment," he said as he wiped up all traces of spilled juice from the kitchen floor.

Gun still in hand, Iris crossed her arms over her chest. "I'm still on administrative. Can't do it."

Back at the sink, Tarker rinsed the rag under the faucet. "That's been canceled. Remington says as far as he's concerned, you're back on the job. We leave for Boston within the hour."

Not certain how to react, Iris remained in the doorway. Since her meeting with the general, she had not worked, and to be perfectly honest, she was getting bored. But was she bored enough to continue to work with a brutal lunatic like Ames?

At the kitchen table Tarker snatched up a pair of coffee cups bearing the logo of a diner down the street, and handed one to her. "Black, just how you like it."

Accepting the coffee, she studied the

man's face. Iris had no idea if he had been told the truth about why she had been put on leave, but she was not about to bring it up. She peeled the cover from the coffee cup and took a careful sip. "I'm surprised he wants me back on the job."

Tarker was drinking his coffee black as well, though from his expression it wasn't his favorite thing to do. "You're good, Agent Green, very good. You're just new to the way things work in Black Box. You'll learn; we all do."

As they faced each other there in her kitchen, Iris realized with some surprise that she had already decided to return to work— but with a new attitude. She and Tarker Ames would function as agents of the Department—Black Box, as he and many others called it—obeying every law to the letter. No longer would she countenance the way Tarker used the job to indulge in brutality for his own amusement. Maybe Black Box didn't mind his being a sadistic bastard, but Iris did. From now on, she would do everything she could to restrain her partner, to balance out the working relationship. It occurred to her that the Department might have partnered her with him for just that purpose, but she ignored the thought. Whatever it was, she was stuck with the arrangement for now, and she'd deal with that.

"Give me ten minutes for a quick shower

and I'll be ready to go," she said, and started for the bathroom.

"Y'know, Green, I almost hate to say it, but I really have missed working with you these past few weeks," Tarker said.

Iris stopped and slowly turned to face him. She said nothing.

"We really complement each other, I think. You're like a yin to my yang. Am I making sense here?"

He took a drink from his coffee, watching her expectantly. There was an insinuation in the man's tone that Iris did not like. Of course, that was nothing new. But she had to wonder how much he knew. His words seemed to echo her thoughts of only seconds before. It wasn't telepathy, and it sure as hell wasn't intuition—not from a baboon like Ames—so she could only imagine General Remington had said *something* to him. Not that she cared, really, if he knew his actions appalled her. That wasn't the bit of truth she wanted to hide from him. No. But there was one thing she could not afford for him to know.

Iris was afraid of Tarker Ames.

His eyes told her nothing.

"I guess I should say thank you, Agent Ames. That's very flattering." She turned back toward the bathroom and felt his eyes on the back of her head, cold upon her neck. "Make yourself at home, I'll only be a few minutes."

"I'll be waiting . . . partner," she heard him say, venom in that last word.

Iris shut the bathroom door and locked it. Just in case.

"Who are you holding for again?" the *Boston Globe* receptionist asked on the other end of the line.

Shane paced the floor of his apartment, the phone held tightly to his ear. "Mary Jane Mulholland," he said, exasperation growing. "Is she there? I've been on hold for close to ten minutes."

"Just a minute, I'll check," the voice said.

An instrumental version of "Smoke on the Water" started to play, and Shane felt as though he was going to start screaming and never stop. He still could not wrap his brain around the fact that Carl Bennett was part of it.

*And I bought his smoke screen*, he thought as he paced. *He lied through his teeth, and I just bought the whole thing*. But at least Bennett had no idea Shane had come back to the office, had overheard him talking to Remington.

There was a click on the phone, and the music stopped.

"Ms. Mulholland?" Shane asked. "This is Shane Monroe—"

"Who are you holding for?" came that infernal voice again.

Shane slammed his sneakered foot down on the floor. "I'm holding for Mary Jane Mulholland. She's a reporter there."

There was another slight pause, then, "Please hold."

As he had raced back from his disturbing encounter in the physics department, Shane had frantically tried to think of someone who might be able to help him figure out what to do about his predicament. His mother was the first person he had thought of, but he had dismissed that thought immediately. What Dr. Bennett was involved with was *wrong*, pure and simple. But it was also confidential, and it involved the government. Shane was not stupid. He knew that if the people Bennett worked for knew that he planned to blow the whistle, things could get ugly. Even dangerous. His mother would realize that as well and, though she would undoubtedly share his horror and disgust at what they'd done, she might advise him to keep silent.

He couldn't do that.

But he also did not want to pull his mother into something that could be dangerous. He had to find someone else. Someone who wouldn't think he was crazy and who could get the information out to as many people as possible.

Shane had met M. J. Mulholland while she was doing a story on Massachusetts public school students with genius I.Q.s for the

*Globe*'s Sunday supplement. It was basically a fluff piece to show that intelligence could be cultivated within the public school system. She'd come to interview Shane while he was setting up his science fair project at Framingham High. He had built solar batteries and rigged them up to power some kitchen appliances that he borrowed from his house. He and M. J. had hit it off right away and had stayed in contact via e-mail for his last two years of high school. Although they hadn't spoken much since he'd started college, she had always said that if he ever came across something that he felt was truly newsworthy to give her a call. Shane figured a conspiracy that included weather control and hundreds of dead innocents fit the bill.

Another grating bit of electronic music was beginning when it was abruptly cut off. Shane was prepared to tell the receptionist yet again for whom he was holding, but a series of loud clicks made him wince and pull the phone from his ear. Had he been cut off? Carefully he brought the receiver back up and listened. There was silence, but Shane knew someone was there. He thought he could hear breathing.

"Hello?" he asked. "M. J., is that you?"

More clicks. In the background he heard static and garbled voices, like someone had a police radio on. Outside his window, a car horn honked.

He heard it over the phone.

Heart hammering in his chest, paranoia spreading through him like wildfire, Shane went to the window and looked out through the plastic mini blinds. On the street, a black sedan had just cut off a yellow Volkswagen Beetle to pull up in front of another dark vehicle with an odd antenna protruding from the roof.

And for the first time, Shane realized that up until now, he had not really been afraid. Anxious, yes, but not afraid. This, though, this was fear.

"Hello?" Shane said, feeling like a child and hating them for that. Still no answer. "Shit," he whispered. He hung up the phone with the push of a button and tossed it on the bed. Then he ran for the door, suspicions running rampant through his head. He had overheard Dr. Bennett talking to Remington and he had no doubt that was who had sent the ominous vehicles down on the street. What they might do to him he had no idea. If they just planned to bully him or even arrest him for treason or something, well, he imagined he could live with that.

But if their intentions were more sinister? He couldn't be here. He couldn't just let them walk in and take him, not until he knew who they *really* were and what they wanted from him.

Shane threw the door open wide, sprinted

down the hall to the stairs, then hurried down two flights to the foyer. As he reached the bottom, Shane eyed the front door. They'd probably have someone watching for him. Surreptitiously as possible, he slid along the wall to a door behind the stairwell. There were bikes stacked in front of it, but he easily moved them aside and opened the door to the basement. Carefully and quietly he closed the door behind him and descended into the cellar's dank coolness. There was a basement entrance—Shane had used it when he'd moved in, to bring in furniture that wouldn't fit through the front—he just hoped his visitors hadn't had time to figure that out.

In the basement he pulled a chain that turned on a single lightbulb. His eyes scanned the piles of boxes, old furniture, and assorted clutter that must have taken many, many years to accumulate. The air was thick with the smell of moisture and heating oil. Carefully he navigated past the furnace to a large wooden door. From above came the creaking of the lobby floor as multiple sets of feet crossed to the stairwell and started up.

Shane fiddled with the bolt and chain that locked the door and pulled it toward him. The door's hinges whined in protest. He froze. Listening. Had they left somebody in the lobby to watch the door? Were they now checking out the foyer, searching for the source of the sound?

He stepped into the dark, cobweb-filled area and pushed open the two metal doors of the bulkhead that would take him outside. He looked up and down the alley before climbing out. A row of large, green barrels partially concealed his exit as he quietly closed the doors after him. The dark sedans had pulled up out in front, so he headed in the opposite direction, to the parking lot behind his apartment building. He crossed the lot and a section of lawn behind it, and then started up one of the roads that went through campus. Shane took a series of deep breaths and tried to look as inconspicuous as possible. He slowed his pace, just another student on his way to class.

There were no shouts of, *Stop! Federal officer.* No screech of tires as they pulled into traffic in pursuit of him. No storm troopers.

Now all he had to figure out was where to go from here.

# CHAPTER SEVEN

*"We can illuminate the sky and deprive the ocean of its terrors!"*
—Nikola Tesla

Shane slunk onto the Hazeltine campus using one of the many side paths that led in from the surrounding city streets. He tried to remain inconspicuous, though he gazed all around him suspiciously, searching for anything that seemed out of the ordinary.

He stopped near the bronze bust of Jeremy Hazeltine, the school's founder, and glanced toward Everson Hall. Today was Wednesday, and he knew Geoff had Foundations of American Literature there. It was lunchtime, and the campus was humming with activity. Class had just let out, and students and faculty streamed from the building into the cool, hazy sunshine.

*Spring's finally here*, Shane thought. *Perfect freakin' timing.*

Two men in dark suits were standing near the stairs to Everson, waiting for something—

for somebody. Shane moved out of their line
of sight and waited.

He tensed when Geoff ambled out of the
building, stopped, and began fishing through
his backpack. The two suits were suddenly
moving toward him. Shane stepped from his
hiding place and was about to yell to his
friend when Geoff's supposed attackers walked
right past him and into Everson Hall, laughing and joking. Geoff pulled a pack of gum
from his bag and stuck a piece in his mouth.
Then he continued on his way, cutting diago-
nally across campus, away from Shane.

*Heading to Spud's for lunch*, he thought.

Cautiously, he began to follow. He could
never figure out why Geoff continued to live
in the dorms when he spent most of every day
at Spud's apartment. He'd once suggested that
the two guys move in together, but they'd just
laughed and said that they would eventually
kill each other.

Shane kept his distance, alert for anything
suspicious. He watched as Geoff turned into
the alley that would lead to the back entrance
of Spud's basement apartment. They all had
keys. Spud's place was the unofficial clubhouse for their circle—which pretty much
consisted of Geoff, Spud, and himself. There
were other guys—and some girls, too—who
hung around with them from time to time,
but not anyone else regular. The truth, Shane
thought, was that he and his closest friends

were not exactly party animals, and he figured most people found them boring, not to
mention more than a little odd.

Geoff was turning the key in the lock
when Shane rushed up from behind.

"Hey, where've you been?" Geoff asked
with a smile as he pushed open the olive
green metal door. "We called last night to see
if you wanted to get pizza, but . . . hey, what
are you doin', man?" Geoff protested as Shane
shoved him into the dark, cool quiet of the
basement.

"We have to get out of the open," Shane
whispered breathlessly. He made sure the
door was closed and locked, then turned back
to his friend.

"Are you very stoned?" Geoff asked, the
hint of a smile on his face.

Shane sighed, closed his eyes, and felt the
jackhammer pound of his heart begin to slow.
It was a relief just to be with someone he
knew he could trust.

"Shane?" Geoff asked, concern in his
voice now.

He opened his eyes, and the words spilled
from his mouth in a torrent of fear. "I
don't . . . I don't know what to do, Geoff. I
think I'm in trouble. I mean really and truly
screwed." He took two deep breaths trying to
stay calm. "It has to do with the research I did
at the Foundation. And why I quit. They
wanted to try to use what I did for . . ."

His mind was suddenly filled with images of Geoff being interrogated. "Damn it, I shouldn't even be telling you this."

Geoff's face wrinkled up with confusion. "I don't get it. I mean, what did you . . . no, look. Even if you're right, you haven't worked at the Foundation for six months. I mean, why would anyone come after you now?"

Shane rubbed his face with his hands. "Bennett. I told Dr. Bennett what I suspected and . . . he was in on it. I went back for some papers I left in his office and overheard him on the phone."

The expression on Geoff's face was dubious at best. Shane didn't know if his friend thought it was all some big joke or that Shane had lost his mind, but it was obvious Geoff did not believe him.

"I'm not crazy," he said grimly. And then he told Geoff the whole thing as quickly as he could. What he had done in the lab, what he had seen on the news, his conversation with Dr. Bennett, the clicking on his phone, the dark cars at his apartment . . .

Geoff shook his head. "Man, this sounds really nuts—"

Shane pushed off the wall. "Listen, I researched this on the Net and I know—"

"I believe you, Shane," Geoff said, laying a strong hand on his shoulder. "This is way too crazy to be coming out of your unimaginative brain."

The teasing fell flat. There was no time for it.

"Let's give Spud the scoop. Maybe the three of us can figure out what you should do." Geoff moved across the basement past the washer and dryer, and approached the door marked 1B. "I think there might even be a lawyer or two in his family."

Shane hesitated. "I don't know. This might be a mistake. I don't want to put you guys in any danger—"

"Shut up, Monroe. We're friends. We're already in this together. Besides, I'm not one of those conspiracy freaks. The IRS may screw people every day and, sure, politicians are pretty much universally corrupt, but the American government does not go around bumping off citizens just to get their kicks." He slipped his key in the lock and opened the door. "Besides, don't we always pull your skinny ass out of the fire?"

A faint smile cracked Geoff's painfully serious features, and Shane followed him. Geoff and Spud were the closest to brothers he'd ever had, but until now, he hadn't truly understood what that bond meant.

The door opened into a small kitchen area with the living room just beyond. The lights were off and the shades pulled, but a movie played on the big-screen TV. They could see Spud in his usual place, the La-Z-Boy recliner in front of the television. The volume was turned down low, and Shane glanced at the screen to see if he could figure out what Spud was watching. Face framed with a clunky pair of glasses, Gene Hackman was in the midst of talking to somebody.

"I thought you had moved on from your Coppola phase," Geoff said as he strolled into the living area. "Didn't you just watch *The Conversation*?"

"*Enemy of the State*," Shane said. He still stood in the kitchen.

Geoff looked back with a confused expression. "What?"

"Will Smith and Gene Hackman?" Shane pointed to the set just as Will Smith came into the scene. "It's *Enemy of the State*."

Geoff looked back at the screen. "Oh, yeah." Then he slapped Spud's arm. "Hey, wake up, the genius has a problem, and we need to—"

A warehouse on the small screen suddenly exploded, filling the darkened room with a pulsing light. Geoff stopped talking and leaned closer to Spud as a chill like spiders with icy legs crawled up his spine.

"Hey." Geoff shook his friend's shoulder.

Spud slumped over, head lolling obscenely to the side.

"Spud," Geoff whispered. "Holy shit, Shane. There's blood." He looked up, terror in his eyes. "There's blood on the goddamn chair!" he called as he slapped his friend's cheeks. "This better not be a joke, man! Be the worst timing, Spud. Spud . . . oh, Jesus, let it be a joke."

Then Geoff swiveled to stare at Shane, eyes wide and haunted. "He's . . . he's cold."

Shane had been frozen, paralyzed with shock, but now he went to join Geoff and saw the blood for himself. It had run down the back of the chair to the seat, and was even seeping into the carpet underneath.

"Oh, no," he said, shaking his head. "No way." But his words were empty, his denial useless. Spud was dead.

"Step away from him, slowly," a voice said from behind them, from the doorway into the back bedroom.

Geoff let out a yelp of surprise, and Shane slowly glanced around to see a man pointing a handgun at them, a silencer screwed onto its barrel. *He was here all the time*, Shane thought. *Probably watching the movie. Watching the damn movie with Spud dead right there, just waiting . . . waiting for me to show*. The gunman was big, stocky, probably mid to late forties and dressed in dark jeans and a loosely hanging brown leather jacket. Shane knew with a sick certainty that this wasn't some botched robbery or home invasion.

"Who the hell are you?" Geoff screamed as he began to move around Spud's chair, chest puffed out with machismo. "You killed him, didn't you? You killed my friend!"

Shane grabbed Geoff's arm. "No, Geoff," he said, a little disturbed by the tremor he heard in his own voice. "He . . . he's got a gun. *Don't.*"

The man straightened his arm and pointed the weapon squarely at Geoff. "Listen to your friend and nobody'll get hurt."

"Is that what you told him?" Shane spat, motioning with his chin toward Spud's body in the chair.

"He didn't do what he was told, and it cost him. The choice was his. Hopefully you two will be smarter." With his free hand the man fished a cell phone from the inside pocket of his coat. He hit a button and put the phone to his ear, the gun still aimed at them.

"Who is this guy, Shane?" Geoff asked in a frantic whisper.

"I . . . I think he's after me," Shane said, hating to admit that he'd brought this catastrophe to his friends.

The man spoke into his cell phone. "This is Bloodhound Five. Subject apprehended. I need a retrieval and clean up team immediately."

Shane bristled at the words that followed.

"Yes, a clean up team. There was an unavoidable incident. One casualty."

Disgust blossomed across Geoff's features. "Unavoidable incident?" he said, his voice climbing. "You shot him in his freakin' La-Z-Boy!"

"C'mon, Geoff. Don't! It'll be all right."
Shane held on to his arm and squeezed. He
wished he could believe his own words.

Geoff suddenly turned on him, his eyes
filled with tears of rage. "What the hell do
you know? From what you said, this is all
happening 'cause of you!" He pulled his arm
violently away from Shane's grasp. "Get your
hands offa me!"

Shane said nothing, the horror and grief of
the scene that unfolded around him too much
for him to bear. Then Geoff pushed him.
Shane stumbled backward, nearly falling into
the television.

The man with the gun moved closer.
"Hey! Knock it off!"

Geoff dove at Shane, and they fell to the
floor in a thrashing heap.

"What are you doing?" Shane screamed as
his friend's fists rained down on him.

Geoff muttered incoherently as he continued to throw punches.

"Stop it, Geoff! Please! You're going to—"

One of Geoff's punches landed on his
chin, and Shane's head snapped violently to
the right. Shane could see the gunman moving toward them as he struggled to turn away
from the rain of blows. Geoff suddenly leaned
into him, his face a twisted grimace, his eyes
wild. Shane thought he was going to bite him,
but instead, Geoff whispered quite sanely,
"Get ready to run."

The gunman loomed over them. He snarled and reached for the back of Geoff's neck. Shane heard the sound of tearing material as the man got a handful of Geoff's football jersey and hauled him up.

"Get off him," the gunman bellowed.

Geoff threw his weight backward, slamming the back of his skull viciously into the man's face. With a sickening crunch of breaking bone, blood exploded from the gunman's nose and streamed down his stunned face.

"Geoff, come on!" Shane roared at him as he scrambled to his feet.

"Get outta here!" Geoff screamed as he grabbed for the gunman's weapon.

Shane scrambled to his feet as the gun went off with a harmless-sounding little pop that punched a hole in the floor and the beer-stained shag carpet. With a shout, he reached for Geoff, but his friend shoved him away. The gunman swore at them loudly, blood streaming down his chin from his nose, and Geoff ducked low and tackled the killer, and drove him down to the floor.

"Get your ass out of here, Monroe!" Geoff snapped. "I'll be right behind you!"

No way was Shane leaving him behind. He glanced around Spud's apartment, looking for anything to use as a weapon to crack over the son of a bitch's skull. His eyes came to rest on Spud's DVD player. It sat on top of the television. Shane lunged for it.

*Pop! Pop!*

Shane froze at the sound. Two shots from the silenced handgun. He turned and saw twin red holes in Geoff's back, blood spattered on the carpet. He lay across the gunman, still grappling with him, but even as Shane watched he grew weaker. His left leg twitched as if it were somehow separate from the rest of his body. But the rest of him was still intent upon the gunman.

Geoff head butted the gunman again, and then once more. Then he slumped on top of his killer, losing consciousness fast. The gunman was dazed, but already his eyelids were fluttering and he was beginning to look around, trying to focus on Shane again.

"Geoff," Shane whispered.

*Get your ass out of here, Monroe! I'll be right behind you!*

But he wouldn't be. Geoff would not be right behind him, and neither would Spud. They were both dead. Through his grief came a surge of hatred for the man with the gun, an animal rage that made him want to tear the guy apart. He promised himself, in that moment, that he would see the man pay for what he'd done. But in order to do that, he had to stay alive.

He had to run.

Shane bolted for the door and grabbed the knob, his hand, slick with sweat, sliding on the metal. Behind him he heard the gunman groan as he began to slide out from beneath Geoff's body. Or at least, that was what Shane imagined he was doing. He did not dare turn around. Again he heard the pop of the silenced weapon, and a smoldering hole appeared in the plaster to the right of the door frame.

*They're going to pay for this,* his fevered mind raged. *They are going to pay.*

He got a grip, yanked open the door, and took off. He ran as if the devil himself were giving chase.

Spud sat in the recliner in perpetual darkness and shook his head with mock disgust. "What the hell are you hiding from, Monroe? Go back to your room, invent a death ray, and we'll all get pizza."

Shane stood before his friend. The room was so dark, he couldn't make out anything but Spud sitting in what he often referred to as his throne of power. "They're after me, Spud. I have to hide or they'll take me away."

Spud nodded his shaggy head and studied the darkness that surrounded them. "No death ray or pizza, I guess. Too bad. You would have made a good death ray."

His friend looked up at him from the chair, and Shane could see blood begin to drip from his hairline down his face. Spud didn't seem to notice.

"You're bleeding," Shane said.

For the first time, Shane noticed Geoff standing there beside Spud's throne. "Yep, Monroe's right. You are most definitely bleeding."

Shane was speechless as he stared at the front of Geoff's New England Patriots shirt. There were two dark holes near the heart and stomach, and the blue of the material was stained a deep, dark maroon.

Spud dabbed at the leakage on his face and looked at his fingertips. He reached behind his head, felt around, and brought his hand back to look at it. His face twisted with disgust. "I think somebody shot me in the head," he said with disbelief.

"Looks like," Geoff said. Then he glanced down at his own chest, examining the holes in his shirt. "Would you look at this? They got me, too."

Emotions clashed in Shane's heart and mind. His grief tore through him and he wanted to help them, but knew he had to run, he had to get away or he would be hurt as well. Frantic, he looked around for a place to hide, but the darkness was impenetrable.

"I'm so sorry," he whispered to the shadows, which seemed to be growing darker, if that was possible. His friends were being swallowed by the inky black. "Guys?" he called as their shapes became more and more indistinct. "I . . . I never meant for . . . I didn't know . . ."

"S'okay, Monroe," Spud said from the darkness. "But if you get a chance, give 'em one for me."

Geoff was barely there. The bloodstains on the front of his shirt seemed to have grown larger. "Did you hear me, Monroe?" he asked. The swirling black moved about his body like smoke.

Shane said nothing, overwhelmed by guilt and sadness as he watched the ebony shadows claim another friend.

"Get out of here now!" Geoff screamed.

Shane turned and hesitated. "But I don't know where to go. I—"

"Run!" Geoff shrieked a final time.

"Where?" Shane asked the gloom desperately. "What do I do?"

*"You stay right where you are,"* a voice that wasn't Geoff's said, *"and we'll be right up to get you."*

Shane awoke with a spastic start, kicking over a yellow bucket filled with a mop and cleaning supplies. His heart pounded against his rib cage as if trying to break free.

He quickly processed his foreign surroundings and remembered where he had spent the night. In the faint light that streamed in under the door of the custodian's supply closet, Shane could just about make out the bags of ice-melt stacked in the corner with three snow shovels, four cans of white latex paint, and some gallon bottles of industrial-strength floor cleaner.

Slowly he stood, careful not to disrupt any of the other precariously balanced items, and glanced at the illuminated face of his watch. It was a little past six in the morning. He reached for the doorknob and listened for sounds of movement outside.

After fleeing the violence that claimed the lives of his two friends, Shane had wandered the streets, staying close to crowded areas, trying to decide what to do. The fact that the last decision he had made caused the deaths of his friends weighed heavily on him. He knew his brain was on the verge of shorting out when he actually considered turning himself in to his pursuers and facing the consequences. He had to rest.

He had wandered back onto the Hazeltine campus. Desperately he searched for a place where he could close his eyes for a few hours. It was when he saw one of the custodians pushing a cart filled with recyclable cardboard out of a side door that he remembered the underground maintenance tunnels.

As part of a prefreshman program, he had spent the summer after graduating from high school working for the buildings and grounds department on campus and had become familiar with the warren of tunnels and storerooms beneath the college campus, a kind of matrix of subbasements lined with pipes, with ceilings low enough that most people had to stoop slightly to pass through. It had been the perfect place to rest and hide.

Now it was still a couple of hours before the first class of the morning and Shane knew it was unlikely he'd be noticed at this hour. Feeling somewhat refreshed, he casually stepped from the closet, stooped low so as not to bump his head on the pipes above, and walked out of the subbasement. His mind was already beginning to formulate a list of people who might be able to help him, people too important and powerful to be hurt.

He remembered his parents had once been fairly close to longtime Massachusetts Senator Robert Michelson. Shane recalled attending a fund-raiser for the old Democrat on Martha's Vineyard when he was no more than seven years old. They'd had pony rides for the kids. On the stairs that led up to the first floor, Shane quickened his pace. *If I can get in touch with him, I just might survive this insanity*, he thought, suddenly feeling the tiniest bit optimistic.

Just as he was about to reach the landing he heard sounds that told him he wasn't alone. Carefully he peered up to the top of the next flight of stairs to see a *Boston Herald* deliveryman filling up a coin machine with morning newspapers. The man whistled as he slammed shut the yellow metal door and gave it a quick pull to make sure it had locked.

Satisfied, he turned and headed for the exit.

Shane hurried up to the newspaper box and felt yesterday's meal of two hot dogs and springwater roil in his belly and threaten to escape as he read one of the smaller headlines on the front page. "College Student Suspected in Two Deaths." Somehow they had managed to get a photograph of him with Spud and Geoff, and the sight of that picture nearly paralyzed him.

With a trembling hand he pulled fifty cents from his pocket, dropped it into the machine, and removed a paper. His eyes skimmed the story, wincing with every inaccuracy. He wanted to curl into a ball and die. It was bad enough that he had a government agency after him, now he had to worry about the Boston police as well. He couldn't stand it anymore. He had to end this.

Shane tossed the newspaper in a nearby barrel and headed outside. He climbed the stairs into a garden area at the back of the campus. He would find a pay phone, call Senator Michelson's office, and arrange to turn himself in. Then hopefully whoever was after him would back off, and this mess could be sorted out.

He walked around Henrickson Hall into the front quad and found it overrun with uniformed police officers. Some were talking with students while others stood surveying the campus and sipping coffee.

Shane willed himself invisible and turned around. He couldn't risk being taken in by them. Then he'd never have a chance to speak with the senator.

He had to find a phone right away.

*C'mon, c'mon,* he wracked his brain, pacing around the garden area. *Where's a safe place with a phone?* It came to him suddenly, and he actually began to think he might soon have something to smile about.

"They'd never think to look for me there," he muttered to himself as he quickened his pace and headed up a path that would take him off-campus.

The brownstone on St. Botolph Street was owned by Hazeltine, and its apartments rented to upperclassmen. Shane stood in the entryway and traced the list of tenants until he found the one he was searching for: R. Junstrom.

He pressed the buzzer, then glanced out though the glass window in the center of the front door as he waited for a response. A police car slowly cruised past. Shane pressed himself against the wall and prayed he had not been noticed. For long minutes he waited, then gradually moved away from the wall and peered outside. They hadn't stopped, but he knew they were looking for him.

Shane pressed the buzzer again, impatient. With his luck, Junstrom had probably already left for class. He was just about to ring a third time when he heard the electronic click of the speaker.

"Yeah?" Ray Junstrom said.

Shane leaned toward the speaker. "Ray? It's Shane. I need your help. I . . . I don't know what you've heard, but I can explain everything. Please . . ." His words trailed off. He did not know what else to say, and so he waited, counting the passing of seconds, before the speaker crackled again.

"Come on up," Ray replied.

The door buzzed, and the lock was released. Shane entered the too-warm foyer and started up the stairs to Ray's second-floor apartment. The door was slightly ajar.

"Ray?" Shane called as he pushed it open and peered inside.

In sweatpants and a T-shirt, hair tousled from sleep, Ray Junstrom motioned for him to enter as he finished up a call and placed his portable telephone back into its charger. "So what the hell is going on, Monroe?" he asked as Shane closed the door and came into the living room. "I mean, the police are after you, for Christ's sake."

Suddenly feeling exhausted, Shane looked for a place to sit. He dropped down on an ottoman and ran both hands through his hair. "The less you know, the better. I just have to use your phone and then I'll be out of here."

"Oh, no. If I'm going to be sticking my

neck out for you, I sure as hell want an explanation," Ray said. The whistle of a teakettle sounded from the kitchen, and he turned toward the room. "Do you want tea?"

"Sure, that'd be great."

Ray took two mugs from the cabinet and placed them on the counter. "So? . . ." He put a tea bag in each mug and turned to face him. "Explain."

Shane moved to a chair at the small kitchen table. "It has to do with a project I was working on at the Foundation."

"Force Majeure." Ray crossed his arms and smirked. "You do realize I've been assigned to that project now?"

Shane nodded. "They wanted me to help them make the project into a weapon, and I turned them down."

Ray grabbed the kettle from the stove and filled the mugs with boiling water. "So there's your first mistake. Why'd you turn them down?"

"I didn't want something that I created to be used for killing people. I couldn't live with that."

Ray came to the table with the two mugs of steaming tea and put one down in front of Shane. "See, that's where you and I differ. I look at it as a job, a way to make some serious money and maybe a little notoriety."

"Thanks," Shane said as he pulled the tea closer. Steam swirled above the cup, but

Shane could only watch it, no interest in the tea itself. Junstrom wasn't his friend, not really, but this was the first time he had felt even remotely safe since the previous day, and now a kind of numbness swept through him. "Maybe it would have been better that way. But I couldn't do it—it scared me. That's why I left. Then I saw this news story and I . . . I put some things together and I realized they'd continued the work without me. And succeeded." He looked up to see that his former rival was grinning. "You think I'm nuts, don't you?"

Ray shook his head. "No, it's not that. They came to me after you left and asked me to duplicate your research in the real world, to figure out a way to manufacture man-made tornadoes outside the laboratory environment."

That horrible sinking feeling in the pit of his stomach returned. Shane stared down at the tea again, watching the swirls. "Please tell me you turned them down."

Ray brought his steaming mug to his mouth. "You'd like that, wouldn't you, Monroe?" he said with a hint of petulance. "You quit and a multibillion-dollar science project gets scrapped. It could never be completed without you. Talk about ego." He took a sip of his tea and set the mug down on the table. "I didn't even think twice before I said yes. On top of all the other benefits to my future, it gave me a chance to be on top for once."

Shane was stunned. "These people are dangerous, Ray. They killed Geoff and Spud without . . ."

Ray wrapped both hands around the mug, not listening. Except for the faint hum of the refrigerator, the kitchen was eerily quiet. "With you gone and then Bennett asking if I'd be interested in working at the Foundation—it was like I'd won the lottery. I was always the whiz kid, the boy genius who made all the papers, got all the attention, had my town—hell, the entire state—predicting I'd make my mark. Do you know what it's like to live in somebody's shadow, Monroe? I never did until I came to Hazeltine. It's awful."

"I . . . I don't know what to say," Shane stammered.

Ray laughed as he stood up and took both mugs to the sink. "I actually started to enjoy myself for a while. With you in a different major, you weren't much of a threat to me anymore. I even started to like you in a screwed-up kind of way." He poured the remains down the drain and left the cups in the sink. He then turned his attention back to Shane. "I should have known it couldn't last forever."

Shane stood. "I'm sorry to have bothered you, Ray. If you'll just let me use your phone, I'll be out of here as soon as—"

"Bennett said I was making excellent progress augmenting your research, that the people funding the project were supposedly very impressed."

Shane held up a hand to silence him. "I don't want to hear anymore. Just let me make my call and I'll get out."

Ray sneered and continued. "The test runs were mostly successful, just a few bugs to work out here and there, although they did lose a few agents in the field because of the unstable conditions."

"Damn it, Ray, just let me use your phone!"

But Ray wasn't listening. His face was flushed with animosity. "As soon as Dr. Bennett told me about the test runs, I went right to work on the bugs. And I would have worked them out. I would have. But Dr. Bennett didn't have any faith in me, Shane. He doesn't think I can figure it out, but he believes that you can. The jerk actually told me the Foundation did not need me anymore because they were going to get *you* back. Can you imagine the gall?"

"They can go to hell," Shane muttered, just as much to himself as to Ray. He stormed into the living room and picked up the phone. He hit the numbers for information and gazed into the kitchen while he waited for an answer.

Ray watched him with an odd smile.

The operator came on, and Shane asked for the number for Senator Michelson's office. "Ray, do you have a pen?"

He didn't move, just continued to grin. Shane swore at him, did his best to memorize the number, and hung up.

"It's funny," Ray said almost dreamily, "I've never been so desperate to have somebody out my life. You're a distraction, and I can't wait to have you gone."

An image flashed through Shane's head: Ray hanging up the phone as he entered the apartment. "What did you do?" Shane asked, stomach churning. "What did you do, Ray?"

Junstrom just laughed. Shane could no longer control himself. He lunged at Ray, grabbed his shirtfront, and slammed him back against the kitchen counter. "What have you done?" he yelled.

"I removed an obstacle from my path," Ray said calmly.

"You son of a bitch," Shane spat as he slammed his fist into Ray's face once, twice, a third time. Ray slumped to the kitchen floor. Shane stepped back, shaking the pain from his hand. His knuckles were raw and swollen.

Blood dribbled from the corner of Ray's mouth as he sat, legs splayed on the floor. He shook his head vigorously in an attempt to clear it and slowly began to stand.

"Didn't think you had it in you, Monroe." He dabbed at the bleeding corner of his mouth and turned back toward the sink. He ran the cold water on a piece of paper towel and placed it against his lips.

The squealing of brakes and the crackling sound of a police scanner carried up from the street below.

"That would be them, I imagine. They're certainly hot for you, Shane."

Primitive flight instincts kicked into overdrive. Shane snarled at the man who had betrayed him and bolted for the door.

"Sorry it had to end like this," Ray called as Shane threw open the door and fled down the hall. "But you have no idea what it's like being second best."

# CHAPTER EIGHT

*"So long as men meet in battle, there will be bloodshed."*

— Nikola Tesla

Carl Bennett climbed out of the backseat of the dark sedan and followed the two federal agents as they approached the apartment building on St. Botolph Street.

"Agent Green, maybe I can talk to him," he suggested to the woman, "get him to turn himself in before this gets out of hand."

She turned slightly and spoke while still walking. "We considered it. But remember, Shane Monroe is suspected of murdering two people. We don't want to put you in any danger."

Dr. Bennett frowned. It seemed incredibly wrong. How was it possible that Shane was a suspect in the cold-blooded killing of his best friends? Bennett had known the boy for years and had never seen even a hint of violence. Although he was pretty agitated during their last meeting. Still, something wasn't right.

"Are you sure this isn't some kind of a mistake? I can't imagine Shane . . ."

The other agent, a man called Ames, stopped short and turned to him. For one who looked so down-on-the-farm wholesome, there was an air about him that filled Bennett with unease.

"Dr. Bennett, we have witnesses who saw Shane running from the apartment where the murders occurred. You yourself contacted our organization and said that he'd been acting strangely."

Bennett nodded reluctantly. "But murder . . . I just don't think—"

"Now isn't the time for you to be thinking, Dr. Bennett. The Department—who funds your research, I might add—needs Shane Monroe whether he's guilty or not. Our job right now is to keep him out of police custody and bring him in unharmed. If we can grab him before the local authorities do, we'll be doing the kid the biggest favor of his life."

Bennett's stomach tightened. He cursed the day he had ever heard of General Maxwell Remington and the unlimited budget he'd offered for research. Silently he watched as the two agents waded in among the uniformed Boston policemen and flashed their government I.D.s. The local cops began to back away. It amazed him how much power the Department had.

*Who do they really work for?* he wondered. *Who do I work for? CIA? NSA? Or do they even really have a name?* With a frightened certainty, Bennett realized that he didn't want to know, that the less he knew, the better.

He remembered how worked up Shane had been in his office the previous day. He wished he'd had the courage to tell the boy that he was right. But he couldn't bear to see the disappointment in the boy's eyes or face the wrath of those who kept his projects afloat.

Agent Ames climbed the stairs and entered the building alone as Green led a group of officers around the back. Bennett was reminded of a Bugs Bunny cartoon where the rascally rabbit pretended to be an entire police force while two cartoon gangsters hid inside a gas stove. "He's not in this stove," he heard Bugs say in that distinctive voice. Hilarity ensued.

At the moment it didn't seem at all funny.

Bennett felt a gentle tap on his shoulder and started. He turned and came face-to-face with a very pretty but obviously upset girl. He recognized her as one of his teacher's assistants. She had a foreign name. What was it? He wracked his brain to remember.

"Dr. Bennett? I'm Nevart Arora," she said.

That was it, he thought, giving her a brief smile and a polite nod. "Of course, Nevart," he said. "Is there something—"

"Is it true what they're saying about Shane Monroe? Did he . . . did he shoot those other students?"

Bennett wanted to answer truthfully, to share his suspicions and doubts, to purge some of the guilt, but he knew the consequences. "That's what they're saying," he replied as they both stared helplessly toward the apartment building and the authorities milling about it.

Tarker Ames stepped into the lobby and approached three waiting policemen. "I'll take care of this, gentlemen," he said, holding up his identification and giving each a peek at his official status as he waved them outside. "If I need you I'll give a holler."

He slipped the I.D. back into his coat pocket and inhaled deeply of the old building's fragrant smells. Buildings like this always seemed to be steeped in the smell of living: countless cooked meals, cleaning products, paint, varnish. He found it comforting and closed his eyes briefly. It reminded him of his grandma's house in Alabama. With some effort he pulled himself away from the pleasant memories and began to climb the stairs to Ray Junstrom's apartment.

Tarker knew that Junstrom had been brought onto the Force Majeure project after Monroe walked. From what he'd read in the file, there was a bit of a rivalry between the two Hazeltine brains. He also knew that his superiors were less than pleased with Junstrom's performance, which explained why the Monroe kid had suddenly become such a hot commodity. Well, that and the fact that there were only two ways to keep the kid from spilling his guts, but the more final of the two would be detrimental to Black Box's latest pet project. So Shane would get to live.

Unless he didn't give Tarker any other choice. That was always nice, when he could honestly write it up in his report that way: *The subject left me no other choice.*

The door was partially open, and Tarker drew his gun. Gently he pushed the door wider and aimed the silenced weapon inside. A man stood by a refrigerator, partially obstructed by the open freezer door. The man, who Tarker assumed was Junstrom, slammed the freezer door closed and put an ice-filled dish towel to his bruised jaw. He didn't seem at all fazed by the agent in the doorway aiming a gun.

"About goddamn time you showed. He just left," Ray said, and motioned to the ceiling with his hand. "I think he went up to the roof."

"And you let him go?" Tarker asked coldly. "Weren't you told to keep him here until we arrived?" *People like this never do what they're told,* he thought in disgust.

Ray glared at him, checkered dish towel pressed to his face. "You're lucky you got a call at all—and would you mind pointing that gun someplace else?"

Tarker didn't like this kid at all. He had a cockiness that reminded him of all the people in his life who thought they were better than him.

"Didn't you hear me?" Ray barked. Here was somebody used to giving orders, and having them obeyed. "I said point that thing someplace else."

*Rich little snot*, Tarker thought. He was glad he'd told his partner to stay outside with the boys in blue. Not only had Monroe proved to be a tad more elusive than they expected, but Tarker was sure that Iris would object to the private orders he'd received to clip any pesky loose ends. Nobody liked a loose end, especially the kind that could come back someday and bite you on the ass.

Tarker lowered the weapon and watched as Ray relaxed.

"Thanks," he said, removing the dish towel from his cheek. "Guns make me nervous, especially when they're pointed at me." He attempted to smile, but winced in pain and put the dish towel back.

Tarker flashed his friendliest good-old-boy grin and raised the silenced weapon again. "I know where you're coming from. If you're not careful, these things can kill you." He fired three shots in rapid succession, two to the chest and one to the head.

Tarker stared into the dead face of Ray Junstrom. The lifeless features of the corpse reminded him of his father.

They always did.

Shane squatted against the rooftop skylight and clutched his throbbing shoulder.

He'd raced up the stairs to the roof only to find his escape blocked by a very old, locked wooden door. He had two choices: wait pathetically and be captured, or break down the door. He chose the latter. He'd seen it done in countless movies and it had always looked easy. With the count of three, he hurled his mass against thc door, and nearly broke his shoulder.

On the third try he'd succceded, splintering the frame and pushing the door open onto the tar paper rooftop.

His shoulder ached painfully as he hid himself behind the raised skylight and contemplated his next move. He didn't have much time. He scrambled to the roof's edge and looked out over the side. There was a fire escape, but he knew he would never get past the authorities surrounding the building.

Shane gazed at the rooftop across from him and figured the distance to be at least ten feet. Though the actual Hazeltine campus was well groomed and almost picturesque, the university was in the middle of the city and did not have nearly enough dormitory housing. More than half the students lived in apartments nearby, and those buildings were stacked one on top of the other in an urban sprawl. This was the first time Shane was glad of that.

*Ten feet.* He knew that was his only way out, and he felt his body tense. *All you have to do is jump*, he coaxed himself, *then get to a phone, contact the senator, and it'll be over.*

He took a series of deep breaths as he walked to the other side of the roof to give himself plenty of distance to build up speed. *I can do this*, he repeated over and over.

He *had* to do this.

Shane was just beginning his run when, from the corner of his eye, he glimpsed a man stepping out onto the roof.

"Shane Monroe," the man bellowed. "Federal officer. Stop or I'll shoot."

He didn't stop. The roof's edge loomed closer and closer. He was going to make it.

There was a strange sound, and then he felt something slam into his back. He stumbled and fell, the palms of his hands sliding painfully across the gritty tar-paper roof. He flailed at the painful invaders in the flesh of his back. Whatever had been shot into him had wires attached.

Shane turned on his side to see the man standing over him holding what looked like a remote control. Wires ran from the end of the device to the two projectiles lodged inside him.

Suddenly Shane knew what it was. The man smiled as he pushed a button on the taser. Electricity shot through his body, and Shane jittered with the force of it, somehow both numb and in agony at the same time. His limbs flailed, and then the world began to go black.

# CHAPTER NINE

*"The spark of an induction coil, the glow of an incandescent lamp, the manifestations of the mechanical forces of currents and magnets are no longer beyond our grasp . . ."*

—Nikola Tesla

Pain brought him up from the darkness and back to the world of consciousness. Shane winced as the harsh light of the fluorescent above seared his eyes. In that moment, pain made up his entire being: his muscles, his back, and even his teeth.

He let out a low moan as he rolled over on his side, his body screaming in protest, and gradually sat up. He gently probed the tender area around his jawline, then ran a finger across his teeth. They felt as though the electricity from the taser was still coursing through them.

Shane gazed around the windowless, brightly lit room. It was made of cinder blocks painted a creamy white and contained only the cot on which he sat, a small metal table, and a single chair pushed beneath it. Resting on top of the table was a bottle of springwater.

His mouth tasted of blood; he had bitten the inside of his right cheek. Stiffly, Shane stood and retrieved the water bottle from the table. The plastic seal was still intact, so he figured it would be safe. He twisted off the cap and took a long pull from the bottle, swishing the water around in his mouth to get rid of the foul, coppery taste.

Shane was screwing the top back on when he heard the faint sound of a lock being turned, and the room's only door swung open. He stared at the two people who strode into the room. The woman he didn't recognize, but the man, who shut the door behind them, was the one from the rooftop, the one with the taser.

"Hello, Shane," the woman said. "I see that you've helped yourself to some water. Good. How are you feeling?"

Shane said nothing, choosing to glare at the two instead. Inside, he was all broken glass, shards of emotion. Geoff and Spud were dead; that asshole Junstrom and Dr. Bennett had turned on him. On the outside, he was just numb. He wanted them to know that it wasn't going to be easy now that they had him in custody. Whatever they said, whatever bullshit they tried to hand him, Spud and Geoff were dead.

It wasn't a game.

"Okay, from your silence I guess you're feeling fine. I'm Agent Green, and this is Agent Ames." She gestured to the man who was standing behind her, and he grinned.

Shane felt the hairs on the back of his neck begin to stand. Ames's appearance wasn't menacing in the least, but a creepiness came off him in waves. Shane made eye contact for a moment, trying to read what might be going through his head. But there was nothing in Agent Ames's gaze to decipher; it was like staring into the eyes of some reconstructed dinosaur on display at the museum. Shane looked away. "Agents of what?" he asked.

Green cleared her throat and sat down on the corner of the small table in the room's center. "We're agents of the federal government, Shane, and you're in quite a bit of trouble."

"I haven't done anything," Shane snarled, "except say no to the people you work for."

Agent Ames chuckled, fixing him with those cold, dead eyes. "What about the three people you murdered, Shane? Did you forget about them?"

It was as if he'd been hit by the taser again. Fury drove Shane to his feet. "I didn't kill anyone, and you know it, you . . ." Then his eyes went wide. "Three?"

"Sit down, Shane," Agent Green said calmly. "Let's talk about this."

He sat, still in shock, as Ames strolled closer.

"Maybe you need your memory refreshed, smart boy." He began to count off the supposed victims on his fingers. "Arthur Wilcox Jr. What was it you all called him again? Spam or something." He lifted another finger. "Geoffrey Cotter, from Michigan—an engineering major, wasn't he? First one in his family to attend college." The third finger. "And let's not forget Raymond Junstrom. Hazeltine's number two student. Your competition, the guy who took your job at the Foundation." Ames waved the three fingers in the air front in front of him. "How's the memory doing now, Shane?"

Shane buried his face in his hands, the rational world continuing to crumble around him. "God," he rasped. Then he looked up at the man again, the corners of his eyes scalded by the tears he fought to keep from falling. "I can't believe it. You killed Ray, too. He was on your side."

"Did you hear that, Agent Green? Kid kills his buddies and now wants to lay the blame on us. Doesn't that just beat all?"

Shane watched the female agent's expression and was surprised to see how disturbed she seemed by her partner's words. Agent Green frowned deeply and studied Ames. Then she set her jaw as though putting a mask over her emotions and turned to look at Shane again.

"We have a murder weapon with your

prints on it. You can't get much more incriminating than that. And besides, why would we want to hurt your classmates?"

Her demeanor made him think that she might not be aware of the whole story, that she actually believed he'd killed Spud, Geoff, and Ray. And Shane had seen the way she looked at her partner, the suspicion there. But it could also be just some twisted mind game to force him to play things their way.

Shane stared at her, trying to figure the woman out. "I have a question for you then, Agent Green—for both of you really. If I'm a . . . a murderer, then why am I here with you and not in jail? Can you answer that for me, 'cause I'd really like to know."

The smirk on Agent Ames's face was infuriating. "You've got a smart mouth, kid. I can bet that's the reason why you're in the fix you're in."

"That's enough, Tarker." Agent Green hopped from the table and pulled out the chair from beneath it.

*What the hell kind of name is Tarker?* thought Shane as the woman sat down across from him.

"Look, I want you to listen to me very carefully," she said. "What I'm about to say could affect the rest of your life."

Shane wanted to laugh. As if his life could be affected any more drastically than it already had been.

"The organization that employs us is aware of important scientific advancements that you've made and is very interested in having you continue your work for them. Do you understand what is being offered to you, Shane?"

He nodded. "I know exactly what's being offered, Agent Green. It's a similar offer to one I turned down six months ago—except that was before my friends . . . before you people murdered my friends and put it on me."

"Shane, please—" Agent Green began.

"Is that how you get people? If they say no, you fix it so it looks like they've committed some horrible crime and you'll make it go away if they come to work for you? Is that it, Agent Green?"

The woman glared at him, but beneath that demeanor she seemed flustered by his tirade.

"Look," Shane said, more softly now. "I found out what the government, or your Department, or whatever, wanted to do with the project I was working on, and I walked. That's all. I didn't kill anybody. I think maybe you believe that. But I think *he* knows it."

In a sudden blur of motion, Tarker Ames hit him in the face. He felt a sharp, stinging pain as his lip split and spatters of blood hit the bedsheets. Shane rocked back far enough to bang his head on the wall, but then he was rising up from the bed, no longer caring what Ames could do to him.

Agent Green was way ahead of him. She jumped between them and shoved Ames backward. "That's enough of that. Touch him again and I'll—"

"You'll what, Iris?" The man stared her down with his dead gaze. "You'll report me to Remington again? Hell of a lot of good it did you last time."

As he wiped blood from his swollen mouth, Shane watched and listened. In the friction between the two agents, he saw opportunity.

"Remington," he said. "That's the guy I met before. You can tell him from me that I'm still not interested. In fact, tell him I said he can go to hell. You want to try to make it out that I killed my friends? Fine. Let's talk about that in court. We'll see what else I have to tell them that they'll find interesting. I'll never work for you people. Never. Got that?"

Agent Green went to the door and rapped twice with her knuckles. "We're done here, Agent Ames."

As the door swung open, Shane saw armed men standing guard outside. Ames walked backward toward the open door, never taking his eyes off him. "For now. Funny though, that never stuff. I remember another science hotshot some years back. Maybe you know him?"

Shane was silent as his tongue moved over the swollen flesh of his lip.

"His name was Don Monroe," Ames growled. "Ring any bells, Shane?"

At the mention of his father, Shane froze. "What do you know about him?"

Just outside the room, Tarker shrugged. "Nothin' much other than he was full of lots of tough talk too. But eventually he saw the error of his ways and developed a mutually beneficial relationship with my employer, that's all."

"What are you talking about?" Shane snapped, throat going dry. He shook his head, pushing away this impossible thing. "You're lying. My father would never have worked for them."

The door slowly closed behind the two agents.

"Wait!" he called after them. "Tell me what you mean by that!"

The lock clicked, and Shane fell back onto the cot, Ames's words echoing in his head like thunder. "He would never have worked for them," he muttered under his breath. But the words sounded hollow, even to him.

"Not you, Dad," he whispered. "Not you."

It had been five years since Iris Green had last smoked, but at that moment, as she stood outside the vacant office building in an industrial park south of Boston, she craved a cigarette in the worst way. She looked up at the star-filled night, took in a lungful of cool, spring air, held it, and then exhaled. It wasn't the smoky goodness of a cancer stick, but it would have to suffice. Even after all this time her body still remembered the nicotine rush she used to get from smoking. It kind of reminded her of this job; all along she had known that smoking was bad for her, but she still kept coming back for the rush.

Iris tried to rub some warmth into her bare arms with the palms of her hands. Everything about this assignment reeked to high heaven—and she had felt that way even before she had heard the kid profess his innocence so convincingly.

*But don't they all!* she thought. *Don't they all say they're the real victims or that they've been set up as part of some vast conspiracy?*

She recalled the look on Monroe's face when Tarker said the third victim's name. She doubted that even Pacino could have done a more convincing job of acting surprised. There were way too many things on this gig that did not sit right with her. Sure, it didn't help that Ames had just tossed out his knowledge of her conversation with Remington. But it was more than that. All they'd been told—or at least all she had been told—was that the Department wanted the Monroe kid to work for them, that he'd gotten himself mixed up in a murder case, and that if he'd come on the job, they'd cover for him. If that was true, it was disturbing enough.

*But what if it isn't true?* Iris was not naive, no matter what Remington and Ames thought. There were times in the employ of one's government, particularly in the covert employ of one's government, when things were going to get messy. But that should not include the assassination of innocent civilians just to get some college kid's cooperation. Even if the kid was Stephen freakin' Hawking, which he wasn't.

Whatever the truth was, Iris was determined to find out.

She glanced at her watch and saw that it was a little after nine. It would take Tarker at least another half hour to get back with their dinner, just enough time to have another chat with young Mr. Monroe.

Back inside the vacant office building she casually made her way to the room in which the boy was being kept. The gnawing suspicion continued to swirl around in her gut as she saw six agents playing cards atop a cardboard box that once held lighting supplies. *Six agents plus two on the door seems like overkill for one college kid*, she thought. *Whatever he knows, it must be pretty damn special.*

"Hey, boys," she said to the two agents stationed outside the door, "I'm gonna take another crack at him without Ames around to screw it up." She smiled, and the two chuckled. Tarker's reputation as a loose cannon was legendary.

One of the guards unlocked the door for her and opened it. "Better work quick, won't be long before John Boy is back with the food."

"Thanks, Eddie," she said, and stepped into the room.

Monroe was lying on the cot, faced toward the wall. She cleared her throat to get his attention and waited to see if he was sleeping.

"Go away," he said, his voice muffled.

"I'd like to talk to you a little more about some of the things you said earlier."

He turned over. She noticed a dark crust of blood on the side of his lip where Ames had struck him.

"Where's your partner? He doesn't want to take another swing?"

"He went to get us some dinner."

Shane rolled over and sat up. He self-consciously combed his fingers through his disheveled head of sandy blond hair. Then he gazed at her, face revealing nothing. She had to hand it to him. If he was telling the truth, he was keeping himself together pretty well while his world fell apart.

"What part of never didn't you understand?"

She strolled to the table and pulled out

the chair to sit across from him. "Look, it's in your best interest to cooperate. Do what they ask, and then everything else can be sorted out. What's so hard?"

He smiled sadly and shook his head. "You make it sound like they're all these benevolent grandparents. Guess what? There isn't going to be a lollipop for me later. Or a cookie, either. They want me to help them build a machine that will create catastrophic weather they can aim like a gun. Don't you get that? The perfect weapon. They can kill people and make it look like an accident. They've already tested the thing, and hundreds of innocent people are dead! But it isn't perfect. It isn't predictable enough for them. They need me for that, and they want my cooperation and my silence bad enough that they've already killed three more people to get it. Now tell me again the part about how they have my best interests in mind. 'Cause I've always liked a good bedtime story."

Fascinated by Shane and repelled by what she was hearing, Iris leaned forward and rubbed her hands together. She sensed she was about to open a big old can of nasty worms but could not stop now that she had begun. "Shane, what if I told you the kind of thing you're talking about is what I took this job to stop, not to be a part of. And that I was starting to think there might actually be something to what you're saying?"

She held his intense gaze in hers.

"What sounds like the truth to you?" he asked.

"It wasn't what you said, it was the look on your face when Ames told you Junstrom was dead."

He nodded. "I thought he was on your side," Shane said softly. Then his face screwed up in confusion. "And I don't know how they could have my prints on a gun. I've never touched a gun in my life."

Iris sat back in the chair and watched Shane. She realized her thoughts on this case were based primarily on what Tarker Ames had told her. She had never actually seen the murder weapon or spoken with anyone about the evidence. She frowned as the lid on the worm can she'd opened was gradually pulled back to show the disgusting, writhing contents within.

Blowing out a short breath, she stood up and paced around the tiny room. She believed him. The whole thing. This was not the kind of crap she had signed on for. *The question is, now what am I going to do about it?*

"Look, just let me talk to somebody outside your organization," Shane said. "Before your partner caught me, I was trying to contact Senator Michelson. He's an old friend of the family, and I think if I could just talk to him, I—"

Iris glanced sharply down at the college

student in the wrinkled clothes. Shane's words cut off abruptly when he saw the look on her face. *What the hell am I doing?* Iris thought. *This kid with the bad case of bed-head could be lying his ass off. He could be responsible for a triple homicide. What if he really is lying?*

"I'm going to have to think some more about this."

"How long am I supposed to stay here?" he pressed.

"We're supposed to transfer you to a farm in West Virginia sometime tomorrow. Maybe we'll get a chance to continue our talk there."

"At least . . ."

Iris raised an eyebrow and regarded him curiously. "At least what?"

Shane would not look at her. "What your partner was saying about my father . . ."

"Oh," she said softly. "That. Not a clue, I'm afraid. Ames would know, that's for sure. But that doesn't mean he's telling the truth."

Iris walked toward the door in a mass of confusion. This kid was between a rock and a hard place, and somehow Iris felt as though she'd joined him there. She was just about to rap for the guard to let her out when she heard shouts and the distant thuds of multiple explosions from the other side of the door.

Astonished, Iris realized they were under attack.

* * *

The room shook with the impact of explosives somewhere in the building. Shane shot up from the bed and moved toward Agent Green, who looked just as mystified as he felt. "What's going on?" he demanded.

"Stay there," she barked as she reached for the gun she wore in a holster at the small of her back.

There came another blast of gunfire and more shouting. Agent Green took a step back and aimed her weapon at the door, even as it burst inward, propelled by a powerful blast of sound and smoke. Agent Green fell backward to the floor, hit by the force of the explosion.

Shane was about to go to her when he caught sight of shapes moving into the room through the smoke, four dark-clad figures wearing gas masks and carrying automatic weapons.

"You're Monroe?" one of the figures asked, his voice muffled by the mask.

Shane froze. *My name. Who the hell are these people and why do they all know my name?*

Agent Green bolted up from the floor, weapon aimed in both hands. "Federal officer, stand down!"

Shane watched with horror as all four invaders pointed their machine guns at the agent, black-gloved fingers twitching on the triggers. "Stop!" he shouted as he lunged forward to get between the men and Agent Green. "Don't kill her."

The men said nothing. The air in the room was becoming hard to breathe, and Shane began to cough.

"Get out of the way, Shane," Agent Green ordered. She, too, had begun to choke on the noxious smoke pouring into the room.

One of the men ushered him out of the way, all the weapons aimed at Agent Green.

"We're leaving. So is Mr. Monroe. It's up to you if you're still alive after we've gone. You can't possibly shoot us all."

Agent Green narrowed her eyes. "No," she said calmly. "But I can sure as hell kill *you.*"

The man did not flinch. "Fine. And you still lose. You'll be dead, and Shane will be gone."

There was a long moment when no one spoke or moved or, Shane thought, even breathed. Then Agent Green put her gun on the floor and slid it across to him. The masked man squatted, slipped the gun into the pocket of his black jacket, then grabbed Shane by the arm and shoved him toward the others.

"Take him."

Then they were pulling Shane out of the room. He tried to see Agent Green through the bodies and the smoke, but in seconds they had left her behind.

"Let's get out of here. Move, move, move!" the leader shouted.

Shane could just make out the shapes of two guards crumpled on the floor, and there were others. Blood pooled beneath several, and he knew his mysterious benefactors had been less merciful to these others than they had been to Agent Green. "Did you kill them?" he asked between coughs.

"Just like they would have done to you once they got what they wanted," said the man who was steering him through the billowing smoke.

"Who are you guys?" Shane began to cough uncontrollably, vomiting up what little he had left in his stomach from the previous day.

"Take it easy," the man said through the thick rubber of his mask, "there'll be plenty of time for twenty questions just as soon as we get you out—"

A single gunshot echoed through the corridor, and the man suddenly let go of his arm and fell to the floor. Through stinging eyes Shane could see that one of his circular eyepieces had been shot out. Shane stumbled back away from the dead body, disoriented in the swirling smoke. He crouched low as he looked from left to right. *Where did that shot come from? Where are the others?* On the verge of panic, he wiped his running eyes with his hand and began to move toward what he thought might be the exit.

"Monroe!" Someone shouted his name

from within the cloud of smoke. When he recognized the voice, his heart nearly stopped.

Agent Tarker Ames, a bag of takeout food
still under one arm, strode toward him out of
the choking mist in what seemed like slow
motion. He had his gun leveled in Shane's
direction, tears from the smoke streaming
down his long, good-old-boy face.

"Stay where you are, Monroe, or I'll put
you down like a dog."

Before Shane could even think about how
he was going to respond, his three remaining
rescuers appeared.

"Move it, Shane! Go!" they yelled as they
pushed him away, firing short blasts from
their semiautomatic machine guns.

Tarker dropped the takeout food and
returned fire as he dove for cover. Two sets of
arms suddenly reached out of the choking fog
and grabbed Shane, dragging him across the
floor. The gunfire continued, and then there
was a single loud thud that he felt hot against
his back and low in the pit of his stomach.

Somebody had used an explosive of some
kind.

Shane could suddenly breathe again.
Through stinging eyes he looked around and
saw that he was outside the building in a vast,
empty parking lot. Greedily he sucked in the
cool night air, coughing as what was left of
the tear gas was forced from his lungs.

Two of the three who had been exchanging

fire with Ames ran from the smoke-filled building. One of them was bleeding from a shoulder wound.

"How many lost?" the man with Shane asked.

"Two," the other said grimly.

Shane heard the wail of spinning tires on tarmac, and a white van barreled toward them from the back of the building. It looked as though it wasn't going to stop, but it did, screeching to a halt with its rear end fishtailing mere inches from them.

Through the dirt- and dust-covered windshield, Shane made eye contact with the driver and the man smiled insanely, giving him the thumbs-up. Shane was dragged toward the rear of the van as its two doors were flung open from inside.

"Wait," he shouted angrily, desolately, as two more black-clad men reached out to pull him inside. "Who the hell are you?"

He was pushed roughly to the metal floor. The doors were slammed shut and the vehicle sped out of the lot, away from the smoking building and into the night.

"Who are *we*?" one of the men asked as he pulled the gas mask off to reveal a young face with a severe buzz cut and intense blue eyes. He bent close to Shane. "Believe it or not, we're the good guys."

# CHAPTER TEN

*"A few years hence it will be possible for nations to fight without armies, ships or guns, by weapons far more terrible, to the destructive action and range of which there is virtually no limit."*

—Nikola Tesla

Shane was pressed to the floor of the van with an oily tarp draped over him, his liberators silent. Tension hung heavy and thick in the atmosphere of the vehicle.

"How we doin'?" the man with the intense blue eyes asked the driver.

"So far, so good," came the response.

They had been driving for well over an hour, and Shane wondered where they could be taking him. He was feeling no safer in the hands of his would-be rescuers than he had with the federal agents. "Where are we?" he asked from beneath the tarp.

"Can't say," blue-eyes answered curtly.

"Are you . . . are you with the government?"

The man uttered a short burst of laughter

that lacked any humor. "Those guys back there? The ones who murdered your friends? They're the government, Monroe. We're about as far to the left as the BBD is to the right."

"BBD?" he asked. "Who—"

"Black Box Department, covert government agency, so many levels above top secret you could be standing in front of them and still not see 'em. I doubt even the prez knows they exist."

"But you do," Shane said.

"Damn straight, and it makes them crazy." Shane couldn't see the man, but from the sound of his voice he knew that he was grinning from ear to ear.

"Approaching base," the driver yelled. "Everything looks clear."

The van had slowed and was traveling down a road loaded with potholes. It bumped and bounced around like some insane amusement park ride. They pulled the drop cloth off of him and allowed him to sit up. The windows had been covered with tape so he couldn't see outside.

"All right, we're here," blue-eyes said as he reached for a black hood and handed it to Shane. "Put this on."

Shane stared at the hood. "Why?"

The man impatiently pulled it over Shane's head. "It's a precaution, in case you wind up back in their custody."

His world went black again. "I'd never tell them where—" Shane protested, his voice slightly distorted by the hood.

"You'd be surprised what you say after they tear off a few of your fingernails with pliers," the man interrupted.

Shane heard him move to the rear of the van. A blast of cool night air caressed his body as the doors were opened. He could smell the ocean in the wind and hear the distant sound of breaking waves. Two sets of strong arms then gripped him and helped him out. When his feet touched the ground, they left him there alone. He could hear the doors slam shut and the rev of the engine as the vehicle drove away.

He was beginning to lose his balance in the darkness and was tempted to reach up and pull the black hood from his face when someone grabbed his arm and guided him forward.

"Over here." Shane recognized the voice of the blue-eyed man.

"I thought you left," he said as he was guided across an area of tall grass.

Shane felt the weeds brushing against his pant legs as he was helped along. They had not walked very far before they came to a complete stop. Shane heard the jangle of keys and a padlock being unlocked. Then there was the whine of an iron-gate being pushed open. From the echo of their footfalls, he thought they had led him into an entry of some kind, possibly stone. Behind him, he heard someone close and lock the gate.

"We're going down some stairs now, so pay attention," his guide said.

"I know this is for security and everything, but it would be easier if you just took the sack off my head," Shane muttered as the man led him down slippery stone steps that seemed to descend forever.

"Quit whining," blue-eyes said even as he kept him from falling. "We could have chloroformed you, but then you'd probably complain about the headache. Deal with it."

Shane decided that it would be in his best interest to keep his mouth shut. They came to the bottom of the steps and began to walk down another corridor. Shane could hear the sound of water dripping from the ceiling above, and it wasn't long before his shoes were soaked through.

They stopped again, and Shane heard the beeping sounds of an electronic keypad followed by a loud whir as an automated bolt lock slid aside. He was led through, and the door closed automatically behind him. Shane immediately noticed a difference in temperature. This room was warmer, comfortable. Through the hood he could hear the faint hum of machinery and the sound of fingers tapping on computer keyboards.

"Good work, Joe," a new voice said from nearby. "You can remove the hood now."

Blue-eyed Joe grabbed at the hood on his head, and Shane reached up to help him pull it off. The hood gone, Shane surveyed his surroundings. He was in an underground bunker. It looked to be like some kind of makeshift command center with people working at computer terminals that ran the length of the room. A burly man with a dark beard stood in front of him dressed in a flannel shirt, fleece vest, and work pants, with heavy black boots.

"I apologize for the cloak-and-dagger stuff, but I'm glad we were in time to help you," he said as he offered Shane a meaty hand. "I'm David Poisson."

Shane frowned and stared at the man's hand, then glanced around again. He was not about to get chummy with some lunatic whose lackeys had just killed a bunch of people. Not even if they *had* freed him.

"What is this place?" he asked. Hundreds of feet of computer cable lay strewn on the floor, and bare bulbs hung from the ceiling to illuminate the underground room.

Poisson dropped his hand. "Welcome to the command center of the Truth Seekers."

"Truth Seekers?" Shane stared at him.

The big man smiled and nodded his shaggy head. He looked around as he spoke. "Kinda hokey, huh? But only at first. Right up until you realize how rare the truth really is."

Shane shook his head, the strangeness of

the whole situation coming back around to rock his world. He thought about Hazeltine, about his murdered friends, about his mother, about Nevart's eyes . . . about all the things he had left behind.

"I can't believe this. How the hell did my life become this?"

Poisson put a strong, companionable hand on his shoulder. "Stay calm, we've all been where you are right now and it does get easier to understand, trust me. It'll all be explained soon enough. I only wish we'd gotten to you sooner. We moved on it as soon as we knew they were after you, but by the time our team got there, you had already taken off. I'm surprised you managed to evade them as long as you did."

Shane shuddered as grief and guilt cut him deeply. "I wish I hadn't run. Spud, Geoff, and even Ray would still be alive. And they weren't going to kill me, anyway."

"You didn't know that. You did what you had to," Poisson said in a reassuring tone. "Nothing you can do to change it now. Move on, that's kind of our motto around here."

"And you're, what, gonna save me?" Shane asked, casting a dubious glance around the room.

Poisson eyed him grimly. "Nope. But we might be able to help you save yourself. If you work with us."

"Work with you. Instead of them. Doesn't

look like I have a lot of choices, does it?"
Shane asked quietly.

"Choice is pretty clear from where I sit.
You're wondering what the difference is?
Here it comes: We're not going to force you to
do anything. And we're not going to kill people you love."

For a long moment Shane let his head
hang down, gaze fixed on the floor. At length
he glanced up at Poisson again, studying the
man's eyes. "I hope you'll forgive me if I don't
just automatically trust you."

Poisson smiled, a sparkle in his eye.
"Good. That makes it easier."

"What does?" Shane asked.

"You're a genius, Monroe. Doesn't mean
you're not also a moron. Not trusting us, after
what you've been through? It just proves
you're not stupid."

Shane's stomach noisily rumbled, and his
hands shot to cover it. "Sorry. It's been a
while since I had anything to eat."

Poisson laughed. "I think we can do
something about that. Come with me to the
kitchen and we'll fix you something." The
large man put his arm around Shane's
shoulder and steered him toward a door
across the command center. "Joe, why don't
you go monitor the usual channels and see
what they're saying about the loss of their
prize."

Joe turned to leave. "Take it easy, Monroe,"

he said, his back to Shane. "I'm sure I'll be seeing you around."

Poisson allowed Shane to pass through the doorway first. "That's Joe Levine. He's one of the latest to join our little band of freedom fighters. He's not much older than you are."

Shane was surprised; he had thought Joe Levine to be in his late twenties, at least. Silently he pondered what Joe could have experienced in his life to cause him to look as old as he did. If it was anything like what Shane had gone through these past few days, he understood how it could take its toll on somebody.

At the end of the hallway they went through a white swinging door into the kitchen area. The walls were lined with high wooden shelves filled with canned meats and soups, and dry foods like pasta and rice. There was an industrial-sized stove and refrigerator, as well as a large double sink. A long rectangular table surrounded by ten or twelve chairs sat in the center of the room, pots and pans hanging from a rack above it. An older man with thick glasses and a ponytail of pure white was sitting at the table alone eating a bowl of cereal. He didn't bother to look up as they entered.

"Would a sandwich be all right for the moment?" Poisson asked.

"Sure, that would be great," Shane

answered, tearing his eyes away from the man to answer Poisson. "Thanks."

Poisson got a loaf of bread from one of the drawers and then pulled open the refrigerator door. "We got ham, cheese, and salami. Any of that sound good?"

"It all sounds good. I'm starved."

Shane couldn't help himself. He turned back to study the man at the table. There was something wrong with him, something missing. The way he moved, his faraway gaze, it was as if he were some kind of machine. Shane was reminded of the automatons from the Hall of Presidents at Disney World.

The man with the ponytail finished his cereal, picked up the bowl, and drank what was left of the milk. "Got a lead on a security guard who was stationed at Dreamland about the time I was let go," he said out of the blue as he placed his empty bowl on the counter where Poisson was making the sandwich. His eyes were still unfocused, staring ahead but not really seeing what was before him. "Think I'm getting close; I can feel it in my bones."

Poisson looked up from the sandwich in progress. "That's excellent, Walter. Keep us posted."

Without another word, Walter left the kitchen.

Poisson put the completed sandwich on a paper plate and placed it in front of Shane.

"Here you go, that should tide you over."

Shane sat down and motioned toward the door with his head. "I don't want to be nosy or anything, but what's his story?"

The burly man pulled out a chair and sat down across from Shane. "Who? Walter? He was a physicist, originally worked for Los Alamos, then for a company called EG&G."

Shane picked up the sandwich and began to eat while he listened.

"He was granted top security clearance and sent to work outside Nellis Air Force Base near Groom Lake, Nevada. The location was nicknamed Dreamland, but you'd probably be more familiar with it by its other name—Area 51."

"Did he see any UFOs?" Shane asked through a large bite of food.

Poisson got up from the table and took a mug from the cabinet. He went to the stove and poured himself a cup of coffee. "They're the entire reason why Walter's problems kicked in," he said, returning to the table. "Seems he saw some things at Dreamland, things he felt should be made public."

Shane had already started on the other half of the sandwich. "And, let me guess, the people he worked for? EG&G, was it? They tried to stop him."

The bearded man took a swig of coffee, then nodded. "You're catching on," he said as he set his mug down. "He was fired—let go for psychiatric reasons, they said. Nobody else would hire him after that, his reputation was ruined—but that didn't stop Walter. He continued to talk to anybody who'd listen."

Poisson was quiet for a moment. "How's that sandwich?" he asked in an obvious gambit to change the subject. "Can I get you something to drink?"

"Water would be fine," Shane responded. "What happened then?"

Poisson rose and poured him a glass of tap water. "They found a way to shut him up. Walter's wife and kids were killed in a suspicious house fire not too long after his last warning. They couldn't get him to shut his mouth, so they took away his reason to live."

Shane slowly put the final bite of his sandwich down onto the plate, his appetite gone. An image of his mother's house had risen unbidden in his mind; his mother's house in flames.

"We'd been monitoring his case. Two months after his family was killed we found him in an Arizona flophouse about to overdose on sleeping pills. We gave him an alternative to death: We asked him to join us—to help us expose the truth—and he accepted."

Shane stared at Poisson, the similarities to his own situation obvious. He swallowed as he pushed the paper plate away. "Were you monitoring me, like you were Walter?" he asked, knowing full well what the answer was.

Poisson nodded his shaggy head up and down. "That we were."

"His story . . . what they did to him, the way his life was changed . . . it sounds like . . ."

Poisson nervously drummed his square fingers on the tabletop. "Yeah, Shane, it sounds like what they've tried to do to you—what they tried to do to a lot of us." He reached across the table and put a large, comforting hand on top of his. "I guess we should consider ourselves lucky that they screw up so much. That is, we might, right up until we begin to realize that these are not incompetent people. And if there are this many people who have slipped through the cracks, how many do you think they went after who didn't get away?"

A chill went through Shane. He thought of his friends, both those who had betrayed him and those who had died because he wouldn't play the BBD's game. He thought of his mother and wondered if she was in danger at this very moment, being watched. And in the back of his mind he could still hear the sneering voice of Tarker Ames as the man implied that his father had been a willing participant in the BBD's operations.

"I don't want it to be this way," Shane said, shaking his head. "I want it the way it was."

Poisson would not meet his gaze. "We'll

see what we can do," he said, standing abruptly and turning back toward the refrigerator. "How about another sandwich?"

His watch broken during the rescue from the BBD, Shane awakened unsure of the time or even what day of the week it was. He had been with the Truth Seekers for a little over a week and had yet to grow used to the monotony of the place. It would be a while, he thought, before he felt like he belonged here. Maybe that would never happen. But after just a few days with them he had decided that they were the real thing. This wasn't a show for his benefit, not with this many people so intense about their work that they barely noticed him.

He sat up, rubbed sleep from his eyes, and put on his sneakers, gazing at the other cots around him. Most were empty, their occupants having risen earlier in the morning to tend to their various responsibilities. *And therein lies the problem*, he thought as he left the makeshift sleeping quarters and stepped out into the hallway. Having nothing to do left him with plenty of time to think and to ponder the new uncertainties of his life. And that was enough to make him lose his mind.

He scratched his head as he headed to the kitchen. Every day was the same: wake up, have breakfast, and stand around hoping to be of use—but no such luck. Most of the people here just glared at him, as if his presence somehow annoyed them.

Shane was just about to push open the swinging door into the kitchen when he heard his name mentioned by a voice within. He stopped to listen.

"Monroe's supposed to be some kind of genius, but I don't see it," a woman said. "Acts more like a kid who got in way over his head if you ask me."

"Poisson isn't talking, but I heard that *kid* supposedly helped to design some kind of superweapon," a male voice responded, "and the BBD's real hot to make him a member of their club. I wonder if he's worth the risk? We've managed to stay hidden for this long, but if they start turning up the heat looking for him, the whole organization's in jeopardy. Let's just hope the boss man knows what he's doing."

Shane felt himself growing angry, a hot pulse throbbing at his temple. He came through the swinging door, pushing it a little too hard and banging the wall inside. He recognized the man and woman at the table just from wandering around the complex. The man was Greg. He was pretty sure the woman's name was Melanie. He glared at them on his way to the refrigerator.

"Morning," he said as he extracted a carton of orange juice and poured himself a glass. He was trying to keep his anger in check, but

after the events of the past week, he had no
room left for frustration and rage. He watched
their faces as he drank some juice. They
looked at each other, then started to gather
their breakfast dishes.

"You know, I'd be worried about me being
here, too. If David was smart, he'd toss my
pathetic genius ass out of here and run for
cover. I'm like a live grenade," Shane said
through gritted teeth. "Dangerous." He took
another gulp of juice, eyeing the two as they
left the kitchen in a hurry. "Have a nice day,"
he called after them.

Joe Levine came in a moment later. He
gave Shane a quick nod as he went to the
drawer for some bread. "Hey. How'd you
sleep? Finally adjusting to your new surroundings?"

Shane downed the last of his juice and
stalked across the kitchen to the sink. He
turned on the water and vigorously washed
the glass. "Oh yeah," he said, voice oozing
with sarcasm, "I'm adjusting just great."

Joe put two slices of bread into the toaster,
then shot him a hard look. "What's your problem?"

"What the hell am I doing here?" Shane
asked. "What is all this? I don't even know
where I am, for Christ's sake. I have a life out
there that I need to get back to."

"Slow down, Shane. What's this all about?
You know it's too dangerous for you to be on

the streets. The BBD has the state covered looking for you. It'd be suicide if you left here."

Shane shrugged. "Well it's either that or be tossed out."

Joe's toast popped from the toaster, but he didn't seem to notice. He stared at Shane, his look serious. "What are you talking about?"

With a sigh of exasperation, Shane ran his fingers through his sleep-bedraggled hair. "Forget it, I'm just frustrated. I get a sense from your fellow Truth Seekers that I'm not really wanted around here."

"You're right," Joe said as he brought his toast to the table. He tore off a piece of crust and popped it into his mouth. "They don't trust you."

Shane came away from the sink to the table and stood with his hands planted on the back of a chair staring down at Joe. "Fine. They don't trust me. I don't trust them. Just let me deal with this on my own. Get me to Senator Michelson's office. I'll explain what's happened and—"

Joe chuckled. "You really don't get it, do you? It comes off you like a stink, and that's why they don't trust you."

"I have no idea what you're talking about," Shane said. Joe was the one person he had thought he could talk to, but now he was not even sure of that.

"Exactly," Joe said. "There's an air about

you, Shane. An air that says what's happened in your life? It's all some kind of mistake, and you can just walk out of here, talk to some senator, and get it all back, just like that." He snapped his fingers for effect. "It doesn't work like that, and when you finally come to realize it, like the others around here have, you'll be on the road to being one of us. But until then . . ."

Joe let his words trail off with a shrug and took another bite of toast.

Horrified, Shane stared at him. "But I don't want to be one of you."

Joe finished wolfing down the last of his breakfast and crumpled up the napkin. "Looks to me like we're still at the beginning of a long stretch of road with you," he said. "With some, it takes a little longer than others. Me? I knew I was screwed the minute the Truth Seekers found me. There was no going back."

Shane was about to protest, to explain again how it was entirely possible to get his life back, when what sounded like school bells began to ring. He gave Joe a quizzical look.

"Operations meeting," he said, shooting the crumpled napkin across the room, where it arced perfectly into the barrel. "Two points, Celtics lead." He pushed his chair back from the kitchen table. "Dave said you're welcome to attend if you're interested."

Shane said nothing as he followed the

man, still smarting from his scathing words. *It doesn't matter*, Shane thought. *No matter what he says, I'm not just walking away from my life.* He thought of the hell his mother must be going through, wondering what had happened to him. It was a guilt that had been haunting him all week, but he did not dare to call her, especially not from here. If what David and Joe and the others said was true, he would be leading the BBD right to them.

The bells continued to ring, and Shane watched as people filed into the hallway from the various rooms of the complex on their way to the meeting place. Again he was reminded of the number of people who were part of the organization called the Truth Seekers. It reminded him of something Poisson had said that first day, about how many people had been captured or killed by the BBD for every person who got away. The thought made him slightly nauseated.

In the conference room it was standing room only. Shane eased his way into the cramped conference room and claimed a spot in the corner. He spotted Joe at the front of the room with David and wondered if they were talking about him.

When David cleared his throat, the noise level dropped considerably. "Thank you all for coming," he said, glancing around the room. "I'll try to make this brief. I know you're all very busy."

He started with a review of the Truth Seekers' various projects around the world and how close they were to achieving their goals. Shane was amazed by the extent of their operations. The kinds of things they knew, and the supposedly covert agencies they were monitoring, made his head spin. As David spoke, Shane studied the expressions of the others in the room, each of whom listened to their leader's words intently. They shared a look, some grave thing in their eyes, that made him think that every one of them had endured something awful at the hands of one of these groups and had survived. He wondered if he had that look as well.

The look of a survivor.

Shane stood behind a woman named Trina as she typed "Tarker Ames" into the computer. He did not have clearance from Poisson to use the group's hardware yet, but Trina had been more than cooperative when Shane had asked her to help him find out more about the guy who had tried to kill him. He had a feeling they didn't want him online just in case he accidentally gave away their location, but he appreciated the fact that they were willing to work with him.

Together, he and Trina watched as the information on the BBD agent appeared on-screen. The data on Ames was from the Truth Seekers' own files on the covert government agency. The database they had compiled on the BBD was extensive.

"That him?" Trina asked.

A frisson of trepidation went through Shane as a picture of the agent appeared along with a profile.

"Yeah. That's him."

Skimming the information over Trina's shoulder, Shane learned that Ames had been born in Alabama in February of 1963 and been raised by his grandmother after his parents were killed in a 1973 automobile accident. Shane felt a bit uneasy as he realized that he and the BBD agent actually shared a life experience. His father, Don Monroe, had also died in a car crash.

Ames had been recruited out of high school by the FBI and continued to jump around from one government intelligence position to another, earning a reputation as a top agent wherever he was assigned. Trina paged down so that Shane could read a little further, and another chill went through him. Ames's psych profile classified him as a sociopath.

*Great,* he thought, *just the kind of guy you want working for truth, justice, and the American way.*

Unable to look at the agent's creepy country boy face any longer, he asked Trina to look for similar information on Iris Green. *There's a face I wouldn't mind looking at,* he mused as Trina typed her name into the file.

"Shane?"

He turned to see David Poisson standing behind him. "Hey, David. Trina was just helping me do some research on the enemy."

David blinked as a picture of Agent Green began to appear on the computer screen. "You won't find much on that one," he said. "She's new. But if she's been teamed with Ames, you can bet she's trouble."

They were all quiet as a college graduation photo of the woman began to download. Shane didn't think it possible that she was as bad as Tarker Ames, but he had been a pretty bad judge of character of late.

"Shane, would you mind coming with me, please?" Poisson said as he walked from the operations room.

"What's up?" Shane asked. He thanked Trina, who waved and went back to the work he had interrupted. Then he joined Poisson, and they went down the hall to the door of the command center. For some reason he felt as though he had done something wrong.

The leader of the Truth Seekers silently punched numbers into the electronic keypad and unlocked the door. Then he motioned for Shane to follow him as he set off down the dank, stone hallway, careful not to step in any puddles there.

"Where are we going?" Shane asked, trying to sound as casual as possible.

They had reached the stone stairs leading up and began to climb.

"Shane," Poisson finally said, "you've been with us for a couple of weeks now. We've done our best for you, tracking the BBD's search for you and the media coverage of what happened at Hazeltine, keeping an eye on your mother for you. But it's time for you to make a decision."

They finished the climb in silence and walked down a hall that Shane figured would take them to the iron-gate and padlock. He could feel the wind on his face now, and it smelled strongly of the sea. He inhaled deeply, happy to be breathing moist fresh air instead of the musty, recycled stuff down below.

They stopped at the chained gate, and David pulled a key from inside his pants pocket. He undid the silver padlock and let the chains fall to the ground. They stepped through the gateway onto a winding concrete path, cracked and overgrown with weeds. He could hear surf crashing somewhere close by and wondered exactly where he was.

The path took them past a large concrete bunker, and as they rounded the side of the gray building, Shane looked out with wonder at the beautiful ocean view sprawled before him. He and David stood mere feet away from a precarious drop to the rocks below. Pulled by curiosity, he walked close to the edge.

"Where are we?" he asked as he peered over the side at a set of wooden steps leading to a small dock below.

"Nahant," David said, a look of absolute calm in his eyes as he stared out over the undulating blue gray sea. "North Shore, less than an hour from the city. Our complex is an old marine biology research station used by quite a few of the bigger colleges over the years. It's been closed fifteen years."

"But how did—"

"We inherit it?" Poisson finished for him. "Using shell corporations and blind business fronts, the Truth Seekers bought this whole place using funds we appropriated from a Miami drug czar who made a deal with the DEA and was allowed to continue trafficking. We hacked into his accounts in the Cayman Islands."

David put his hands in the pockets of his fleece vest. "Sad part is, there was so much money, he didn't even notice it was gone." He pulled his attention away from the hypnotic rhythm of the sea and turned to Shane. "And that's part of the reason I brought you up here."

He motioned toward an old picnic table on the verge of being swallowed by the overgrowth. The two walked over and sat on the benches across from each other.

Shane gazed out at the peaceful view. "How is it possible that nobody knows you're here? There have to be homes nearby. How do you keep hidden?"

Poisson plucked one of the long weeds from the ground and placed it in the corner of his mouth. "It's not that they don't know we're here. They know all right. They just don't know what we're all about."

"So what, they think you guys are some kind of marine research group or something?"

The leader nodded a little, chewing on the end of the green stalk. "Something like that. We're no threat to their day-to-day lives, so they leave us alone. It's disinformation, Shane. That's what it's all about."

Shane pulled a weed from the ground as well. "And if the BBD should find you? What then?"

David didn't even have to think about it. It was obviously a contingency that had been planned for. "We're packed and setting up our new digs someplace else before they even figure out our old address." He tossed the weed to the ground as if throwing a spear. "The Truth Seekers have eyes and ears all over this country, and our numbers are growing every day."

"Is that what you want to talk to me about," Shane asked, "joining you guys?"

A seagull screeched overhead. Poisson looked up, shielding his eyes from the hazy sunshine.

"You've seen firsthand what most people think is fiction, the stuff of best-sellers and action movies. But you know better now, don't you? You got a tiny glimpse of what's really going on behind Joe America's back."

Shane was silent as he got up from the table.

"The Truth Seekers need people like you, Shane. We need people who can see reality, no matter how bizarre, and deal with it. You were pretty resourceful on the run. I don't think many of my operatives could have done better—"

Shane spun around to face him, fists clenched, indignant. "I can't believe you just said that. This isn't some kind of game. People died because of me—because of what I know."

David sighed. "I'm sorry. I didn't mean to sound insensitive." He got up from the picnic table and approached Shane. "But it doesn't change the fact that what I said is true. The Truth Seekers need you, all those people out there who have no idea of what's really going on in the world, they need you."

Shane turned back to the ocean. It calmed him. "I'm really grateful for what you people did for me, but I'm not part of this. With or without your help, I'm going to get my life in order and things are going to go back to the way they used to be." Reluctantly, Shane faced Poisson again. "I appreciate everything you've done for me, but I'm sorry, I can't do this. It's not for me."

The Truth Seekers' leader stood in stony silence, gazing past Shane, past the ocean sprawl to something beyond. "I'll bet you're not even aware of how big a part the BBD has already played in your life."

Grief spiked through Shane then, and he felt a hard knot form in his stomach. "If you're making reference to my father, I know all about it. Agent Ames got quite the thrill out of telling me my dad worked for them."

David scratched his chin through the thick forest of beard. "I don't know what they told you, Shane, but your father never worked for the BBD."

Shane stared at him. "What do you mean?"

"I've seen records that show your father was approached by the BBD, but he refused to work for them. He turned them down flat, even threatened to expose them."

The knot in his gut gave way then, and a wave of relief washed over him. "I knew it," Shane said, his fists clenched, "I knew he would never work for them. Ames just said that to try to convince me."

"No. He wouldn't work for them, Shane." David hesitated, cleared his throat. "That's why they killed him."

The silence after those words was broken only by the sound of the surf crashing nearby. Shane gaped at David, shaking his head slowly. At length, he took a step back, as though he might run. "My father died in a car accident."

Poisson nodded in agreement. "Yeah. He did. Thanks to the BBD. He threatened to expose them, and they killed him for it. He wasn't the first, nor will he be the last."

Shane sat down heavily, his legs no longer able to support him.

"I'm sorry you had to find out this way, but—"

Shane looked up at Poisson, eyes alive with anger. "But you thought it might help me decide to join you. Am I right, Dave?"

David began to leave. "You have an awful lot to digest right now. Think about it and we can talk later."

Shane looked out over the roiling water. In a matter of a few minutes the sky above had gone a steely gray. *Storm coming*, he thought as he watched the sun gradually become covered by the invading dark clouds. The seagulls above dipped, weaved, and wailed mournfully as if this were the last they would see of the life-giving sun.

Then he laughed softly, grimly, to himself. *Got news for you, kid. Storm's already here.*

Shane jumped to his feet, wiping sand from his backside as he ran to catch up with Poisson. "David, wait up."

Poisson was just about to close the gate. He stopped and peered back at Shane through the wrought-iron bars.

"Looks like you've got yourself a new Truth Seeker."

# CHAPTER ELEVEN

*"It signifies the subjugation of natural forces to the service of man . . ."*
—Nikola Tesla

Tarker Ames strode the silent hallways of the prison wing of the Walpole Psychiatric Hospital, every step heavy with purpose. Closed in July of 1985 for renovations that never seemed to come, the wing now provided the perfect place to care for the only enemy survivor of the raid that had set Shane Monroe free.

An old man with a shock of white hair and sagging bloodhound eyes stood in front of one of the rooms smoking a cigarette. A stethoscope was draped around his neck like a winter scarf, and he looked up as Tarker approached.

"How's our patient today?" Tarker asked as the physician dropped the smoldering remains of the cigarette to the white and black tile floor and stepped on it.

"He's conscious but still on the ventilator,"

the old doctor said, his voice thick with mucus.

Tarker caught the stale stink of whiskey wafting off the man and felt his stomach lurch in revulsion. He noticed the tremor in the physician's hands and wondered how long it had been since his last drink.

He often speculated about why the Department didn't employ a better class of professional, but was well aware of the answer. In the case of the doctor, he had had a run of bad luck with a new drug designed to eliminate morning sickness. It was tested and deemed safe by the pharmaceutical company that he held controlling shares in. Unfortunately the new wonder drug caused severe birth defects in the babies of the women who used it. The Department had an interest in some of the other drugs being developed by the company, so they made a deal with the doctor, and his legal problems miraculously went away. The doctor owed the Department and would do just about anything to be sure his old problems stayed far away from him.

"I told your partner I'd come back later and check on his progress," the old man said, casually gesturing to the closed door behind him. "I have some errands to run and then—"

"My partner?" Tarker asked, at first confused.

"Yes, she's inside with the patient."

Tarker shoved by him, practically knocking the doctor over in his rush to get into the room. Iris Green rose from her chair alongside the hospital bed, startled by his sudden entrance.

"Agent Green," Tarker said, his eyes darting from his partner to the prone figure beneath the sheet. "What are you doing here? I thought you were watching Monroe's mother."

She seemed flustered by his arrival. "I was, but I thought our suspect here might be more useful."

The old man sniffled in the doorway, and Tarker turned to glare at him. "You still here?" he growled. "I thought you had a date with a bottle."

The physician's face grew an angry red. *Almost as red as his nose*, Tarker mused.

"Thank you, Doctor," Iris said from across the room.

"Yeah, thanks, Doc," Tarker added as he slammed the heavy security door in the doctor's face and walked toward the figure on the bed.

His fingerprints had identified him as Thomas Stanley, twenty-five years old, from Philadelphia, once arrested for writing a threatening letter to the president. He appeared to be asleep. What wasn't covered by the white sheet was wrapped in thick gauze bandages. An accordioned plastic tube trailed from his mouth to a machine by the bedside that hummed with mechanical life as it helped him to breathe.

"What have you learned?" asked Tarker.

"Nothing. He drifts in and out of consciousness. I don't think we'll get much from him today."

Tarker stepped closer to the bed and produced a pad of paper and a pen from his back pocket. "Let me try," he said as he tossed the items onto the man's chest.

Stanley's eyes flickered open and looked up at him.

"Look at that," Tarker said with a smile, "he's already bright eyed, bushy tailed, and ready to talk to us. Isn't that right, Tommy boy?" Tarker asked in his friendliest tone.

The man's eyes bulged at Tarker, his lips moving around the plastic guard that held the breathing tube in place. He reached up, snatched the pad and pen from his chest, and let them fall to the floor.

"Oh, I see how it's going to be," Tarker said as he bent over and picked the paper and pen up. He walked around the bed to stand beside the respirator. "Let's try this again," he said as he placed the notepad back on Stanley's chest.

"What are you doing, Agent Ames?" Iris asked, caution in her tone.

Tarker smiled. "She's kinda pushy, don't you think, Tommy?" he said, his hand reaching up to casually stroke the plastic tubing allowing the man to breathe. "But I'm a sucker for that kind of woman. How about you?"

He squeezed the plastic closed, and the machine began to beep loudly. Stanley struggled and clawed at the tube in his mouth. Iris lunged toward Tarker as he released the tube. The alarm stopped, and Stanley's body relaxed as the machine once again pumped air into his starved lungs.

"Stop it, Tarker. He's the only real lead we have. Let him recover a bit and then we'll question him."

"We don't have that kind of time," Tarker replied as he again grasped the tubing.

Stanley's eyes bulged with fear. Tarker bent the tube in half. The alarms tolled, and Stanley's fist beat upon the mattress.

"Let's start with an easy one. Who do you run with, Tommy?"

Stanley began to convulse as his body was dangerously deprived of oxygen. Tarker eased his grip on the tube and let the airflow resume. He glanced at his partner, who stood grimly across the room and started to squeeze the plastic again. This time Stanley fumbled for the pad of paper and the pen. With a frantic hand, he began to scrawl.

Tarker managed to hold his enthusiasm in check as he watched the man write and then hand him the pad.

"The Truth Seekers," he snarled. "The

general ain't gonna be too happy when he hears about this." He grabbed hold of the air tube. "Now we're getting somewhere. You wouldn't happen to have an idea as to where your little terrorist pals are holed up, would you?"

Stanley closed his eyes and shook his head as Tarker deprived him of breath.

"I'm not going to stand by and watch you kill that man," Iris said with new defiance.

Tarker looked at Thomas Stanley writhing in agony. "Then I suggest you turn right around and walk out that door, 'cause something tells me this ain't gonna be pretty."

The white Renovations Inc. van pulled up to the curb behind a dump truck in front of a powder blue Dutch Colonial on Morse Street. Workmen swarmed over the rooftop, tearing up shingles and tossing them into a Dumpster below. Shane gazed out the passenger window at the home he grew up in, the home that he desperately missed.

"She said she was going to put a new roof on; looks like she was serious."

Joe Levine leaned forward in the driver's seat to look out Shane's window. "Lucky for us she was—gives us the perfect cover. That's why we chose this in the first place. Make it quick, all right? Get in there, explain the situation to Mommy Dearest, and get out. No more than ten minutes, Shane. Got it?"

Shane caught his altered reflection in the side mirror and was startled. He wasn't used to seeing himself with chestnut brown hair and a goatee. The facial hair was only a week old, and it made his chin itch, but it had grown in much thicker this time.

He took a leather wallet from the dashboard, opened it, and looked again at the photo license claiming his name was Robert Dexter. "What if they run the plates?" he asked Joe, who was disguised in dark glasses and a black curly wig.

Joe studied the rearview mirror. "Our hackers have it under control. They'll be monitoring radio frequencies and picking up cellular communications for a three-block radius. If these guys figure out you're here, or even run the plates, we'll hear it. But let's not have it come to that, okay? Get yourself in and out without BBD surveillance taking notice."

Shane stuck the wallet in his back pocket, placed a Red Sox cap on his head, and grabbed a clipboard. "I'll try my best," he said as he got out.

"There is no try. There's do and do not," Joe said, staring at him through the reflective lenses of his sunglasses.

Shane could see twin images of himself standing outside the door. "Funny," he said with a grin as he slammed the door closed, "I don't remember Yoda wearing shades."

As he turned to face the house, he studied the information on the clipboard and marveled at the Truth Seekers' attention to detail. The paperwork was on Renovations Inc. stationery. He flipped through the multiple sheets while, from the corner of his eye, he checked out the cars on the street. He didn't notice anything unusual, but that didn't mean they weren't there.

With a glance back at Joe—who pointed to his watch—Shane began to walk toward the house. There was another van parked in the driveway, and an older gentleman with an amazing gray-and-white handlebar mustache was poking through tools in the back of the vehicle. He turned around holding what looked like a mutated crowbar and came face-to-face with Shane.

"Hey, Bob Dexter from Renovations Inc. Is Mrs. . . ."—Shane glanced at his clipboard for effect—"Monroe at home?"

"She's inside," the man said in a gravelly voice that could only have been perfected by years of smoking and drinking whiskey. He pointed the monstrous metal tool at the back entrance and walked off to rejoin his fellow roofers.

Shane glanced around the yard and then at the four steps that led up to the back door. Waves of nostalgia washed over him. How much of his life had been lived in this house?

He felt like some kind of ghostly being returned to haunt the place that meant so much in life.

He climbed the stairs and rapped on the glass of the back door before opening it. "Mrs. Monroe? Mrs. Monroe, it's Bob Dexter. I'm here about the renovations?" he called out as he stepped into the kitchen.

As always, the coffeemaker was gurgling with life on the counter, and he wondered what number pot this was. His mother had a serious coffee addiction. There was a large stack of mail in the center of the small circular kitchen table, his mother's glasses on top. Everything looked as it should have, and for a moment Shane almost believed the past month was just some kind of crazy nightmare and that he'd be waking up in his bed upstairs after coming home from college for the weekend.

"There must be some mistake," his mother said as she came into the kitchen from the back of the house. There were dark circles under her eyes and a kind of hollowness to her features. She might have gone about the business of her life despite Shane's disappearance, but one look at her showed him that it was only to have something to do. Nancy Monroe looked like little more than a ghost of herself.

"I didn't call anyone about renovations. I scheduled the roof repair ages ago, and I know

I mentioned I might want to do some renovation, but this is . . . right now I just can't. . . ." Her words trailed off, and she pressed her lips tightly together. "I'm sorry. This is a very bad time for me."

Shane put a finger to his lips to silence her. At first her expression was indignant, then fearful, and then recognition dawned. He wondered how much she had cried over the past few weeks, and the knife of guilt twisted in him. There was nothing worse than making your mother cry.

He kept his finger to his lips and walked across the kitchen to the stove. "Sorry. Must have got my wires crossed. The guys did mention you might be interested. I hope I'm not rushing you or nothin' but business is kind of slow and I could make you a sweet deal."

He switched on the fan in the hood above the stove, and the kitchen was filled with its roar. "If they're listening," he said, leaning close to his mother, "this should pretty much drown out what we're saying."

The two embraced, and Shane was overwhelmed with emotion. They pulled away from each other, and he tried to give her a reassuring smile. Her face twisted up in an odd mixture of confusion, anger, and relief.

"What the heck is going on?" she asked, her voice growing louder as panic attempted to take control. Her eyes reddened, but she wiped at them and did not cry.

Shane motioned for her to keep her voice down. "I don't have much time," he said, and quickly related the events of the last three weeks.

When he finished, she was enraged. "I lost your father far too early, I'm not going to lose you as well. This kind of thing can't happen in America. I'll call Jim Michelson right now. They won't get away with this—"

"Mom," Shane interrupted. He squeezed her hand. "It's too late for that. Not with the way the BBD has twisted the story in the media. The Truth Seekers are kinda out there, I know. But this is so far beyond what . . ." He stopped and shook his head.

"I just have to believe that these guys know what they're doing and that they can help me. I just want you to know that I'm okay. You go on acting like you haven't heard from me, and you ought to be all right."

Her eyes welled with tears, and she pulled him to her. "That's crazy talk, Shane. We're going to fix this. They're saying you're wanted for questioning in the murders of those boys. If you talk to the papers, get the media involved, they won't dare come after you."

"I wish that were true, Mom. But they'll just spin it into the story they want. It's what they do." Shane hugged her back, then awkwardly broke the embrace. His time was running out.

"I have to go." He slowly stepped back

toward the door. "I don't mean to scare you, but if we think you're in any danger, we'll want to move you someplace safer. Keep a bag packed. Just in case, you know, something happens."

Nancy Monroe stared at him as the reality of the situation sank in. She shook her head, still trying to deny it, but at last she composed herself. "Let me come with you now. I can't bear not knowing what's happening to you."

He shook his head. "I can't do that to you, Mom. I'm not going to let them steal your life away from you, too. Not unless we don't have a choice."

"They've already taken it," she whispered, so softly that he could barely hear the words. "You find a way to keep in touch with me. I don't care how dangerous it is. You do it."

Shane reached for the screen door latch and pushed open the door. "Don't worry about a thing, Mrs. Monroe," Shane said, resuming his charade, away from the sound distortion of the stove fan. "My crew can complete the job in no time. I'll work up the estimates by the end of this week and get back to you."

"Thank you, Bob," she said, choking on her words, going along with the game as tears began to stream down her face. "You have a good day."

Shane chanced one more look at his mother before heading up the driveway to Joe and the waiting van. She stood on the steps and mouthed the words, "I love you."

"Same to you, Mrs. Monroe. Same to you."

He got back to the van as Joe clicked off his cell phone. "Everything go all right?" he asked.

Shane slumped in the passenger seat, drained. "Let's get out of here."

Joe put the van in drive and pulled away from the curb. "Good idea. We've got a lot to do before tonight."

Shane glanced his way. "Why, what have you got planned for tonight?"

Joe watched the road, eyes twinkling. "How do you feel about breaking and entering?"

Iris Green slouched in the seat of her unremarkable sedan and watched as the white van pulled up in front of the Monroe house. No bells or whistles went off in her head; trucks and vans had been coming and going from the house all week. Marked Renovations Inc., this one appeared no different from any of the others.

She closed her eyes briefly, her recent lack of sleep beginning to have its effects, and saw the image of Thomas Stanley flopping around in his hospital bed as he struggled to breathe.

Her eyes snapped open again, but the horrible picture did not go away. In the back of her mind she still saw him heaving and thrashing, his hand frantically searching for the notepad and pen, the sound of the respirator alarm almost deafening. And the most horrible image of all, Tarker Ames's peaceful face as he squeezed the respirator tube open and closed, the man's very life in his grasp.

To her shame, Iris had left the room. She wondered now how long it had taken for Stanley to finally die? Had it been a few minutes? An hour? Two days? Every time she closed her eyes she saw the helpless man being murdered at the hands of her partner.

In an attempt to distract herself she picked up a small pair of binoculars from the seat beside her. Iris studied the back of the van that had just pulled up. *Just do your job*, she thought. *For today, just go with the flow*. Eventually, she would have to figure out how to extricate herself from the BBD without ending up like Thomas Stanley. But she needed time to sort things out.

For no real reason other than to combat her anxiety, to redirect her attention, Iris picked up her cell phone and called in a trace of the license plate. She hung up; they would call back in a moment with the results.

Iris thought about her last conversation with Shane Monroe. She'd interrogated murderers in her tour with the FBI, and there was always something about them—a weird body tick, a certain look in their eyes. No matter how strongly they protested their innocence, the guilt was always there like some kind of caul over their faces. But no matter how hard she tried to find the sign, all Monroe seemed guilty of was being pissed off and scared.

*What do you know, Shane?* she thought. *What makes you so damn valuable to them?* Iris was determined to find the kid before Ames did. She wanted to know why the Department had pulled out all the stops to bring him in.

"It's not supposed to be like this," she muttered to herself. Her mind skipped through memories and images from her early days in the academy when she couldn't wait to get out and save the world. *Look at me now,* she thought. Her partner had murdered in the name of some shadow agency that supposedly existed for the good of the country, and she had walked out of the room so she would feel less culpable.

That was bullshit. She was culpable. She could have stopped it. *But at what cost?* And that was the truth of it. Iris had been afraid of what would happen to her if she tried to stop Ames. It cut her to the core to confess that to herself. She had always thought that when push came to shove, she would do the right thing, be the hero.

Iris slammed her head against the headrest

in frustration. Her eyes ached from lack of sleep, and she rubbed them. Thomas Stanley was still there waiting in the darkness—still dying.

She quickly opened her eyes and stared through the windshield at the peaceful Framingham neighborhood around her. Somebody had gotten out of the van with a clipboard and was heading up the drive. Iris picked up her binoculars for a closer look, but his back was to her as he moved out of view.

The cell phone chirped, and she picked it up. "Green."

It was the Department calling with the results of the plate trace on the van. They reported nothing out of the ordinary. The plate was legitimate, and Renovations Inc. had been in business since 1985.

Since she already had them on the phone, she decided to play it safe. "Do me a favor and take a look at their financial and tax records. I'll wait." She could hear the sound of fingers moving over a computer keyboard as she watched the roofers on the Monroe house.

Her answer came moments later. Internal Revenue files showed tax returns for Renovations Inc. filed for the last four years, but nothing before that. That didn't make much sense unless . . .

Iris broke the connection and picked up her binoculars. It could have been an IRS filing error, or possibly even some kind of computer glitch. But what if it wasn't?

The man with the clipboard was heading back to the van at a pretty good speed, and this time she could see his face. The hair color was different, and he had a goatee, but there was no mistaking Shane Monroe.

Iris picked up her phone, her thumb hovering over the auto-dial back to home base, and then thought better of it. She tossed it onto the seat beside her. The van was leaving. She waited a few seconds before starting after them.

If she was ever again going to feel good about what she was doing, she had to bring Shane Monroe in safely, so that the question of his innocence could be addressed.

And she had to do it without the violent interference of Tarker Ames or the BBD.

It was a little past three in the morning, and Shane sat in the passenger seat of the white van, the Renovations Inc. sign having been replaced with the far more colorful insignia of Fabonio's Pizza. Joe Levine was behind the wheel, and another Truth Seeker named Roberta sat in the back. All three of them watched through the windshield of the van as a fourth member of their team, a guy named Max, rapped on the glass door of the Cambridge Research Foundation. From this vantage point they could just make out the guard who sat behind a high desk beyond the plateglass windows at the front of the building.

Max wrapped on the glass again. The guard must have been dozing because he quickly jumped to his feet. Max held up a pizza box to display to the guard through the glass. Between that box and the matching Fabonio's shirt and cap, there could be no doubt what Max's purpose was.

The guard moved around the desk, hiking up his pants to cover a prominent potbelly, and ambled toward the door. He unlatched the door, pushed it open a crack, and stuck his jowly face through it. "What do you want?" he snarled, loudly enough that Shane could hear him through the partially open window of the van.

Max looked at the white box and then back to the man. "Pizza delivery," he responded, sounding a little disgusted that he had to explain himself.

"Who's it for?" the guard asked.

"Wait a sec, I got the name right here," Max told him as he reached inside the box and removed a small, silver spray canister.

"What's that?" the guard demanded.

Shane watched as Max put the spray nozzle beneath the guard's nose and depressed the plunger. There was a loud hiss, and a moisture-filled cloud enveloped the man's face. Shane was amazed at how quickly the gas took effect. The security guard's eyes rolled back in his head, and Max had to catch him so the man would not crack his head on the floor. The Truth Seeker slid the guard gently to the ground, his foot still propping the door open.

"Move," Joe said as he popped open his door.

Shane and Roberta followed him out of the van and they hurried over to the front of the building where Max was already dragging the unconscious guard back through the door. They had prepared for this raid on the lab for days without Shane's knowledge. His new associates had schematics of the floor plan, surveillance of the guards on duty, and records of local police response time. At the last moment they had asked Shane to draw a map of the layout of his lab and explained that unless he came along they would never be able to be certain if they had gotten everything.

As far as he was concerned he had no choice. He had created this tech. Given a chance to take it away from the people who were misusing it, he could not turn his back. Now, heart thundering in his chest, hands clammy with anxiety, he only hoped that he was not an anchor to Joe and the others, that he did not do anything to screw up their operation.

"What is that stuff?" Shane asked as Max stashed the unlabeled spray can inside his jacket.

Behind the desk, out of sight of the street, Max kneeled beside the security guard and checked his pulse. "It was developed by the military a few years back. They spray it from helicopters when they need to incapacitate large numbers."

"It's almost never been used domestically except on a couple of small towns when they've had to remove extraterrestrial wreckage from crash sites," Joe added casually. "Pretty powerful stuff. He should be out for the rest of his shift."

"Extraterrestrial wreckage?" Shane asked.

"And that's just the half of it," Joe replied, his tone suggesting that the conversation was over.

They sat the guard in his chair and let him slump forward on the desk. He looked very much the way he had when Max had first rapped on the window.

They hurried to the elevator, where Max and Roberta got to work and Shane stared at them in fascination. Though he had been with the Truth Seekers several weeks, he had only just begun to pay any real attention to what they did. Although he was certainly well versed in computers, his field was really physics, and so some of the technology that they had at their disposal—most of it, he suspected, was either stolen or liberated from some covert agency or another—was foreign to him. Case in point, he stared mesmerized as

Roberta slipped a card key into a slot beside the elevator. Once upon a time, Shane had had a card that would have unlocked it. But attached to the card Roberta was using was a black plastic box the size of a pager. A red light blinked on the top, but otherwise the device was featureless. It could have been anything.

What it was, Shane now knew, was a locking sequence decoder. It would download an infinite series of number combinations into the locking mechanism until it found an access code that the security system recognized.

"C'mon, baby," Max muttered, staring at the tiny device. As though responding to his words, the tiny light on its black surface turned green.

The elevator chimed cheerfully, and the doors slowly slid open.

"Ain't technology grand?" Roberta asked with a bright smile as Max retrieved the card key and they all stepped inside.

"Go ahead, Shane," Joe said. "This used to be your playground."

Shane leaned forward and hit six. They waited in silence as the elevator rose, and then the doors slid open on the sixth floor.

Joe gestured for Shane to get out first. "We're following you."

The aroma of fresh paint assailed him as he stepped out onto the sixth floor. "It's completely different," Shane said, looking up and down the hallway. "They've remodeled the entire floor." Shane turned a corner and pointed to a small office space. "That used to be the entrance to the lab, and the environmental control chamber was behind it."

"Did you think they wouldn't try to hide it?" Joe asked.

Shane glanced at him in surprise. "You knew they'd changed it?"

The other man shrugged. "What else would they do? I mean, on the off chance that you told your story to someone who believed you? It was what we expected, and our sources confirmed it."

"But you didn't mention it to me," Shane replied.

Joe only smiled. The expression said a great many things, not the least of which was that Shane might be running with the pack at the moment, but that did not make him a part of it. He was working with the Truth Seekers, they were helping him, but he was not one of them.

He frowned. "I don't get it. If they wiped my data and moved the project—"

"They didn't wipe it. They just moved it. Your friend Dr. Bennett still has an office here. We want to get what we can from that and then frag his hard drive. We couldn't hack it from outside the firewall they've got here, but from inside it's a different story. Plus, Roberta here's going to e-mail a virus to everyone in Bennett's address book that will do the same to them. We can't be sure that will have the kind of impact on the Force Majeure project that we'd like, but it might."

Shane stared at him. "You had all this planned. And . . . I'm glad. I mean, you're way ahead of me. But I figured the lab was still here, that that was why we were hitting this place. Nobody thought to mention the plan to me?"

Roberta and Max looked anxious. Joe waved them on, and they ran down the hall toward Dr. Bennett's office. Then he turned to regard Shane coldly. "Don't take offense, okay? But you're an unknown quantity, Shane. You could rabbit on us—"

"I'm not going anywhere," Shane argued, frustrated.

"But you could. Or they could grab you up, no matter how well protected we've got you. Eventually, if you stick around, I figure you'll end up a larger part of this operation than you ever wanted to be. You're a quick study, with more street smarts than the typical egghead ever gets credit for. But for now, the less you know, the better for all of us, you included."

Joe turned and went down the hall after Max and Roberta. Shane wanted to push the subject, but didn't know what else he would have said. The tone of Joe's voice had made it clear there was no room for argument. With a buzz of frustration and annoyance going around his head, he set off after the others.

Bennett's office was still there, but it was locked. Max did not hesitate a moment. He hauled back and kicked the door in, splintering the wooden frame.

Roberta went right to the computer on the desk and turned it on. Shane glanced around, always surprised at the difference between this place and Bennett's stuffy academic office at Hazeltine. He recalled his interview here when he first applied to work for the Foundation. He'd been extremely nervous going in, but Carl Bennett and the rather jovial atmosphere of the man's office had quickly put him at ease. Bennett loved Warner Brothers cartoons, and this room was a tribute of sorts—filled with toys, statues, and Dr. Bennett's prized possession: a framed animation cell of Bugs Bunny signed by animator Chuck Jones.

"Looks like we got ourselves a password problem, folks," Roberta said, staring at the screen. "I've tried half a dozen ways to bypass, but there aren't any back doors. I could probably figure it out eventually, but I don't think we have that kind of time."

Shane moved around the desk with the others to stare at the screen. *What would someone like Dr. Bennett use for a personal password?* Shane took note of the cartoon paraphernalia on display all over the office. A tiny statue of the Road Runner on top of the monitor caught his attention, and he remembered the night they had celebrated their success. *Last stop, the apartment of Shane Monroe—super genius.* Dr. Bennett had imitated the Coyote from the Road Runner cartoons. Bennett had done that imitation often.

"Try *super genius,* two words," Shane instructed Roberta.

The woman turned and looked at him, then at the others. She hesitated until Joe nudged her back.

"Go ahead. Try it."

Her fingers flew across the keys, and she smiled like a kid at Christmas when Carl Bennett's private files opened before her. Roberta pulled a blank CD from inside her jacket pocket and slipped it into the burner tray.

"Well, we're here. So howzabout we just copy everything," she said with a mischievous grin. She manipulated the mouse on the Tweety Bird pad, and a cartoon image of papers flying from one folder to another appeared on the screen.

"Now to get online," Roberta muttered.

Once again, her fingers danced over the keyboard. When the demand came again for a password, Roberta entered the same one. A moment later Bennett's computer began to retrieve its new e-mail messages.

"We're in," she said.

They breathed a collective sigh of relief.

Shane noticed something at the bottom of the screen and leaned in closer to the monitor. "What's that?" he asked, tapping a flashing red dot in the far corner of the screen. "It wasn't there before."

Roberta looked at the screen. "Crap. We tripped an alarm." She glanced guiltily at the others. "Sorry. I looked for the obvious stuff, but I didn't think to check if there was a safeguard on the files themselves. It's the copying that did it."

Joe swore, glancing quickly about the office. "Let's take what we've got and move on outta here, people." He turned back to Roberta. "Dump the virus into the system. Now. We're about to have company."

Working swiftly, Roberta plucked the CD from the burner tray, then inserted another from a case she had taken out of her inner jacket pocket. She slipped the new disk in, and immediately a new window opened on-screen asking if she wanted to install and run the application Roberta had named "Typhoid."

She clicked on *Yes*, and the screen flashed quickly through several windows. The smile on Roberta's face was chilling to see. Shane wondered if the virus would spread beyond those people in Bennett's address book, wiping the hard drives of not just hundreds, but many thousands of people on the Net. He decided he did not want to know.

"Move," Joe barked.

Roberta got up from Bennett's desk and followed the rest of the group to the door. "We didn't get all the files—but that's better than nothing," she said.

Shane hung back. A kind of silent rage had been building in him as his memories of Carl Bennett—and of this place—cut into him. He let Roberta pass him and stood staring at the autographed Bugs Bunny animation cell. He hauled back and drove his fist into the center of the picture, breaking the glass and sending the piece crashing to the floor. He hissed and shook his hand at the stinging pain that came from the cuts that now crisscrossed his knuckles.

"You coming, Monroe," Joe asked from the hall, "or are you staying to greet the authorities?"

Shane hurried from the office and saw that the others were not heading for the elevators. "We're taking the stairs?" he asked as he caught up to Max. Roberta and Joe were already shoving open the door to the stairwell.

"We may get out of here before the cops arrive," Max replied as he shoved the door open and held it for Shane to pass. "But we can't risk being on the elevator when they get here. We go all the way to the basement and hope we're gone before they get organized."

Shane hustled down the stairs after Joe and Roberta, their footsteps echoing off the concrete

walls. Max followed close on his heels. It
occurred to him that if he ever did decide that he
wanted to be a part of this group he was going to
need to start doing a lot more thinking ahead.
There was no *Mission: Impossible* sliding-down-
elevator-cable-or-on-ropes-out-the-windows
escape for them. The Truth Seekers were good
at what they did, but this wasn't a movie.

No, their best chance of eluding the police
was the basement. When he had first started
at the Foundation, Shane recalled, he had
helped some of the lab assistants bring in a
shipment of new computers through a garage
door that led out onto a loading bay in the
back alley. Joe and Poisson must have seen
that on the schematics of the building and
planned it as their escape route if anything
went wrong. But . . .

Shane frowned as he rounded the next
landing and started down toward the third
floor. "What about the van?" he asked.

"Screw the van," Joe Levine snapped from
below him.

Max laughed. "The van's clean, Shane.
We'd never have left it out there if it
weren't."

They raced down the last few flights of
stairs. At the bottom, Joe opened a heavy door
into the basement. With caution, he led the
group through the semidarkness, past the various cooling and heating systems and electrical stations.

"Looks like the coast is clear," Joe said as he led them up a slight incline toward the closed, sliding door. He glanced at his watch. "Given the typical response time around here, I'm guessing they're hitting the lobby and finding Sleeping Beauty up there right about now. It'll be a couple of minutes before they get a unit to look back here.

"Shane, you want to get the door?"

For a moment Shane only stared at the garage door. He knew they could use the decoder to figure out what the numerical sequence was to unlock and open it, but it would be faster if he could remember. It surprised him to find that he did.

"As long as they haven't changed it since," he replied as he punched the simple code 4-3-2-1 into a keypad on the wall. After a moment, the door hummed to life and began to slowly ascend. Shane looked toward Joe. The Truth Seeker was watching him and smiling.

"What?" Shane asked him.

Joe shook his head, moving closer to the door as it rose. "I had my doubts, Monroe, but I think you're gonna work out just fine."

"Thanks," he replied. Then he shook his head with a soft chuckle. "I think."

The alley outside was well lit, and they leaned back into the shadows cast by the Foundation building. Shane scanned both ends of the alley.

"All right, we split up, now. Less conspicuous that way," Joe instructed them. "Other than Shane, they're not going to know who they're looking for. Individually, in cabs or buses or on the T, nobody's going to give us a second look." He turned to Shane. "You have the cash Poisson gave you. Get back to the base when you can. Don't rush. Do *not* get caught."

"Not really on my list of things to do," Shane said dryly.

Roberta and Max nodded in agreement.

"See you soon," Joe said, and then he turned and started off down the alley, using the shadows for cover.

Max and Roberta followed and, after a moment, Shane did as well. One by one, they waited at the corner, and when the coast was clear, took off in different directions. Joe went north, weaving in between some parked cars. Roberta headed south. Max scaled a chain-link fence and disappeared into the darkness. Obviously they had all been part of other missions like this and knew full well how they were supposed to play it out. It was all new to him, however. And though he found it terrifying, there was also something exhilarating about it.

At the end of the alley he peered around the corner. He did not want to follow any of the others, but unless he wanted to hide in the big blue Dumpster across the street, he did not have much choice. After a moment's hesitation, he went north, crossing the street and picking up the collar of his jacket against the cool night breeze. He started for the subway station two blocks away.

As he passed the Dumpster, he heard the scuff of shoes on the pavement behind him and turned, panic surging up inside him, heart hammering, to find himself staring down the barrel of Iris Green's gun.

"Hey, Shane," she said. "Nice night for a walk."

# CHAPTER TWELVE

*"If we could produce electric storms of the required ability, this whole planet and the conditions of existence on it could be transformed."*

—Nikola Tesla

Iris Green watched as Shane slowly raised his hands.

"You could do without the dye job," she said as she studied him. "But I like the goatee. Makes you look older."

Somewhere not far off, car doors slammed. Iris glanced back toward the mouth of the alley Shane and his friends had just snuck out of. The last thing she wanted was for the Department, or even the police, to interrupt this conversation. She gestured along the street with the barrel of the gun. "Walk with me," she said, moving up beside him and holding the gun close against her abdomen.

"Can I put my arms down?" he asked.

Iris arched an eyebrow. "Who told you to

raise them? Just don't try going for my weapon and we'll be best friends, okay?"

"Deal," Shane said, a forlorn look on his face.

They fell into step beside each other and started away from the Foundation.

"I'm going to give you three minutes to explain yourself," she told him. "Go."

Shane didn't need any more prompting than that. "I won't tell you anything about the people who took me out of your custody—"

"You don't have to. I know exactly what they are," she interrupted. "The Truth Seekers, terrorists responsible for the deaths of at least four Department agents. So far you're not exactly winning me over, Shane."

He froze there on the sidewalk. Then Shane Monroe turned and glared at Iris with a kind of disdain she had never felt from anyone but Tarker Ames. "I don't have to win you over, lady," he said angrily. "I haven't done anything wrong. You and your friends in the Black Box Department? You're the bad guys here."

"That's . . . that's ridiculous," she said slowly, pursing her lips.

"The truth hurts," Shane muttered. "And you're eating into my three minutes."

Iris stared at him. All of a sudden the scared college kid had grown up a little. She wasn't sure if she liked that, but she certainly respected it. "Go on," she said, and then they fell into step together again.

"I had nothing to do with the deaths of those agents," Shane said. "That raid was just as much a surprise to me as it was to you. I'd never even heard of the Truth Seekers until after they freed me. But an awful lot has become clear since I've been with them."

Iris scowled. "I suppose you're going to tell me that you had nothing to do with the break-in I just caught you running away from, or maybe you were forced to help at gun-point?"

"You don't have a clue what you're talking about, do you, Agent Green?" Shane asked. "The Truth Seekers have been the only people I've encountered since my life went to hell that actually seem to understand what's going on. You sure don't. Yes, I was helping them destroy computer files back there, hoping that might stop the BBD from killing more people with the technology that I helped create. If that's a crime, fine, I'm a criminal."

"BBD?" she echoed. "You mentioned that before. The Black Box Department. The BBD is nothing but the product of paranoid minds that think everybody and everything associated with the government is out to take away their personal freedom."

The image of Tarker Ames squeezing Thomas Stanley's air hose flashed before her eyes. She quickly wished the disturbing imagery away.

"The organization that I work for exists to protect the citizenry of the United States from dangerous technological advancements," she continued.

"Who are you trying to convince?" Shane asked. "Me, or yourself?"

The sounds of the tortured Truth Seeker's gasps as he'd struggled to stay alive echoed in Iris's ears, mingling with her words, and she knew that everything she had just said was complete and utter bullshit.

"I can guarantee your safety. I want to get to the bottom of this as much as you do, Shane, and I promise you'll never be out of my sight."

Shane grunted as he lunged forward and grabbed the wrist of her gun hand. Iris shouted a warning but was stunned as he turned her hand so that the weapon was pointed at his own chest—specifically his heart—and leaned into the barrel. He locked eyes with her.

"You want to bring me in? You want to guarantee my safety? You want to hold me in custody while you investigate my story, find out who really killed my friends and why they're after me now? You might as well shoot me now. 'Cause in their hands, one way or another, I'll be dead soon enough."

Iris tried to pull away, but Shane held on.

"That's . . . that's absurd! Let go of the gun. I'm a federal agent, Shane. I can *protect* you."

"You know what they'll do to make me work for them—and I won't do it. I'd rather die."

She felt his grip weaken and pulled her gun hand away. "Aren't we being a little dramatic?"

"I would have said yes a month ago. But that was before I helped develop technology the government could use to manipulate the weather, to create storms that would kill people, Agent Green. Sounds crazy, doesn't it? But I know it's true, because I did it. I did it. Do you have any idea how that makes me feel? People have already died, including some of my friends, and all of that is on my head, one way or the other. I have to live with that.

"And the BBD killed my father.

"You want to think I'm paranoid, feel free. But dramatic? You can go to hell, lady. With all that's happened to me in the last month, I think I'm taking things pretty well."

Iris lowered her weapon, the gun suddenly very heavy in her hands.

"They have to be stopped," Shane said. "I've read the Truth Seekers' files on them. I know what they've done over the years. The way you act, it's like you have no idea. You've got this perfectly benevolent vision of the people you work for. Here's the harsh truth, Agent Green. You're not one of the Knights of the Round Table. That's just a legend. Myths aren't real, but the rumors, especially the most paranoid ones? They're all true."

Iris swallowed and was surprised to find her throat dry. Images of Tarker Ames and General Remington flashed through her mind, and she wished with all her might that she could reverse her life and go back to her days with the FBI. They weren't all happy, but at least she had known where she'd stood.

"I won't deny there may have been some abuses of power, but—"

"Did you not hear me when I said they killed my father?" Shane snapped.

Iris shook her head. "How can you know that? I've read your file. Your father's been dead for years."

"They wanted him to work for them, and he refused. He threatened to expose them and he was murdered. The BBD made it look like an accident, but they killed him."

She could have denied it. She could have looked him straight in the eye and told him that the terrorists he was working with were using him, feeding him false information—but she couldn't. It just sounded too much like the truth.

Iris brought her gun around her back and holstered it. "Get out of here, Monroe." She didn't want to look at him. She didn't want him to see the shame in her eyes.

"Come with me," he said, not moving.

"With the Seekers' help, we could expose—"

Iris looked at him, filled with rage fired by disgrace. "Go! Before I change my mind and haul your ass into custody."

He began to walk past her and stopped. She felt herself tense. If he asked her again to join him, she wasn't sure what she would do.

"Thanks," he said quietly, and continued on his way. He turned the corner and was gone.

Iris reached down and turned the volume up on her walkie-talkie. She wasn't the least bit surprised to hear them calling her. She had been out of radio contact for several minutes.

"Agent Green, do you copy?" a voice said. "Agent Green, this is Agent Pyer—"

"I'm here, Pyer. I thought I saw something, but it turned out to be nothing. Everything's quiet. Looks like they got out through a loading dock exit."

There was silence and then a crackle of static before Pyer spoke again. "Yeah, nothing here, either. Looks like they got away clean this time. But I wouldn't worry. From what I hear, this case'll be pretty much over by morning, anyway."

"What's that supposed to mean?" Iris asked in alarm.

Again there was static, and she stepped out of the alley hoping to improve the reception.

"Word is they've found the Truth Seekers' nest. Agent Ames is putting together an assault team as we speak. It should all be hitting the fan within the next few hours."

Static roared from the device, and she turned it off altogether as she hurried back to her car. Her thoughts raced. She'd let Monroe go only to have him return to the very place where it was the most dangerous for him to be.

*What the hell do I do now?* she thought.

The answer was painfully hard to accept: Absolutely nothing.

Tarker Ames stepped languidly down from the cab of the metallic green Range Rover and surveyed the tranquil marshland around him.

"Agent Ames?"

Tarker had noticed someone approaching out of the corner of his eye. Now he turned to find a man dressed in full combat gear with grenades of various sizes hanging from his jet-black flack vest and an assault rifle hanging over one shoulder.

"Commander Wayne Maddan," the man said, adjusting his helmet before he reached out to grasp Tarker's hand in a firm shake. "We're just about ready to begin."

Tarker let go of the soldier's hand and looked out over the expanse of marshland. He could see the gray stone shape of the supposedly abandoned marine biology station squatting among the tall grass like some kind of strangely angled toad. "Excellent," he responded cheerfully.

"Each team will be wearing one of these," Commander Maddan said, tapping a tiny video camera taped to the side of his helmet. "If you'd like, you can go to the communications station and watch the operation from there."

"That won't be necessary, Commander," Tarker said, fixing the soldier in his cold gaze. "I'll be accompanying your team."

The soldier's expression grew tight. "Sir, please. It's completely unnecessary and quite dangerous for you to—"

"I'm aware of the danger, Commander," Tarker interrupted. "Now, if your people will loan me the proper attire, I'll suit up and we can get this show on the road."

Maddan's face reddened, and his voice dripped with sarcasm. "Will there be any other special guests joining us, sir?"

"No. I would have brought my lovely partner along, but I doubt her heart would be in something like this."

The soldier abruptly stormed off in the direction of a large black van, leaving Tarker with thoughts of his partner. Tarker recalled Iris's horror as he interrogated the Truth Seeker prisoner back at the hospital. She hadn't even stayed long enough to see the fruit of his arduous labor. Thomas Stanley had lasted longer than Tarker would have expected, but eventually he had given up the most important information, the location of the Truth Seeker base. It was obvious that Iris thought he was some kind of monster, but Tarker knew that it was in his heart to be merciful. When Stanley had told him what he wanted to know, Tarker had killed him quickly.

Tarker was becoming concerned about his new partner. It bothered him to think it, but she was soft, and in this job that could be dangerous—especially to him and the Department.

A gull shrieked overhead, and Tarker gazed into the powder blue sky at the bird that seemed to hang in space, defying gravity. *It really is peaceful here*, he thought with a heavy sigh.

It was a real shame that a place as beautiful and tranquil as this was about to be sullied by so much bloodshed and violence.

A real shame.

Shane took a long draft from the bottle of springwater before he pulled out a chair and joined Max, Roberta, and Joe around the large kitchen table.

"Good to see you made it back," Joe said as he ate the final remnants of his breakfast.

"When did you guys get here?" Shane asked.

"About an hour and a half ago," Max replied.

Shane leaned back in his chair, smiling tiredly. "How did you get from Boston to Nahant in under an hour? I took the T to Haymarket, caught a bus to Central Square, cabbed to the Bayside Restaurant, and walked the rest of the way." He took another swig of water. "Let me guess, you guys have perfected teleportation and beamed yourselves back here."

"Teleportation, now that's something we should really be looking into," David Poisson said as he walked into the kitchen.

Joe leaned over and patted Shane on the shoulder. "You're still a novice, Monroe. Maybe in a few months you'll be ready for some of the more complex mysteries that—"

David laughed and cut Joe off. "Yeah, like Car Theft 101."

"You stole a car?" Shane asked, taken aback.

Joe, Max and Roberta shrugged in unison.

"Yeah, but it was for a good cause," Joe said. "We did look for you."

Shane set his water bottle down on the table. "Yeah, well, for a while there, I didn't think I'd be making it back at all."

That got their attention. Joe had picked up a napkin from the plate in front of him and begun to tear it into strips. Now he stared at Shane. "Did they see you?"

"Remember that BBD agent I was talking about—Green?" He hesitated, unsure if he should tell them. But it was too late now. He had begun. What was that old saying? *In for a penny, in for a pound.* The same was true, he supposed, of his relationship with the Truth Seekers. "Well, she caught me right outside the alley and then let me go."

Joe's face twisted up in confusion, his blue eyes twinkling with nervous energy. "Now wait a minute, a BBD agent had you and then let you just walk away?"

Shane nodded as he screwed the cap in his hand back onto his water bottle. "She was one of the agents that had me when they first picked me up. Even then I kind of got a vibe off of her, like she had some doubts about the way things were going. I got the impression she didn't even know what the people she works for really do. Tonight, she gave me a chance to talk to her, and I think it freaked her out, what I was saying. Hey, she let me go, right?"

Joe looked as though he were going to jump out of his skin. "This isn't good, David, not good at all."

"Hold on, Joe," David said calmly. "Let Shane finish before we go into panic mode."

Shane was confused by the sudden tension. Then it struck him, and he started shaking his head. "No, you guys. Listen, I wasn't followed, okay? I mean, not that I'm some expert, but with what I had to go through to get back here . . . and, anyway, I'm telling you, Green is spooked by all this. She seems on the up and up."

But Poisson was obviously unsettled. "She seems to be, Shane," David said. "That doesn't mean she is."

A heavy silence fell upon the room then. Shane shifted uncomfortably as the others all gazed at one another. Though David seemed merely anxious, Joe was obviously pissed off, and that made Shane feel stupid, which only made him angrier. They hadn't met Agent Green. Who were they to judge?

The silence was interrupted by the abrupt, piercing squeal of an alarm bell. Shane's eyes went wide, and his thoughts raced. *No*, he thought. *No way.*

Poisson swore. "Perimeter alarm."

He rose and rushed out of the kitchen toward the command center. The others followed him hurriedly. Shane felt numb as he went along with them. Just outside the kitchen door, Joe pushed past him. "You should have thought of this, Shane," Joe said. "She let you go so you could be followed back here."

Shane was about to object, but the words wouldn't come. What if Joe was right? What if he had led the BBD right to their doorstep? He followed the others to the control center, trying not to think about the repercussions from such an action. Trying, and failing. His clash with the BBD had already cost the lives of his best friends. *How many more people are going to die because of me?*

He felt nauseated.

The control center was a flurry of activity as he entered. He spotted David and the others in a far corner of the room and headed toward them. They were standing behind a short, round-faced man who sat at a control panel. All were staring up at a bank of video monitors mounted on the wall.

"What do we have, Mike?" Poisson asked.

"Perimeter breach in the north sector," Mike said as he manipulated a small toggle on his control board to change the views.

A dark shape darted across screen number three. Then more intruders appeared on several of the other monitors.

"Oh, boy," Mike muttered. "Trouble."

Shane wormed his way closer.

Without a word, David turned and strode toward the support column in the center of the room, where a small plastic alarm box was located. Grimly, he smashed the plastic casing with his fist, then slammed the palm of his hand against the big red button. Instantly a deafening claxon filled the air, and Shane was caught up in a tide of scrambling Truth Seekers.

He saw Joe preparing to leave and grabbed his arm. "What now?" he asked, a horrible feeling churning in his gut.

Joe stared at him with cold, blue eyes.

"War," he said, and he strode from the room with an ominous purpose. "It's war."

Shane held the automatic weapon as if it were a deadly snake whose venomous bite might be fatal. All around him Truth Seekers grimly checked and rechecked their weapons as David finished handing out guns from their hidden arsenal.

"Problem, Shane?" Joe asked as he came to him with a similar weapon slung over his shoulder. They were like enormous pistols with fat, perforated barrels and long cartridges jutting from their bellies. On the back of each weapon was a metal stock that folded out.

"I . . . I have no idea how to use this."

"Not much to it." Joe raised his own weapon, fitting the metal stock against his shoulder. "Walther MPL. Used by German police and border guards before the Berlin wall came down. We have some K-50Ms and some Uzis—even some Armalites—around, but this is good for you. Selective fire. You're less likely to shoot all of us by mistake."

He reached for Shane's weapon and flipped a catch on the side. "Make sure the safety's off, aim, and shoot the bad guys." Joe handed the weapon back. "You screwed up, Shane, but you didn't know. We shouldn't have left the area without you. Let's just hope we're all alive to bust your chops about it later."

"Welcome to the Truth Seekers," Shane muttered as he gazed at the instrument of death in his hands.

Joe punched him in the shoulder reassuringly as they followed the others back toward the control center. "That's what I was gonna say."

They had just stepped through the doorway when the outside security door exploded from its hinges with a sound like thunder. Shane saw the first casualties of war go down in broken heaps, too close to the force of the blast. The others ran for cover, toppling computer tables to use as shields.

"This is it, people," David bellowed as he marched into the room, an assault rifle cradled in his large arms.

For a moment, everything was silent, the sense of expectation so thick in the air, it was almost palpable. Smoke poured in from the ravaged doorway, and then Shane saw dark shapes swimming within it. The BBD assault force fired first as they streamed into the room clad in black jumpsuits, face masks, and helmets like some kind of alien invasion from one of the countless science fiction movies Shane had watched with Spud and Geoff. Except these attackers did not fire ray beams courtesy of some Hollywood special effects studio. What these invaders fired was real and could kill a person in an instant.

He watched the attack unfold in a weird

kind of slow motion. Truth Seekers fired their
weapons from behind overturned office furniture. BBD soldiers fell in the deadly rain of
bullets as more agents emerged from the
smoke to take their place. Men and women
he had learned to call friends danced obscene
jigs of death as automatic gunfire tore
through their bodies.

Shane jumped as a powerful hand gripped
his shoulder and pulled him to the floor just
as the wall behind him dissolved in an angry
swarm of bullets.

"Wake up, Shane!" David hollered above
the sound of gunfire and the screams of the
dying. "If you want to see these sons of
bitches pay, you have to *fight*!"

"I . . . I don't know if I can . . . *kill*."

"Then stay down and don't move until I
tell you to!"

David pulled him down further behind an
overturned computer station, then popped up
and began to spray the room with bullets.

"They're falling back," David said as he
pulled the empty clip from his weapon and
snapped a new one home.

Shane peered cautiously over the table at
the control-center-turned-battleground. Bodies
of Truth Seekers and BBD agents alike littered
the ground, mingled as they never did in life.

*Death is the ultimate equalizer,* Shane
thought. He'd heard that somewhere before
but could not remember where.

It was then that he spotted Joe across the room. He seemed to be having a problem with his weapon; the firing mechanism or the clip or something was jammed. In frustration, he threw it to the ground and signaled to David that he was going to try to retrieve a gun from one of the fallen BBD agents. David vehemently shook his head, but Joe was already moving.

"Idiot," David muttered as he aimed his own weapon over the barrier to cover him.

Joe was just pulling a machine pistol from the grip one of the dead agents when Shane caught a flash of movement from the doorway. He gasped as something landed in the center of the room, something that sputtered and smoked.

"Stun grenade, get down!" David screamed as they dove to the floor.

"Cover your ears and keep your mouth open!"

The grenade exploded and sent a deafening shock wave through the enclosed space. Shane felt as though his head had been wrapped in foam rubber and then whacked with a shovel. He struggled to regain his footing.

Next to him David was blinking and shaking his head.

"Joe . . . ," Shane said.

They peered from their cover to see Joe lying unconscious on his back in the center of the room and black-garbed BBD agents slowly coming through the doorway, weapons trained on every corner, every shadow. Shane was overcome as the fear, anger, and frustration of the last few weeks suddenly exploded within him. He grabbed the automatic weapon by his side, and with a scream of rage, squeezed the trigger.

Three of the black-garbed agents went down while the others scrambled for cover. They wore Kevlar body armor, he knew, and so they were probably only injured. Part of him wished he could hurt them more. BBD agents poured into the room and began to concentrate their fire in Shane's direction as he continued to click on empty rounds.

"We've got to get out of here!" David yelled above the din as he dragged Shane back to the floor.

"What about Joe?"

"He knew the risk. We leave now or all we've done adds up to nothing. They win. Do you want that, Shane?" David asked as he began to crawl toward the long hallway behind them.

Other Truth Seekers were already dragging themselves down the hall, and Shane began to follow, but something pulled him back. He couldn't leave another friend to die. He glanced toward Joe.

The room was now filled with BBD agents, and one stood over Joe, weapon pointed down at him as he slowly regained consciousness. Shane felt his heart pound. There wasn't much time. Quietly he aimed his weapon at the figure looming over his friend and pulled the trigger.

Nothing. In the chaos, he had forgotten that the clip was empty.

The agent removed his helmet and looked around. It was Tarker Ames. Shane felt the knot of rage in his belly tightening. Geoff's last words echoed eerily in his mind:

*"Get outta here, Shane. Get outta here now. Run!"*

"Not this time," he said softly.

His gaze locked on Joe and the down-home country boy face of Tarker Ames, he leaped from his cover, roaring as loud as he could, and scrambled across the room toward them.

He saw the soldiers take aim with their weapons and recognition bleed across Agent Ames's face.

"Hold your fire!" Tarker commanded.

It was exactly what Shane was hoping for. They still needed him.

He reached down and scooped a cylindrical device from the flack vest of one of the dead BBD agents as he charged past. He knew it was some kind of grenade. He pulled the pin and tossed the smoking explosive at Tarker as he dove for the floor.

The agent raised his weapon in response and fired, but it was too late. The grenade exploded with a flash of phosphorescence that ignited

Ames's hair and tossed him to the floor.

Shane managed to crawl to Joe in the confusion. His friend was stunned, blood oozing from his ears.

"C'mon, get up!" Shane screamed as he pulled the man to his feet and half dragged, half carried him toward the safety of the hallway.

Bullets rained down around them, and Shane was sure they would die, until David appeared in the entryway. He let loose a spray of gunfire that slowed the enemy and covered their retreat.

"The kitchen!" he hollered. "I'm right behind you!"

Shane and Joe stumbled into the kitchen. He was shocked to see that the large refrigerator unit had been pulled away from the wall to reveal an entrance to a tunnel. He pushed Joe down into the tunnel and then followed, careful not to step on his fingers as they climbed down the metal ladder. Shane glanced up to see David standing over the hidden entrance. He could hear the leader's labored breathing as he slid the heavy refrigeration unit back into place over the hole, hiding their escape route.

Shane continued his descent deeper into the earth as the entrance above was covered, and their retreat was plunged into total darkness.

# CHAPTER THIRTEEN

*"Higher electromotive forces were attainable with apparatus of larger dimensions."*
—Nikola Tesla

Jon Ledin adjusted his safety goggles before he picked up the large tree limb and dragged it over to the wood chipper. He fed the gnarled appendage into the gaping maw of the machine, watching as whirring blades ground the limb to so much sawdust and spit the remains into the back of the covered pickup truck it was attached to.

Sweat beaded on his forehead, and Jon wished he had listened to his landscaping partner and done this particular job yesterday, when the weather had been cooler. But Jon had talked Vinny into taking the day off for some gambling at Foxwoods Casino. Blinking away the sweat that stung his eyes, he wished that Vinny had had a little more willpower than he did.

Jon ran a gloved hand over his face and checked his watch. It was well after noon, and his partner had yet to return with their lunch. He debated on whether to call it quits for now, but decided to work until Vinny came back. He turned to haul another limb from the remains of the ash tree they had cut down that morning, and practically jumped out of his skin. A man was standing beside the pile, and it startled him.

Jon walked over to the chipper and shut it down. "Can I help you?" he asked. His eyes were drawn to a nasty red scar on the right side of the man's face. He was wearing dark sunglasses, but Jon could see the edge of a gauze patch that covered the man's right eye beneath the smoky lens. It was really pretty creepy. Whatever had scarred his face had tried to get at his eye as well.

The man removed a small notepad and pencil from his pocket. He flipped back the cover. "You're Jon Ledin, right?" he asked with a faint southern twang.

Jon could feel himself begin to panic. The guy had to be here about the unpaid traffic tickets.

"Look," he said with a heavy sigh as he pulled his work gloves off and placed them on top of the chipper, "I have every intention of paying those fines, but business hasn't been—"

"You're a friend of Shane Monroe? Classmates in high school, right?" the man interrupted.

Jon was momentarily confused. He'd heard

that Shane had been in trouble with the law recently, but why would the authorities be talking to him? "Yeah, he's a couple of years younger, but we still hung out."

The man put his notebook away. "Do you have any idea where Shane might be?"

Jon thought for a moment, trying to remember the last time he'd seen Shane. It was probably about the year after he'd graduated, at the Thanksgiving football game. They had exchanged E-mail addresses, but Jon had never gotten around to sending him anything.

"Nope. Haven't seen him in over a year. I heard he was in trouble, is that what this is about?"

It was warm, and the man carefully removed his sunglasses. He took a handkerchief from his front pocket and wiped the sweat from under his undamaged eye. "Something like that. I'd like you to send him a message for me," he said as he slipped the handkerchief back into his pocket.

Jon laughed. These law enforcement types didn't like to take no for an answer. "I just told you, I don't know where he is. I'm sorry, but I can't help you."

He didn't believe what they were saying about Shane, anyway. The thought of such a good guy committing murder was ludicrous. He turned away to retrieve his gloves. As far as he was concerned, the conversation was over and it was time to return to work.

The blow to the back of his head was abrupt and painful. Something cracked, and a spike of pain went through his skull. Everything began to spin, and Jon found himself facedown in the dirt. His head throbbed from the force of the blow as his vision started to dim at the edges.

He tried to stand and again he was struck. His body sagged to the ground. The chipper roared as it was turned on, and he was grabbed from behind and roughly hauled to his feet.

Jon had heard of this kind of thing before, read it in books, seen it in the movies. When the cops didn't believe you were sharing all the facts, they attempted to scare the truth from you. *Son of a bitch!* he thought. *I'm telling the truth.*

"What are you doing . . . ?" he wheezed, nauseated from the blows to his head. "I . . . I swear I don't know where he is."

The man's drawling voice was in his ear now. "I told you, I need you to send a message to your buddy, Shane."

He spun Jon around to face the gaping maw of the wood chipper. Jon struggled, but the man was much too strong for him.

"Please," he shrieked, thrashing in the man's grasp as he was pushed closer to the machine's hungry mouth. "For God's sake, how . . . how can I help . . . if I don't . . . ?"

"You're doin' just fine," the man said in a

leisurely tone as he pushed him toward the chipper.

Instinctively, Jon's arms shot forward to halt his descent and were grabbed by the maw of the ravenous machine. He shrieked in agony and shock as the torn-up remains of his limbs were spat into the back of the covered pickup in a scarlet, bone-flecked spray before the safety mechanism cut the power. Then darkness claimed him, and Jon surrendered to merciful oblivion.

Iris Green was summoned from the Royale Plaza Hotel to an unfinished office building in the Copley Square section of Boston. She entered the incomplete structure through a revolving door and stopped to watch four workers in hard hats finish attaching a section of wall.

She was sure she had the wrong address until she caught sight of an older man dressed in a dark, three-piece suit waving from a bank of elevators. She walked toward him, cautiously picking her way through construction debris.

"Agent Green?" he asked as she drew closer. "The Assistant Director is expecting you on the twelfth floor."

"Thank you," she said as she stepped into the elevator he had been holding for her.

As she ascended, she thought of all the strange places she had met with her superiors recently. It was odd not to have a base of operation, but with an organization like the Department, which really wasn't supposed to exist, she could understand why they didn't have a clubhouse. If anything, it made meetings interesting.

The elevator doors opened on a huge expanse of incomplete office space. General Remington stood in the center of the room reading a file, his large and menacing German shepherd standing alert by his side. The dog turned its large head toward her as she stepped from the elevator.

Tarker Ames was looking out over the city through a wall of floor-to-ceiling windows. He turned and walked toward her, and she struggled to control the shudder that passed through her. She had heard about his injury, but this was the first time she was seeing it. The flesh on the right side of his face was burnt a deep, mottled red that stood out like a beacon against the paleness of his skin. He wore a black patch over his right eye. "Hey, partner," he said with a smile. "I've missed you."

The smile was devoid of any warmth, and she did her best to imitate it in return. "I'm sorry about your injury," she said, feigning concern.

"Nothing a bit of plastic surgery and a good glass eye won't fix," Tarker said with a shrug. "I'll be seeing about it just as soon as this Monroe thing is put to bed."

"How is your search for the Truth Seekers progressing, Agent Green?" General Remington asked as he finally looked up from the file.

She felt Ames's good eye on her as she prepared her answer. "Nothing yet, sir. We're questioning local realtors for any large properties sold or leased over the last five years. We're also checking out a number of obscure abandoned properties."

What she didn't reveal was the result of her own private investigation into Shane's allegations that the Department had murdered his father. Iris didn't like what she had found. The Department had indeed approached Donald Monroe, and not only had he refused to join them, he had also threatened to reveal the existence of the shadow organization. Obviously that had been a big mistake on his part, for two weeks later he died in a fiery car crash. It was all there, documented in the Department files.

Remington strolled closer to them, the large dog following its master. "And your progress, Agent Ames?" he asked, intruding on Iris's thoughts.

Tarker placed his hands behind his back and cleared his throat. "We obtained a copy of Monroe's e-mail address book. As you can see from my report, I've managed to visit several of his local contacts and . . . persuaded them to send Monroe . . . messages."

Iris didn't care for the sound of that. Cold fingers of dread tickled the hair at the back of her neck. "Can I ask what you mean by that?"

"See for yourself," Remington said as he handed her the file.

Tarker continued on with his report, but Iris wasn't paying attention. Her legs felt weak as she opened the file to find a computer printout and several newspaper clippings. Names were highlighted on the printout, and for each of those names, a newspaper article recounted a horrible death.

"Excuse me, General," she said, her anger and revulsion on the rise. The dog began to whine as if sensing her hostility, and the general reached down to scratch behind its ear. "Yes, Agent Green?" He glared at her, challenging her to respond.

"Is this . . . is this what I think it is?"

Tarker laughed softly and shook his head. He sidled over beside the general, and then Iris knew exactly how this meeting was going to go.

"What do you think it is?" Remington asked.

Iris bristled, stood up straight, and glared right back at the general. "Well, sir, it looks like the Department is killing innocent people just to get Shane Monroe's attention. We're supposed to be working in the national interest, and that doesn't really seem like it's in the best interests of the nation to me. Sir."

"What the hell do you know about what's in the best interests of the nation, Agent Green?" Remington snarled.

Despite her resolve, Iris flinched.

"Monroe is capable of perfecting a very powerful weapon. Beyond that, his mind is an extremely valuable tool. One that could be very dangerous if turned against this country. If he should fall into the hands of the enemy . . . I shudder to think of the repercussions."

*That's it*, Iris decided, *they're all insane*. Everything Shane had said was true. She stared past the general at the spectacular view of the city. She didn't even realize that she'd begun to speak, the voice—her voice—sounded flat, as if synthesized by a machine.

"So you kill enough of his friends and he'll come out of hiding to save the ones who are still alive. Is that the plan, General?"

She focused her gaze on the older man who was calmly patting the head of the panting animal. She looked at Tarker. He was gently touching the black patch that covered his ruined eye.

"Why haven't you gone after his mother, then? I'm sure that would bring him running," she said, poison in her words.

Tarker let out a good-natured laugh. "That a girl," he said. "Now you're starting to think like a professional. See, General, I told you she'd catch on eventually."

She couldn't believe what she was hearing. They were so cold, so casual, as if they were discussing the weather for the weekend.

Remington continued to pat his dog. "We haven't touched Nancy Monroe because she's our ace in the hole."

Tarker strolled closer. He stood in front of her now, closer than she cared for. As his good eye stared, her gaze was drawn to the scars on his face.

"We're keeping a real close eye on Mommy Monroe," he said. "She's gonna help us catch that bad little boy of hers. Once Shane catches wind of what's been happening to his friends, he'll have to save her, won't he? Just think of her as a big old piece of cheese in the middle of a mousetrap."

The scarring was hideous, as if the badness that Iris knew existed inside of him was somehow bubbling up from the core of his pitch-black soul.

Lucas Yelverton had never fancied himself a religious man. Even after he formed The Brotherhood of White Freedom and built the White Freedom Compound in Arkansas for his 125 followers, Lucas shied away from the belief that there was one all-powerful force looking out for them. But that didn't stop those who followed his teachings from looking upon him as some kind of savior.

Yelverton sat behind the large, oak desk in his basement office and calmly contemplated his future. He thought of himself as a leader, a man of strong principles, a man who believed in fighting for what he wanted. He wondered how hard the enemy would fight when their polluted way of life began to crumble all around them.

The country was on the verge of moral collapse, the once mighty white race on the precipice of becoming the minority in a politically correct mockery of a world. That was why he had formed the Brotherhood, why he had gathered his followers in Arkansas.

He pulled open the desk drawer at his belly and removed a folded map. He spread it open on the desktop. "Historical Places to Visit with Your Family!" was written in cartoon lettering across the top. He looked over the multicolored map of the United States and wondered which state would be the first to fall.

His well-manicured finger traced the roadways connecting state to state, and he smiled. The Brotherhood had waited long enough. On a cold winter's night, a little over a year ago, Lucas had become impatient with the speed in which Western Civilization was declining and had decided that it was up to him to jump-start the inevitable.

It was simple, really, a way to strike fear

into the impure hearts of most Americans. Explosives planted in the backs of rented vans parked at historical sites across the country. The bombs would be detonated, and the decadent people of the United States would realize that a death knell for their polluted culture had been rung and it was time for the supreme white race to rise up from the ashes like a phoenix reborn.

Tomorrow the vans would leave the compound driven by families who realized the truth of his words and agreed it was time to take back what had been stolen from them. The weather reports said it would be a glorious day, perfect to mark the beginning of the end.

As if on cue, a powerful crack of thunder shook the compound to its very foundation.

*That's odd*, he thought as he put away his map. He didn't recall hearing anything about thunderstorms in the forecast for today.

Yelverton left his office and climbed up the stairs to the first floor. Again, there was a deafening thunderclap and this time he saw the white flash of lightning that illuminated the room at the top of the staircase.

The sun had been shining brightly when he'd entered the main house no more than a half hour ago and it wouldn't set for another two hours, but right now it was so dark in the room, it was as if night had fallen.

He tried a lamp and realized the power was out.

Yelverton made his way carefully to the front door as the rain began to beat unmercifully against the house. *Like the hiss of a thousand serpents,* he thought to himself as he opened the door. *The weather forecasters really screwed up this one.* He stepped out onto the covered front porch. The wind howled around him. He could see several Brotherhood members standing on the lawn, mesmerized by something in the distance. He tried to get a glimpse of whatever had drawn their attention, but the sloping roof of the porch blocked his view.

Lucas Yelverton left the porch, his hand before his face to shield his vision from the relentless wind and rain. *What's so fascinating that they'll stand in the downpour to watch it?* The wind blasted across the compound, the air warm and dense with moisture, heavy and close around him. A kind of shiver went through him. Yelverton frowned and reached up to touch the back of his neck, where the hair was standing on end, prickling with static electricity.

"What the hell?" he muttered as he proceeded down across the lawn to join his brethren. *Maybe it's a sign,* he thought as he lifted his head to gaze in the direction in which they stared. Perhaps it was a rainbow or some other atmospheric anomaly that could be looked upon as a harbinger of good luck for the Brotherhood's holy mission.

Yelverton watched with growing wonder as the curtain of rain parted in the distance and a monster emerged, a white boiling tube of swirling wind and debris. And it moved inexorably toward the compound, his followers, and himself.

Lucas Yelverton didn't fancy himself a religious man, but as he and those who looked upon him as leader were sucked up into the swirling vortex, he felt, more than any other time in his life, that he finally had a true understanding of the wrath of God.

Shane stood in the trash-strewn alley near the back entrance of the abandoned movie theater on Tremont Street. He clutched a newspaper and slowly turned his face up to the falling rain.

Every time it rained, it felt to him as though the city were getting a fresh start. The rainfall washed away the grit and the grime and left every thing new again. If only it could do the same for him.

How could his life have changed so dramatically—so drastically in such a short period of time? A little over a month ago his biggest concern was if Spud was going to make them watch *The Postman* again during their Friday night movie marathons. He smiled at the thought of his dead friend defending the Kevin Costner movie as a modern-day classic that had yet to be embraced by the world.

*Look at me now,* he grimly observed: wanted for murder, pursued by a covert government agency, crawling through sewer pipes with a group of conspiracy theorists who think the "new Coke" campaign was an evil corporation's plot to take over the world.

Shane lowered his face and sighed. He looked at the front page of the water-soaked *Boston Herald* and felt his heart sink. The high school photograph of Jon Ledin had begun to smudge from the rainfall, turning his friend's smiling face into a grotesque blob of gray. The story said that he had been killed in a bizarre accident at his job. This was the fourth acquaintance of Shane's in the last week to meet an untimely death. The virus of change called the BBD that had so affected his life was beginning to spread to others. It had to stop.

Shane sensed that he was no longer alone and turned to see Joe Levine standing just outside the graffiti-stained door, lighting a cigarette.

"David sent me to be sure you're all right," he said as he shook out a match and tossed it to the ground.

"I didn't know you smoked," Shane said as he looked away from his friend and concentrated on the rusted metal Dumpster and stacks of wooden pallets that littered the back alley of the once spectacular Monarch Movie Palace.

"Only when I'm stressed," Joe responded. "Can you guess I'm stressed?"

"They're killing more of my friends," Shane said gravely, "not even friends, really—acquaintances. People who I was kind of friendly with in high school but since college . . ."

Joe sucked on his cigarette, smoke obscuring his face. "Yeah, well, they killed a bunch of my friends last week, too. Or did you forget that part?"

Shane nodded. "I know. I'm sorry. I guess sometimes you can't help being selfish. Or, at least, I can't."

"Nah, I understand. We all get that way. These were people in your life. But are you sure? I mean, how do you know you're not just being paranoid?"

Shane glared at him. "Paranoid? Isn't that like the pot calling the kettle black?"

Joe shrugged. "Just thought I'd ask. No matter how much we'd like to blame them for all the bad things in our lives, the BBD can't take the rap for everything."

Shane held up the saturated newspaper and shook it at him. "A high school friend died the day before yesterday when he *fell* into a wood chipper. And that's just the latest one. It's them. They're trying to force me out of hiding."

"Wood chipper," Joe mused. "Ouch."

Shane threw the newspaper to the ground.

"That and what they did to that militia in Arkansas . . ."

Joe snubbed the life from his cigarette on the brick wall. "It's wrong, no question. And we've got to stop them. But I can't say I'm going to cry over a little army of bigots with assault rifles."

"That's not the point, and you know it," Shane said. "If they can do it to those racist militia guys, they can do it to anyone. They get away with it because the idea of somebody controlling the weather is so ridiculous that it overshadows the coincidence of such happenings." He stepped closer to Joe. "Which is why I've been thinking."

Joe gave him a cautious look and pulled up the collar of his jacket. "Uh-oh, should I be worried?"

Shane shook his head. "No, but they should be. I have to destroy the technology I helped create, but I'm going to need the help of the Truth Seekers. I say we take the fight to them."

Joe was silent, digesting his words.

"And when would we be planning on doing this, considering half our people are dead and most of our equipment was destroyed or impounded?"

"Soon," Shane said, "but first we have to pick up my mother."

# CHAPTER FOURTEEN

*"Recently I have obtained a patent on a transmitter with which it is practicable to transfer unlimited amounts of energy to any distance . . ."*

—Nikola Tesla

Iris sat in the Royale Plaza bar sipping from her third scotch and soda in less than an hour. She set the drink down on the napkin and placed her hand atop the manila folder. She was well aware of its contents but couldn't bring herself to read the specifics of the Department's latest efforts to draw out Shane Monroe.

*It's murder,* she thought, *cold-blooded murder, plain and simple.* She brought the drink to her mouth again and finished it off with a shudder.

The waitress walked by the booth and reached for Iris's empty glass. "Would you like another?" she asked softly.

Iris looked up, distracted. "No, no, I've had enough. Thank you."

The waitress smiled, placed the bar tab and a pen in a plastic tray on the table, and walked away. Iris picked up the pen and signed off on the bill.

She snatched up the folder and slid it into the leather satchel on the seat beside her, careful not to let any of its poisonous contents spill out. She slid across the red vinyl seat and left the bar.

As she stood waiting for the elevator she made up her mind. In the morning, she would resign from the Department. She just couldn't do it anymore. She had tried to work within the system, tried to play by the Department's rules, but what she had discovered was that the Department had no rules.

She left the elevator on the eighth floor and walked down the hall to her room. Feeling a bit buzzed she decided the best thing now would be a hot shower and a good night's rest. In the morning she would rise early and try to figure out how she was going to protect herself against an action she knew could prove fatal.

Iris fished the card key from her bag and slipped it into the lock. The tiny light on the door lit up green, and she turned the knob and entered. That hotel room smell wafted out to greet her with the coolness of the air-conditioning. The room was dark, and her hand slid along the stucco wall for the switch to turn on the lights. Finding it, she hit the button. Nothing.

Years in law enforcement had made her extremely cautious and just a bit paranoid. Iris immediately felt herself become more sober as adrenaline began to pump through her veins. There was a lamp on the dresser near the TV stand, and she cautiously moved through the darkness toward it.

She heard the intruders first. There were two and they came at her from around the corner of the wall that separated the sleeping area from the bathroom. One grabbed her arms from the front, and the other put his arm around her throat and went for her gun. They were silent except for their breathing.

Iris ducked forward, throwing the attacker behind her off balance as she kicked back and drove her heel into his kneecap. The man went down hard, his squeal of agony music to her ears. The one holding her arms was trying to pull her closer to restrain her, but she would have none of that. She lunged at him, driving her forehead into the taller man's face. He grunted with pain and let go of her arms, stumbling backward. She could see his shape well enough in the dark to know where to aim her punch and delivered a powerful right cross that hurled the man into the heavy wooden armoire that held the television set. She sensed the man behind her as he struggled to stand, and spun in a roundhouse kick to the side of his head. She heard the satisfying thud of his skull hitting the wall.

A lamp in the corner suddenly bathed the room in light. Iris spun in its direction, prepared for yet another attack, and stopped when she saw Shane sitting at the desk. He was holding a gun pointed directly at her.

"You set me up," Shane said.

It only took her a moment to realize what he was talking about. The raid on the Truth Seeker compound in Nahant.

"No," she replied sharply. "I didn't. They found you without my help. Think about it for a second. You know how bad they want you, how bad Remington wants you. Sure, they want the rest of your buddies, too. But not the way they want you. If they knew I'd let you walk away, even if it was to try to tail you, I'd have a bullet in my head right now."

Shane looked uncertain, lines creasing his forehead.

Iris glared at the man who was attempting to stand by holding on to the armoire. She turned for a moment to check the other, who had leaned back against the wall and was clutching his leg.

"Sorry. I'm not very big on company these days," she said. Then she turned to Shane again. "Believe me or don't, nothing I can do about it."

He stood, the gun still pointed in her direction. "Where's that psychopath you call a partner?"

She crossed her arms. "If he'd been with

me"—she nodded toward the injured Truth Seekers—"those two clowns would be dead." Iris walked to the foot of the double bed and sat down. "How did you find me?"

"It wasn't too hard, actually. The Truth Seekers have a list of dummy corporation names used by the BBD. They just hacked into the databases of the hotels in the area looking for guests who registered with one of their bogus credit cards. You're currently employed by the Huntington Corporation. What do they do again? Oh, right. Import fish. Into Boston. I'm surprised they get away with that one."

Iris nodded slowly, impressed with their resources. She slipped off her loafers and brought her feet up onto the bed to sit Indian style. "You going to shoot me? Because if you are, I'd rather we not waste time on small talk."

He looked down at the weapon and then back to her. "It's the only guarantee I have that I'll be able to leave this room when and how I want."

She massaged a cramp in her feet, not even bothering to look at him as she responded. "I won't try to stop you."

From the corner of her eye she watched as the young man placed the weapon down on top of the desk. "I was getting tired of holding it, anyway," he said. "It's funny, they don't look that heavy in the movies."

"What do you want, Shane?" she asked, massaging the other foot.

"We need your help."

"Meaning you were never convinced I'd set you up in the first place," she said. "I think I'm flattered." Iris closed her eyes and leaned her head back. "I've helped you enough. Do you know how much danger I've already put myself in for you?"

He nodded, his expression one of under-standing. "And I appreciate all that you've done." He pointed to the other two Truth Seekers who both stood by the bathroom keeping their distance. "They do too. But we're tired of running, Iris, tired of hit-and-run missions that do nothing more than annoy the BBD. The next time we hit, it's going to be hard. I gave them a weapon. Now I want to take it away."

A shiver went through her, but she kept her face expressionless. "Why are you telling me this? I work for the organization that you're planning to attack."

"Why did you let me go?" he asked, his voice eerily calm. "You know what they are. I don't think you want to be a part of that."

She said nothing as he continued to stare at her.

"Do you?" he asked as he sat back in the chair. "Or will you help us, Agent Green?"

She thought about her decision to resign—and realized how foolish that was.

What chance would she have of walking away from the Black Box Department with her skin intact? "What if I say no?"

Shane reached over and picked up the gun from the desk. He stood and shoved the weapon into the rear waistband of his pants. "I guess we could always leak the story of you letting me go to Remington. Or, better yet, Ames."

Iris unfolded her legs. "That won't be necessary."

He moved closer and looked down at her. "You'll help us, then?"

As she looked at him, it struck her how much he had changed from the college kid who had nearly fallen apart in her custody long weeks before. With a sigh, Iris lay back and gazed up at the white ceiling and remembered how she had done the same in her bed as a little girl, imagining all kinds of fabulous things in the imperfections of the white plaster ceiling. She had felt at peace then, confident that everything was right with the world.

Iris longed to feel that way again. She knew that she never would. But there had to be something better than this. "I'm in."

Tarker Ames carefully removed the black eye-patch from his face and gazed at his scarred visage in the hotel mirror. He picked up the warm facecloth that had been soaking in the sink and dabbed at the mottled red skin. The dead right eye stared at him like a bulbous, white growth from the swollen flesh of the socket.

"What are you lookin' at?" he growled at his reflection before breaking into an ear-to-ear grin.

Carefully he reached up and touched the milky orb, feeling nothing but the pressure from the poke. The eye reminded him of that time in his life that proved most formative. It had come immediately after his parents had been killed in a horrible car wreck. *Just like Monroe's daddy*, he thought. Tarker had been ten years old. The first night of the wake, the funeral director, a ghoulishly pale man with jet-black hair named Mr. Carroll, had spoken to his bereaved grandmother in a hushed whisper.

There had been an atmosphere of accumulated sorrow in the place, as if all the people who had ever paid their respects to a loved one had left a little bit of their sadness behind. But he had no plans to contribute to the morass of sorrow, for at that moment in his short life, he felt nothing but relief and satisfaction.

"This is gonna scar the boy," Mr. Carroll had said.

It had been all he could do not to laugh.

Now Tarker gazed at his reflection in the overly bright lights of the hotel bathroom.

Shadows fell across his face, making him look like one of the temporary residents of the Carroll Funeral Home. He remembered how they had looked that night, resting in their caskets.

His parents.

No one paid him the slightest bit of attention, so he wandered the various hallways, peeking into viewing rooms filled with the overpowering scents of flowers and grief. He stood in the doorway of the room at the end of the hall and stared at the two coffins, a framed photograph from their wedding resting on a white Romanesque pedestal between them.

He entered the room and studied the picture. How joyous they'd seemed. He tried to remember if there was ever a time in his ten years that he had seen them smile. But all he could remember were the sneers of disgust and teeth gritted in rage before he was struck.

He stood for a moment, looking from one parent to the next in their fancy wooden boxes, and savored the quiet.

Tarker happily recalled the moment he'd come to realize that he rather enjoyed the two being dead. He never doubted his decision to tamper with the brakes in their car. Not for a minute.

What was it his father used to say to him after he'd had one too many drinks? "Look at you," he'd growl, his breath stinking of tobacco and cheap whiskey, "you're no son of mine. If there'd been two in the litter, I'da drowned you and kept the other."

His mother had been no better, her frightened silence serving only to invite his father's never-ending abuses. He had once asked her why she let his father hurt him. "Better you than me," she had replied. *Better you than me.*

On tiptoes he had peered into his father's coffin. They had dressed him in his blue suit, the one that he proclaimed to have worn only to weddings and funerals. A powerful chemical smell wafted up from the corpse and tickled his nose, making him want to sneeze. He smiled down on the waxy countenance of Floyd Ames.

"How'z it feel, Daddy?" he had asked. "Look at me when I'm talkin' to you, boy." He had reached down into the casket and tried to pull open his father's eyes and found that beneath the lid they were covered by a pair of flesh-colored plastic cups. There was resistance, but not enough to deter him. He wanted to look into his daddy's eyes. He pulled the caps off with a wet, sucking sound and looked into the opaque, gelatinous orbs.

"Should'a been nicer to me, Daddy," he had said. "Now look at you, look at you both."

Decades later, he stared at his own milky white eye in the hotel bathroom mirror, and remembered his father. "Not so worthless now, am I?" he whispered to the empty room.

Tarker dried his face with a fluffy white terry cloth towel, the softness of the fabric sending spasms of pain through his face. He didn't mind the pain. It helped him focus on the job at hand.

The portable phone on his nightstand began to ring, and he walked from the bathroom to answer it. "Yes?" he asked as he placed the phone to the undamaged side of his face.

Tarker grinned as he heard the voice on the other end. "Well, hello there, haven't heard from you in a dog's age." He stopped and listened, and his heart began to race and his hands to sweat.

"When will they be trying this?" Tarker asked, his voice tight with anticipation. He snatched up his watch from the nightstand and glanced at the face. "That doesn't leave me much time. Thanks for the heads up."

Calmly he placed the phone down and began to dress.

Iris counted to three, rapped her knuckles against the back of the surveillance van, and waited. The door slowly opened, and the vaguely familiar face of a young, handsome agent peered out at her. Fogg, she thought his name was.

"Agent Green?" he asked quizzically.

Behind him, four others sat around various forms of surveillance equipment in the back of the vehicle. Iris glared at Agent Fogg and put on her most serious game face.

"We have to move the subject right now."

It was as if the man had been slapped. He looked to his fellow agents, then back to her. "Move her? We haven't heard anything from Agent Ames about . . ."

Iris gave her best disgusted sigh, turned from the van, and began to walk toward the Monroe house. "You're hearing it from me. We've got intel that the house is going to be hit tonight and we can't afford to have the woman anywhere near the action."

She stopped and turned back. Fogg was standing outside the vehicle, and the other four agents crowded into the doorway watching her. "I'm going to need all of you to secure the perimeter."

They only stared at her. It was time to get tough. "Look, do you want me to get Agent Ames on the phone and you can explain to him why the subject hasn't been moved?"

Clearly, none of them wanted that. All five of the surveillance agents followed her across the street and up the driveway to the back of the house. "Sit tight. I'm going in. I'd like to try to do this quietly, without a fuss. But if she gives me a hard time, you can carry her out wrapped in a carpet for all I care."

As she spoke, she saw multiple shapes

emerge from the shadows of the backyard in her peripheral vision. With silent stealth, the figures moved toward the five Department agents. The ease with which her former comrades were taken down filled her with equal parts dread and awe. The Truth Seekers were far more capable than she had expected. Three of the BBD agents were taken down using a kind of aerosol gas that worked better than anything she had ever seen. The other two put up a struggle, but it was brief. In seconds, they were unconscious.

"Don't kill them," she said as they were dragged into some of the surrounding shrubbery.

"Don't worry about it," she heard a Truth Seeker say. She thought it was the one named Levine. "We leave the murder of innocents to the BBD."

*Touché*, she thought as one of the darkly clad figures came toward her. They were all wearing black face masks, but he pulled his off as he reached the back steps.

"So far, so good," Shane said as he climbed to the back door.

Iris didn't say a word as she followed. She didn't want to jinx it.

The kitchen was dark except for the light from the ventilation hood over the stove. Shane paused to get his bearings, and something whizzed past his face. He jumped back, falling into Iris, who had just stepped through the doorway.

"Mom, it's me!" he yelped as he threw up his hands to ward off another blow from the frying pan.

Nancy stopped in mid swing, gradually lowering her cooking weapon. "Shane?" She dropped the heavy frying pan with a clang and hugged him. "Are you all right? I've been so worried."

He hugged her back, sinking his face into the corner of her neck. "Remember I told you there might come a time when we'd have to move you to someplace safe?" he said, his voice slightly muffled. He pulled away from her embrace and looked into his mother's eyes. "Well, it's time."

She held his gaze for a bit, then nodded. "Who's she?" Nancy asked as she noticed Iris standing silently in the doorway.

"Iris Green. She's one of the good guys."

Iris smiled weakly and gazed at her watch. "We're pushing our luck. We need to get out of here quickly."

Nancy turned and strode from the kitchen.

"Mom?" Shane called after her.

She returned moments later with a duffel bag slung over her. "What's that Boy Scout motto?" she asked as she adjusted the bag strap. "Be prepared? I knew it was only a matter of time. I told work I might have to leave town unexpectedly for a family emergency."

Shane looked from his mother to Iris. The former BBD agent looked pleased.

"So, shall we get out of here or what?" Nancy asked.

They didn't waste any more time. His mother was the last to pass through the back door, and Shane smiled sadly as she locked it behind her.

"Don't worry," she said, "this'll always be our home. We'll be back."

Shane did not respond. He doubted she was right about that, but he didn't have the heart to tell her.

Joe Levine and the others stepped from the shadows of the backyard. "What the hell took so long?" he asked, tension in his voice. "The surveillance team has been incommunicado for more than five minutes and that's bound to concern somebody."

Shane escorted his mother past Joe. "We're ready, Joe, just call David and tell him to bring the van."

They were halfway down the driveway when they first heard it. A low-level hum, followed by a sudden blast of wind.

"Shane?" Nancy asked, concern in her voice.

He looked at Iris. She didn't say a word, but slowly drew her weapon from its holster. The incessant hum grew louder, and then he saw them. They were small, about the size of a Volkswagen, darting around the night sky like dragonflies over the surface of a pond. Helicopters. Small, black helicopters.

"Take cover," Iris screamed.

Shane heard the rapid-fire sounds of automatic gunfire. He watched with horror as two Truth Seekers standing by his mother began an obscene dance of death. *Annie and Kyle*, Shane thought. Not his friends, but they had come to help him save his mother, anyway. Bullet holes erupted like tiny blood-filled volcanoes across the fronts of their bodies.

"Dear god," he heard his mother say as he grabbed her and pulled her to the side of the house for cover.

"Damn, Monroe! They want you bad if they broke out these babies," Joe said as they drew up beside him.

Iris crawled over, weapon in hand. "This isn't good. Those are stealth choppers, strictly black ops."

One of the choppers flew low strafing the side of the house and driveway with a rain of bullets.

"Why hasn't anyone called the police?" Nancy asked, disbelief in her tone.

Iris scanned the sky. "If your neighbors are smart, they'll stay inside with the curtains closed. The guys flying these bugs don't care who they shoot, and the police were probably warned to stay away." She glanced at Nancy. "You know, government business."

The humming of one of the craft's engines grew louder.

"We have to get out of here if we're going to live to see tomorrow. They'll shoot this house into toothpicks to get at us."

The craft opened fire again, and the sounds of glass shattering and bullets chewing through wood filled the night. Iris cocked her head slightly to the left, listening as the gunfire abruptly ceased. She ran out into the driveway in a crouch and aimed her weapon up at the sky. "He's empty, cover me!" she screamed to the others.

On reflex, Shane pulled the gun from inside his vest.

"When did you start carrying a gun?" his mother asked.

"Since people started trying to kill me," he said, standing up with the others and firing into the sky.

The chopper closest to them seemed surprised by their sudden aggression. It started to ascend, but Iris was relentless in her attack, taking careful aim and emptying her entire clip into the mirrored bubble of the cockpit. The craft began to fly erratically.

The other two crafts moved in on opposite sides of the wounded copter. They fired their weapons as the Truth Seekers again sought cover. Shane heard the bark of a handgun and turned to see Iris shooting her weapon at another of the black helicopters.

"Iris!" he screamed, "get out of there!"

But she continued to fire, her expert marksmanship cracking the mirrored windshield of a second craft. To avoid any further damage, the chopper pilot was forced to veer out of her line of fire—right into the side of the damaged first helicopter. Their wildly spinning rotors struck, shattering the blades on both crafts as they tumbled from the sky like marionettes, their wires cut by a malicious child.

The helicopters crashed, one landing atop a neighbor's car. Shane watched as Iris turned to face him, smoldering weapon still in hand, her posture slumped as if drained of energy.

He began to walk toward her when the first of the black helicopters exploded in a fiery ball that hurled him backward to the ground. He heard his mother calling his name from somewhere off in the distance, nearly drowned by a persistent ringing. Shane struggled to his feet and ran to help Iris.

"Better move our asses, the other one's probably going to—"

The second downed chopper blew, taking the Ford Taurus with it. The force of the second explosion helped propel them up the driveway where the others waited in relative safety. Shane and Iris hung on each other gasping for breath, their lungs seared by the heat of the conflagration.

His mother came to him, pulling him

away from the former BBD agent. She
touched his face lovingly, and then moved
around to the rest of his body checking for
any serious injury. "Are you all right? Any
pain?"

He smiled at her concern, though he was
haunted by the deaths of Annie and Kyle.
"I'm fine, Doc. Why don't you check out the
other patient?"

His mother was checking out the still
stunned Iris Green when Joe stepped forward.
He was putting a cellular phone back into his
pocket.

"David'll be here any second. Follow me,
right now. We hit the street and wait for
pickup."

"What about the other helicopter?" Shane
asked. "There's still one left."

Iris moved away from Nancy. "That
baby's gone. They'll leave the cleanup to a
ground crew. If Poisson's coming for us, Joe's
got the right idea."

Shane caught Joe giving the woman an icy
stare. It was obvious that she had yet to earn
the man's trust, but it was more than that. On
this op, Levine was calling the shots—or at
least coordinating in the field for Poisson—
and it was obvious he didn't like the idea of
Iris having an opinion about *anything*.

The air was thick with black smoke and
the noxious smell of burning fuel. The
mournful wail of sirens could be heard in the

distance, in no hurry at all. At the end of the drive they peered down the stretch of road unobstructed by twisted metal and fire. A Chevy Blazer was heading toward them. David Poisson had arrived.

The truck banged a sudden U-turn and came to a screeching halt in front of them. The sirens were closer now. Shane opened the door to let his mother inside, followed by Joe and the other surviving Truth Seekers. He touched Iris's arm, gently urging her to get into the truck, but she seemed distracted, staring into the billowing smoke and fire.

"What is it?" he asked.

She didn't respond immediately, tilting her head, listening. "I thought I heard something."

Iris was just about to climb into the Blazer when they all heard the gun of an engine and the screeching of tires. They looked through the back window as a car drove through the flaming wreckage of the black helicopters and sped directly toward them, its front afire as it screeched to a fishtailing stop.

"Get out of here," Iris yelled as she backed out of the car. She reached into her pocket and removed a full clip of bullets, ejected the empty one from her gun, and slammed in the new.

"Get in!" Shane yelled, leaning out of the vehicle. "We can make it."

Iris was walking toward the car now.

"Don't worry about me," she said without turning around. "This is something I have to do."

Iris felt her stomach tighten and her blood run cold as Tarker Ames opened the door and stepped from the burning car.

"Would ya look at this mess?" he asked with mock amusement as he moved around the vehicle. His hands were empty, but that didn't make her feel any more safe.

"What in the name of hell is going on here, Agent Green?"

She thought about lying to buy the others some time, but decided that it wasn't worth the effort. Instead, she raised her weapon and pointed it at the man with the burned face and the eye-patch. "That's far enough, Ames," she said planting her feet and squinting down the barrel of the gun. "Get back in your car and leave. I'm only going to tell you once."

Tarker looked at his car. The windshield and front hood were still smoldering. "My car is on fire, Agent Green. I can't leave here in a burning car. It isn't safe." He put his hands into the pockets of his jacket.

"Take your hands from your pockets slowly," she barked.

Tarker pretended to be frightened as he slowly removed his hands. "What's happened to you, Iris? I remember when you were or of the good guys. What was it that turned you?"

She didn't want to answer, but the words just spilled from her mouth. "I thought I *was* one of the good guys. I've learned different. Get out of here, Ames. Leave before I'm forced to do something I might regret."

Tarker smiled, his good old boy looks made alarmingly disturbing by the addition of the eye-patch and scars. The fires continued to burn behind him, and for a split second she imagined that she knew what it was like to be in hell and come face-to-face with the Devil.

"It's kinda sad when a good agent goes bad," he said with a sneer. "I've seen it happen before, but never to an agent that had so much promise—or was as pleasin' to the eye, if you catch my drift."

She felt nauseated as he smiled at her. She jabbed the gun in his direction again and hissed, "Go, now."

He started to back toward his car, arms raised in mock surrender. "You know what the sad thing about you is?" he asked.

She heard the faint clicking sound of some kind of mechanism springing to life and watched as a small pistol shot out from beneath Tarker's sleeve and into his hand.

"You don't even realize you're dead."

Tarker brought his weapon to bear and began to fire. Iris did the same, squeezing off multiple rounds even as one of Tarker's bullets found her shoulder and sent her flipping backward to the pavement made unusually warm by the still-burning wreckage. The pain was excruciating, and she fought to stay conscious.

In the distance she could hear the roar of an engine moving quickly toward her.

*Did I hit him*? she wondered. Was he behind the wheel of his flaming car on his way to run her down? The gun was still in her hand, and she tried to raise it but her arm was numb. Then her eyes focused on the body of Tarker Ames lying very still by his car. Equal parts joy and terror shot through her as she realized what she had done.

The gun slipped from her hand and clattered to the ground as the Chevy Blazer pulled up alongside her.

The door swung open and Shane leaned out, hand extended. "Now can we get out of here?" he asked.

She was going to say yes. She wanted to thank him for staying despite the danger to them all. But all she could manage was a pathetic grunt as somebody turned off the lights in her head and she fell deeper into the waiting arms of darkness.


Nancy Monroe wandered from the dilapidated rest room of the old Monarch Movie Palace, vigorously rubbing the moisture from her hair with a bath towel.

The unpleasant rotten-egg smell of hair

dye was still in her nostrils, and she left the bathroom to escape it and to find a mirror. She'd often wondered what she would look like as a brunette but had always been too conservative to try. Now she didn't have a choice.

She walked up two small wooden steps, passed through a doorway, and found herself on a stage, an enormous curtain of velvet behind her covering what was left of the old movie screen. Nancy looked out over the body of the theater and marveled at the activity. Most of the seats had been removed, and the floor was covered with all kinds of computer equipment. It reminded her of NASA mission control, the way the people—what was the ridiculous name Shane called them? Truth Seekers?—the way the Truth Seekers went about their frantic business.

She gave her hair another rub with the towel and then ran her fingers through it. It was drying nicely. She found the side steps and descended to the floor. There were floodlights set up all around the perimeter of the theater, their power supplied by multiple generators that purred in the dark corners of the auditorium like sleeping jungle cats.

"It looks good," a voice said behind her.

Nancy turned to see Iris Green coming toward her. Her arm was in a sling, her wound sutured and bandaged.

"Thank you. How's the arm feeling?"

Nancy stepped closer to examine her handi-
work. "Not much call to look after gunshot
wounds in pediatrics, but not too bad of a job."

"I won't be bowling for a while," Iris said
with a playful grin, "but it's good. Don't
really need the sling, but I want to rest the
arm until I need it. Thank you."

"It boggles the mind, doesn't it?" Nancy
asked as she and Iris watched the Truth
Seekers work.

Iris sighed. "I couldn't agree more. Three
months ago I would have arrested them all for
any number of capital offenses—but now,
well, I guess I've had a change of heart."

With a startling abruptness, Bryan Cole, a
heavyset guy who was the organization's preeminent hacker, let out a scream of victory. He
got up from his computer station, shook a fist
in the air, and started to dance. Other people
moved over to see what he had done.

"The man . . . the one you . . ." Nancy
didn't want to say the word.

"Shot?" Iris asked.

"Yes, the one you shot. I thought I heard
Shane say that he was your partner."

It was like watching a dark cloud pass
over the sun. "He was, but only for a short
time."

Nancy started to fold the damp towel, her
dyed hair pretty much dry. "I'm sorry it had
to come to that."

Iris looked at her, the stare incredibly

cold. "Don't be. If I had to kill the son of a bitch again I wouldn't give it a second thought." She abruptly changed the subject. "So, are you ready to disappear for a while?"

Nancy headed toward a small section of seats that hadn't been removed. Iris followed, and they sat.

"I don't have any choice in the matter," Nancy said. "If this BBD would try to get at Shane through me, it's best that I get out of the way."

Iris chuckled. "I'm not sure that most mothers would be so understanding."

Nancy laughed as well. "So, what's next? Where am I going? Any idea?"

Iris craned her neck and looked past her to the other side of the theater. "I think I'll let your son explain it."

Nancy turned in her seat to see Shane walking toward them, her duffel bag over his shoulder. "Thank you," she said to Iris as the woman stood to leave.

Iris stared, clearly confused. "For what?"

"For trying to help my son. Thank you."

Shane let the heavy bag slip from his shoulder to the floor. "Ladies," he said.

"It's not necessary, but you're welcome," Iris said with a gracious nod.

"What'd I miss?" Shane asked.

"Not a thing," Iris said as she turned to leave. "Fill your mom in on what happens next and I'll catch up to you later."

"So, what now?" Nancy asked, turning to Shane.

He knelt beside the duffel bag and unzipped it. "You're going to Canada for a while," he said as he reached inside and produced an official-looking envelope. "Think of it as that much needed vacation you're always talking about taking."

He handed the envelope to her. She opened it and glanced at the contents.

"Gloria Nihoff? Is that who I am now?" she asked as she thumbed through the new birth certificate, driver's license, and various credit cards.

"New identity courtesy of the Truth Seekers." Shane stood and brushed dust from the knees of his jeans. "They want to get you out of here as soon as possible, so you'll be leaving within the hour."

She rested the envelope on her knee. "We'll be driving there, I imagine?"

Shane nodded. "Yeah, they figured it would be less conspicuous than flying. You'll be traveling with Arthur and Joyce. They're pretty nice, but whatever you do, don't bring up any movies made after nineteen thirty-five. Arthur thinks they're all crap and—"

"What about you? Where are you going to be?" Alarm bells went off in her head.

He looked away. "I'm part of this now. The Black Box Department has taken almost everything from me—which is why I want to get you somewhere safe before I start taking back."

Nancy put her arms around her son's waist and she held him as she had when he was young. And Shane didn't fight it at all.

"You can't blame yourself for what's happened, Shane," she said close to his ear. "You did what you thought was right, and these are the repercussions. There was no way you could have known. Don't beat yourself up over it."

Shane cleared his throat. "Do you understand why I'm doing this?"

She squeezed him tighter, enjoying a closeness to her child that she had forgotten. "You're doing what you think is right. It's the same thing he would have done."

Nancy let go of her son and looked into his eyes. He looked so much like his father right now, it almost hurt her.

"I love you, Mom," Shane said as he took his mother into his arms.

"Of course you do," the newly christened Gloria Nihoff said in the embrace of her son. "Why else would you be sending me on such a nice vacation?"

Tarker Ames eased himself into a chair in the back of the surveillance van. His chest hurt like hell, and every time he took a breath it felt like somebody was sticking a hot bayonet in his side.

He started to unbutton his shirt. Again, he counted the cluster of bullet holes around his heart. "That was some mighty fine shootin', Iris," he muttered as he pulled the shirt apart to reveal the Kevlar vest beneath.

"Mighty fine," he said as he started to pluck the four flattened bullet slugs from the indented surface of the bulletproof material. "It's a good thing I decided to be extra cautious on this one. Somebody upstairs must be lookin' out for little ole Tarker Ames."

A speaker among the communications and surveillance equipment began to crackle and sputter, the faint sound of what might have been a voice could be heard behind the white noise.

"Is that you, Lord?" Tarker asked with a smile. He placed the lead slugs down on the counter beside a half-empty cup of Dunkin' Donuts coffee and began to unstrap the vest.

The speaker again made noise as if in response. "If you're curious about how I'm feelin', I'd have to say fair to middlin'." He dropped the heavy vest to the floor.

Tarker winced as he pulled up his white T-shirt to examine the angry red welts, which were starting to turn a far darker shade. "It's gonna' be a while before these start to fade."

He quickly looked to the speaker. "Not that I'm complainin', Lord."

Tarker let the undershirt drop back down over his bruises and leaned his head back against the chair. "But I think I might'a busted a rib or two." He winced.

He closed his good eye and sighed, ashamed of his performance tonight, ashamed that he hadn't compensated for the loss of his right eye, his aim being badly thrown off.

The speaker buzzed and hissed, and somewhere in the electric ether a voice said what sounded like *yes.*

"Glad you agree," he said, a smile of amusement on his face despite the pain. "But don't you worry about me. The next time I see Iris and her new friends there's going to be an awful lot of dyin' goin' on. Of this I can assure you."

There was a knock at the van's doors.

"Yes?" Tarker said as he shifted in his seat. Multicolored explosions of pain danced before his eyes, and a sheen of sweat broke out upon his brow.

Both doors swung open, and Agent Fogg peered into the darkness. He looked jaundiced and nauseated, obviously still feeling the effects of the H-17 gas the Truth Seekers had used on him. *Pansies just don't have the guts to finish a job.*

"Agent Fogg," Tarker said. "How goes the cleanup?"

"Fine, sir," Fogg responded, his speech still slurred. "The media and the neighbors are being fed a story about the FBI pursuing white supremacists who were planning a series of terrorist attacks on Boston during its Fourth of July celebrations. Of course the supremacists were killed when they tried to escape in a helicopter and it was shot down."

Tarker nodded. That, too, sent spasms of pain through his body. "Excellent. Any leads on the Blazer?"

Fogg shook his head in slow motion. "No sir, the smoke from the copter crash was pretty thick. Nobody saw a thing."

"And seeing how you were still in the bushes catching up on your beauty sleep, I'd—"

The portable phone at his side began to chirp. With his single eye he glared at Fogg, unhooked the phone from his belt, and placed it against his ear. "Ames," he said.

The voice on the other side was harsh, dry sounding. He could make out the sound of a dog panting in the far background. He knew who it was immediately.

"Agent Ames, you are to stand down from your current placement and await reassignment."

He leaned forward in the chair, oblivious to the pain that now wracked his side. "Come again, General? I don't think I quite heard you right."

General Remington's voice, full of authority, blared from the phone. "Being hard of hearing is not one of your problems, Agent. You heard me the first time."

Tarker jumped to his feet. He could feel his broken ribs grind together as he moved. He wanted to shriek in agony, but there were other, more important matters to attend to.

"Sir, I don't think you understand. I'm close, very close to—"

"You've screwed up one too many times, Tarker. I'm sorry, but you're beginning to draw attention to our activities and that is not a good thing."

"But sir, I—"

"That's all, Agent Ames. Stand down."

The connection was severed and Tarker let the phone in his hand slowly fall from his ear. *How can this be?* His mind raced. *Remington can't be serious; it's gotta be some kind of mistake.* Maybe he just needed some time to get over the loss of two of his helicopters.

And then it hit him. The gravity of what had just transpired between him and his superior, intermingled with the severity of his physical injuries, sent him to his knees. He held on to the side of the chair to prevent himself from falling onto his side.

"Agent Ames?" came Fogg's voice from the van's doorway. "Are you all right, sir?"

Tarker held on to the chair, the excruciating intensity of each breath a living testament to the human body's endurance. He was about to answer, to tell the agent to bring a doctor to help him with his pain, when the sounds from the nearby speaker distracted him.

At first he was unsure of what he was hearing hidden among the hissing and the crackling of white noise—and then he knew what it was for sure. He had been mistaken earlier. It hadn't been the Lord that was with him in the van tonight.

Tarker continued to listen to the sounds coming from the speaker very carefully. The bad eye behind the patch began to throb with the frantic beat of his heart.

Laughing—he heard laughter coming over the airwaves, and he knew who it was that found his pain so humorous.

"Shut up," Tarker hissed through gritted teeth as he clung to the chair like a life preserver, solace in a sea of agony.

But the words had no effect, and his father continued to laugh at him from beyond the grave.

# CHAPTER FIFTEEN

*"The principle is this: a ray of great ionizing power is used the give the atmosphere great powers of conduction."*

—Nikola Tesla

In the long run, it was easier to figure out the location from which the BBD was running the Force Majeure project than it was figuring out how to get in. Benson Air Force Base had been closed down in the late 1990s as part of a series of military facility shutdowns caused by federal budget cuts. The town of Billerica was half an hour or so northwest of Boston and had a heavy concentration of blue-collar workers.

When the Massachusetts Transportation Authority quietly bought up the property from the government, they had apparently figured nobody would notice. Logan International Airport in Boston was locked in by the harbor and the cluster of cities around it. Every time the suggestion of a new runway to handle increased air traffic came up, the

screaming was deafening. Massport figured
they could turn Benson AFB into a satellite
airport to handle overflow from Logan.

But the people in Billerica weren't any
happier than those down in Boston and
Revere and Charlestown. So Benson AFB just
sat there, weeds growing up through the pavement like some abandoned drive-in theater,
chain-link fences rusting, broken windows
collecting dust, waiting for someone to come
along and rescue it—up until recently, when
neighbors had begun to complain of planes
flying in and out.

At the edge of the tree line, perhaps fifteen feet from the fence, Shane knelt on the
soft ground and gazed along the perimeter of
the base through a pair of night-vision goggles
that were too tight around his head. Either
the tightness of the strap—which he'd tried to
loosen to no avail—or the night-vision itself,
had given him a low-grade headache that
would not go away.

There was very little activity upon the
grounds of the base itself. Every five to six
minutes a Humvee would rumble by carrying
a trio of soldiers in unmarked fatigues. That
was what gave them away. These guys were
not U.S. Air Force or even army. The very fact
of their anonymity—with no identification
on their uniforms—marked them as Black
Box Department operatives.

With the night-vision goggles, Shane's

vision was magnified enough that he could see the stubble on the driver's chin and the unlit cigarette that poked from behind the ear of the guy riding in the back with a rifle slung across his lap. But he could also see the cars in the central parking lot, arranged in front of a single, squat, three-story building. Whatever activity was going on, it was inside there. They had watched for a long time, and nobody had come or gone from any of those buildings, not even that focal point, which he suspected had been set up as de facto laboratories, out of which the BBD could build, maintain, and transport the mechanisms for the Force Majeure project.

Just thinking about it now, as he watched that faceless building, made him shiver. That last strike, the one on the racist militia compound in Arkansas, had been too incisive. All along they had wanted to capture him alive so that he could continue to work for them, perfect and imperfect science. But unless the attack on the militia was pure luck, it looked like the BBD had figured out how to better aim their weapon.

Which probably meant they didn't need him anymore. They might not be so keen on keeping him alive.

A small click came over the headset he wore. "Shane."

It was David Poisson's voice. Shane frowned slightly and glanced over his shoulder. Poisson was only a few trees away. The goggles magnified everything, and Shane blinked at the blurred images as he pushed them up onto his forehead.

"What's up, boss?" he asked, speaking quietly into the headset.

Poisson gave him the thumbs-up. "Looks like we've got some activity at the gate."

Shane offered Poisson a satisfied grin, but wasn't sure if the guy could see his features. It was dark, and the trees overhead made the shadows somehow deeper. He glanced around at the others gathered there in that little patch of woods. Iris Green was there of course, in a jumpsuit she'd borrowed from Hayley Booth. Hayley was there too. Shane didn't know her very well, but David and Joe said she was the best at this kind of thing. Joe Levine was in the tree above Shane's head, also with night-vision goggles on. His pack was on the ground by Shane and, almost as though summoned by Shane's thoughts, Joe started to climb quietly down the oak's limbs.

"Good thinking," Joe whispered. "We needed a diversion they'd never think was a diversion."

His voice was loud and clear on the headset, but though he was only a few feet away, Shane doubted he would have heard Joe without it. Shane nodded, pleased that his idea had panned out. He felt like he was becoming more a part of the organization, but more

often than not he still felt like a liability.
Helping him had cost the Truth Seekers a
great deal, but then, not helping him might
have cost the world a great deal more in the
end. Still, it was nice to feel as though he had
contributed something.

"What kind of turnout do we have?"
Shane whispered.

Poisson ducked his head, hand over his
mouth, but Shane could not hear him on the
headset now. He had switched channels.
David was the only one in touch with the
entire team. It was simply less confusing that
way. They had three squads on the ground,
including the one Shane was with. The second was perhaps a hundred yards farther
along the perimeter, and the third was nearer
the front gate. They were there ostensibly for
observation only, but for backup if it came to
that. The rest of the Truth Seekers—a lot of
them were techs or simply noncombatants—
were back at their temporary base or already
relocated to one of the other facilities they
had around the country.

After the shit hit the fan on this one,
nobody was going to be able to remain in
Boston very long. Shane figured the only reason the BBD had kept the project here in the
first place was because Benson AFB was the
nearest practical location to operate out of.

"Substantial," Poisson's voice whispered
in his ear. "The front team reports at least

sixty people, not including media. Vans with cameras from Channel seven and the local Fox affiliate."

*Yes*, Shane thought. It had been a simple thing for the Truth Seekers to filter out a story by phone and e-mail that Massport officials were planning to meet with state and city representatives on the premises to finalize the deal for Benson to open as a commercial airport. The rumor was illogical—why would they meet at nine at night at the base rather than in city hall or down at the statehouse in Boston? But some of the locals were on guard, expecting something underhanded because there had been aerial activity around the base recently, and so they had come out to make sure nothing got slipped past them.

Shane only hoped they would be safe, that they would figure out that nothing was going on and head home. Otherwise . . . well, otherwise, they might be in danger, and he did not need that on his conscience. Still, they had needed a diversion, and now they had it.

Poisson moved across the soft earth without a sound, crouched about halfway between Shane and Iris, whose arm was still bandaged but who had left her sling behind. David gestured to Joe Levine, who put a hand on his pack and nodded in return. Two full minutes ticked by, and the engine of a Humvee growled loudly not far off. A moment later it came into view off to their right, prowling the

edges of the runways. Adrenaline rippled
through Shane, and he felt the weight of the
two Heckler and Koch semiautomatic pistols
he wore, one holstered under each arm.

This wasn't going to be a night for sleep gas.

The Humvee rolled by. When it reached
the far end of the compound and turned right,
headed toward the front gate, it began to
speed up. The fields and runways were suddenly bathed with red and blue as a bar of
lights began to spin atop the vehicle.

Shane glanced at Poisson, who smiled
and nodded. With a nervous fire burning in
the pit of his stomach, Shane pulled his
night-vision goggles down again and focused
on the front of that squat main building. Less
than a minute passed before the two guards
at either side of the front door went up the
steps, only to be stopped by a trio of men
coming out. One of them held a clipboard in
his hand and looked very much in charge.
The five of them hurried to an open Jeep,
climbed in, and tore across grass and pavement on a beeline for the front gate, unmind-
ful of whatever damage they might do to the
fields.

"Go," Poisson whispered.

Shane said a silent prayer of thanks to
God for Bryan Cole, the hacker who had
tracked shipping documents from the
Foundation building in Cambridge to Benson
AFB. Iris had been further unnerved by this

information, yet more proof that the Department was involved in horrifying covert ops far beyond what she had imagined, and what she had been privy to. Bryan, though, had relished the challenge of discovering the location. Shane was glad the man wasn't a field operative, back home safe and sound, undermining the dark secrets of world government with his brain.

Bryan had also been the one to hack air force and Massport files to confirm that when it had been run as an air base, Benson had relied on its human resources for security. On their home soil, in a place like Billerica, Massachusetts, nobody saw any real need to spend the budget on perimeter alarms or security cameras and the like.

The Black Box Department was obviously well funded, and they had plenty of manpower—not to mention at least two more Hornet helicopters, which now sat in a hangar at the back of the base. But other than the boys in the Humvee and the guards at the front of the building, and probably a platoon or so of men living in a barracks on the grounds, they made little effort to guard their location. Probably under the assumption that too much military presence would alert the townspeople to unusual activity, and that was attention they didn't want to draw.

With the perimeter guards and the main security at the central structure dealing with nosy reporters and irate, misinformed neighbors at the front gate, the only thing separating the Truth Seekers from the BBD was a twelve-foot chain-link fence topped with razor wire.

Shane reached up and clicked a switch on the side of the goggles and the magnification disappeared. The night-vision facet was still in use, however, and he could see all around him as though he were on the field at a night football game, under the lights.

Joe Levine had pulled two pair of bolt-cutters out of his pack and he handed one of them to Hayley. The two of them rushed across the space between the tree line and the fence with remarkable silence and began cutting the chain link. They worked as quietly as they could, but each cut released some of the tension in the fence and made the metal pop and ring.

Thirty seconds, no more, and then Poisson waved to Iris and Shane and the two of them rushed forward. Around the perimeter of the fence the rear team would be doing the same, though the front team would remain in place as observers.

"Move it," Poisson muttered into the headset. Though the words would be heard by all of the members of their little squad, Shane felt as though they were meant specifically for him.

Joe Levine pushed through the fence

ahead of everyone else. He and Hayley had
cut it so that it hung like the doggie-door
Spud's parents had on their place. Thoughts of
his dead friend made Shane grit his teeth and
nod impatiently while Joe lifted the flap of
fence and Hayley shoved the pack through.
Then she held it up while David, Iris, and
Shane slipped through, and Joe slipped the
pack onto his back, bolt-cutters already
stowed.

"Go. Night-vision. Front team reports
guards fully engaged at the gate. No further
activity at our target location."

The five of them ran then, and to Shane it
seemed to take forever. His chest burned as
they sprinted across one runway after
another, then a field and a stretch of parking
lot, until at last they slipped between a pair of
buildings, one of which was an office structure of some kind and the other of which had
the look of a mess hall or maybe some kind of
recreational building. *Could have been a gym
at one time*, Shane thought.

They paused there and again glanced
around at one another. Joe wore the night-
vision goggles just as Shane did. The others
had only their eyes. Shane slipped past them
along the building and peered around the
edge. They were fifty yards from their objective. The front steps were still abandoned, but
at any moment more sentries could appear
from inside, either to take over or to head

down to help quell the townspeople who were still up in arms.

But that wasn't going to last forever.

"Clear," Joe's voice whispered in his ear.

Poisson waved them on, and they ran again, soles of their shoes slapping the road that curved through the base. Shane had suggested just going right in the front door, but Joe had argued against it. Yes, what they were doing was tantamount to a kamikaze run, and they'd certainly have the element of surprise. But if they could manage to get a few minutes in which to search the facility for the Force Majeure project equipment, both the transportable setup and whatever laboratory they might still have set up there, well . . . going through the front door would not give them even that much time.

As they ran, Shane glanced up and saw an array of barometric and meteorological instruments atop the building. They gleamed in the starlight, brand-new, without the tarnish of everything else on the abandoned base. Not far away from it, also on that same roof, was an old-fashioned weather vane that looked as though it had been there forever. The wind gusted, and the weather vane twitched slightly.

Then they were behind the building, and Shane couldn't see it anymore.

Their objective was larger than it had looked from off the base. Shane had seen the schematics—yet another gem Bryan had dredged up from Massport files—and given the sheer square footage, he ought to have realized its size. But now, up close, it seemed even larger than that to him. It was like a small hospital, and it made him wonder exactly what the air force had used it for.

There were actually three doors in the back, all of which had small lights above them that glowed down on gray pavement. None of them had guards, or even doorknobs, but they did have locks.

"Emergency exits," Shane whispered.

"Yeah," Iris replied, her voice steeped in sarcasm. "Well, I think this qualifies."

"Everyone study the floor plan?" Poisson asked.

There were only nods in response.

"Use stairs only. Do not go through the first-floor foyer. We hit the basement right off and start room by room. Ignore bathrooms, maintenance, and small offices. They'll need a large storage room or a lab."

None of this was new to them, but Poisson seemed to need to say it. *And*, Shane thought, *maybe the rest of us need to hear it, to steel ourselves.*

A moment later a cluster of shadows appeared at the far end of the building, six other members of the Truth Seekers. Hayley Booth raised a hand to them and brought it down like the starter at a NASCAR race.

Then she reached into Joe's pack again and brought out a handheld metal instrument that looked like a cross between a handgun and a drill. She pressed its tip against the lock, where the key would have gone, and glanced at Poisson.

"You realize if this thing's alarmed, they'll be on us in half a minute."

Poisson grinned. "That's why God made Kevlar, darlin'. That's why God made Kevlar." He wore an assault rifle on a sling around his neck and raised it in both hands as he took up a position behind Hayley. Iris and Joe drew their weapons as well. Shane was the last to do so, and the nine-millimeter hand-gun felt cold in his grip.

The leader of the Truth Seekers stared at Shane a moment, then glanced around at the others. "Listen up. Monroe's here because he knows this tech inside and out. That means he's protected at all times. Clear?"

Shane dropped his gaze. He did not like the idea that they all had to look out for him. On the other hand, he figured it did give him much better odds of coming out of the whole thing alive.

"Do it," Poisson whispered, but Shane did not hear him on the headset. The order was carried to the back team, who were perhaps 150 feet away.

Hayley pulled the trigger on the instru-ment in her hand, and a thick drill bit turned and dug into the lock on that emergency door. A second later, though, it froze as if it had locked up, buried in the metal. Then a jagged-toothed metal tube extruded from the mouth of the thing like a particularly vicious socket wrench. With a metallic whine and a spray of sparks, it slid through the metal where the locking cylinder sat in its housing, then simply cut the lock out as if coring an apple.

"Wow," Iris whispered. "Where can I get one of those?"

Hayley smiled as she stepped back and dropped the lock-drill into Joe's pack. David Poisson stepped forward, raised his leg, and kicked the door in.

Shane flinched, waiting for an alarm, but there was only the bang of metal against concrete and the clang as the remains of the lock fell to the floor. There was a moment as if none of them knew what they were supposed to do next, and then David rushed in, covering both sides of the hallway with sweeps of the barrel of his assault rifle. Iris was next, and she proceeded with a kind of unnatural calm, her eyes slightly narrowed, as if she was suspicious of every doorway. Shane figured that was a good way to be.

He followed next, and Hayley and Joe brought up the rear. David led them down a corridor at a wild pace. If a BBD agent had stepped into the hall in front of them they likely would have silenced the man by simply running him over. But they saw no one. Shane wondered how the backup team was doing on the other side of the building, but he could not think too much about it. His mind was focused on the sounds around him.

A single shout came from a junction in the corridor ahead. Someone must have heard their entry, either the whine of the drill or the bang of the door. No way were they going to be lucky enough for that to go unnoticed. But almost as soon as Shane heard that shout, Poisson came to a metal door with a red exit sign gleaming above it. He pushed through the door and then stepped aside, and they all disappeared into the stairwell.

More shouts came from the hall, but Shane thought they sounded more curious than anything. The door clicked shut behind them as the Truth Seekers moved down the stairs toward the basement. They went more slowly now, so their footsteps would not carry up to the corridor they had just departed. If the other team remembered the floor plan, they should be descending an opposite stairwell on the other side of the building. Despite their matrix of information sources and the talented hackers like Bryan Cole in their employ, the Truth Seekers had not been able to discover where in the building the Force Majeure project had been relocated. As a result, Poisson had called the mission a "search and destroy." Now that they were inside, the teams would work inward from either side and meet in the middle. If they hadn't been found out by then, they'd start upstairs.

Then the gunfire would begin. There were explosives as well, at least a few small hand grenades that Poisson had clipped to his belt. But nobody had given any of those to Shane, and he was glad.

Joe and Iris hit the bottom of the steps one right after the other, and automatically took up posts on either side of the door. Poisson and Hayley came down behind Shane, who pushed his goggles up onto his forehead as he reached the landing. He glanced back at David, who nodded and used his gun to motion Joe forward.

*No way to tell if anyone's on the other side,* Shane thought as Joe pulled open the door.

A trio of black-garbed BBD operatives leveled automatic rifles at them from about three feet away.

Shane froze. He felt the others stiffen around him as well. All four of his comrades had their weapons trained on the hallway, but no one fired. Shane was glad. Had anyone pulled a trigger, Joe would have been dead on the spot. For a long moment, the opposing forces only stood there facing one another, gun barrels unwavering.

Then, out in the hall beyond Shane's field of vision, someone spoke.

"I knew you'd come around eventually," said a gruff, male voice.

It had been a very long time since Shane had heard that voice, but he recognized it immediately: General Remington.

"We're here to end this, General. Not to help you massacre even more people," Shane replied grimly.

The old man moved into Shane's field of vision, standing behind the BBD agents. "Oh, it's going to come to an end tonight, no question about that. In fact, I'm not even sure I need you alive anymore." His gaze ticked toward Iris. "Hello, Agent Green. Why don't we go upstairs and speak to the director? We'll let him decide exactly how long all of you are going to live."

"What makes you think we're going anywhere with you?" Iris snapped, her own hatred for the man obvious.

"Arrogant son of a bitch," David muttered. "Tell your men to drop their weapons or you're all dead."

General Remington's eyebrows went up and he smiled. "Mr. . . . what was it? Poisson, yes? I like fish. That's how I remember your name. The fish man. Feel free to fire on us at any time, you cocky little puke. Maybe you'll get lucky and one or two of you will be left standing when the smoke clears. But how long is that going to last? And even if you do, I promise you that young Mr. Monroe will be the first to die, and you can't do what you came here to do without him, can you?"

"We can if we just blow the whole building," Hayley spat, enraged.

"That's exactly what we should have done," Shane said bitterly. "To hell with the body count."

Remington chuckled softly. The BBD agents merely stood there, aim unwavering.

"You wouldn't have gotten past the fence," the general said. "The only reason you got this far was because you weren't carrying high explosives. I must congratulate you on your ruse at the gate, though. Using the Massport thing, the neighborhood annoyance factor, that was excellent thinking."

Shane stared at him, mouth dry. Something about his tone, the choice of words, had started a thought worming its way through his mind. It coalesced a moment later, and Shane swore under his breath.

"You knew we were coming," he said, voice breaking.

In the space between the Truth Seekers and the BBD agents, Joe Levine swung the barrel of his assault rifle around and leveled it so that a single burst would have cut Shane and Iris in half.

"Jesus, Joe," Poisson whispered, incredulous.

"That's not my name," Levine replied. "You'll never know my name."

Shane stared at the man, his friend whom he had never really known, and pieces of the puzzle began to click into place. That was how the BBD had known they were going to break into the Foundation that night. He and the others had barely escaped. But the BBD had a backup plan—a raid on the Nahant compound—made simple because someone had tipped them off to the location of that base.

"You traitorous bastard," Shane snarled through clenched teeth. "Do you have any idea how many people are going to die because of you?"

Levine shrugged. "It's nothing personal, Monroe. I was deep cover, supposed to get the locations of all the Truth Seeker cells. Deep cover means you play along, no matter what. But when things started to get serious with you, I figured giving you up was more important than keeping my cover. Got a little war wound out of the deal, too. Maybe they'll give me a Purple Heart."

A shudder went through Shane, and his grip tightened on the nine-millimeter in his hand. He had never wanted to kill anyone. Defend himself, yes, but not to kill. But right then, if other weapons had not been trained on him, he might have shot the man he knew as Joe Levine dead in his tracks.

Levine smiled and stepped out the door to stand with the other BBD agents. "At least

your mother got out safe. Once they knew
they were going to get you, they agreed to
leave her alone. You owe me for that one."

A sick churning in his gut made Shane
want to vomit, but he realized that the man
was right. That did not assuage his disgust
and hatred even the slightest bit.

"Enough of that," General Remington
instructed. "Come out. We'll go down to the
main stairs and up to the lobby that way.
Drop your weapons and keep your hands
where we can see them. I have agents moving
on the other half of your little invasion team
as we speak. You've no way out."

After a moment, Poisson lowered his gun.
"Do it," he said. "Drop your weapons."

Shane heard defeat in David's voice, and it
terrified him. But he put his nine-millimeter
on the floor, then removed the other and set it
next to its twin. He was afraid of the guns in
front of him, of the bullets in them. Shane
Monroe was afraid of dying. But he knew that
whatever was going to happen now, it was too
late to stop it.

The storm was rolling in.

The lobby of the building was a two-story
rotunda. At the back of that vaulted foyer the
second-floor corridor became a kind of half-
circle balcony that overlooked the main
entrance, with a set of stairs on either end
leading down to the tile floor. Though the

skylights above were black with the darkness beyond them, the entire rotunda was well lit. The second-floor balcony offered an excellent view of the proceedings below.

Tarker Ames crouched behind the waist-high balustrade and watched as General Remington and a squad of BBD operatives led Shane Monroe and his cronies into the foyer, where twenty-one additional operatives, all armed, waited with Carl Bennett and Theodore Larch, the withered old man who was the director of the Black Box Department.

*The endgame. Checkmate,* Tarker thought. *And you bastards tried to cut me out.*

After what the Monroe kid had done to his face—his eye—after all he had gone through to run the little punk into the ground, no way was he going to let them finish this without him. Tarker stared down at them and saw the way Iris Green stood near Monroe, like she was some surrogate mommy, or worse yet, his girlfriend. He had told Remington a dozen times that she was too holier-than-thou for the job, that she would only bring headaches and hard decisions. But Tarker was not happy that he was right.

Right about now, he wasn't happy about anything.

The only bright side, if there was one, was that nobody could argue with him about

Green anymore. Iris had done them a favor, taken away the hard decision, when she threw in with these conspiracy losers. Now they had to kill her.

A slow smile spread across Tarker's face. Iris was going to die, and so was Monroe, and there was no way the Department was going to keep him from being a part of that. No way.

Another five Truth Seekers were herded in from the back of the lobby then, all at gunpoint. Tarker hunkered down a bit lower, only slightly concerned that someone would glance up at the balcony and notice that the two sentries were missing. It had been a shame that the BBD boys had had to die, but Tarker wanted his arrival to stay unnoticed until he decided to reveal himself, and the sentries had been in his way.

Even now, his knee nudged the corpse beside him on the ground. He had broken the sentry's neck, not paying any attention to the man's identity, barely even registering Hank Whitney as a guy to whom he still owed money for a football pool two years' past.

Down on the floor, Shane Monroe spotted his old mentor. The look on the kid's face was heartbroken, priceless.

"Dr. Bennett?" Shane said hesitantly. "God, Carl, I knew you were in this, but not how deep."

Bennett said nothing. One of the BBD

agents slapped Monroe in the back of the head as they were shuffled into the rotunda. Director Larch clasped his hands as if praying and rested them against his chest.

"Well, well," the director said. "So this is the infamous Shane Monroe." He glanced at Bennett. "Super genius? He looks like just another little punk to me. And you, Agent Green. Ah, what a disappointment you turned out to be."

Iris glared at him. "I know. I'm all broken up about it too."

Larch focused on Shane again. "You've had a good run, Mr. Monroe. But it's done now. General Remington tried to take you under his wing. It's a shame you didn't listen to him."

"Sir, if I may . . . ," Bennett began hesitantly. "It may still be beneficial to keep him alive. There are still people Shane cares about. If he could be coerced into pursuing new avenues of research . . . it's just, I think we've only just begun to tap the kind of breakthroughs that might result if Shane's attention was focused on the sorts of things we'd like to see it focused on."

General Remington cleared his throat. "You really think he'd ever play ball?"

Monroe said nothing. Tarker liked that. The kid just glared at all of them without saying a word, waiting to see how it was going to play out. Iris looked a little green around the gills, like she might be sick. The other Truth Seekers alternated between sullen and scared. Poisson, their leader, though, he was wide-awake, alert, watching for an opening. Tarker figured he might have to shoot Poisson first.

Larch pointed to Levine, the snitch who had infiltrated the Truth Seekers. "What about you? You have thoughts on the matter?"

Levine shrugged. "He doesn't want to die. Doesn't want his mother to die, either."

At that, Monroe muttered something under his breath that Tarker couldn't hear, even with the amazing acoustics in the rotunda. But he figured he got the gist of it from the hatred on the kid's face.

"If we decide to keep Monroe alive, Agent Ames will have to be retired. His stake in this is too personal," Director Larch said. "He'd never accept it willingly."

Tarker stiffened.

Remington actually laughed. "Not a problem, sir. Ames is a loose cannon now. When a dog goes rabid, there's only one way to deal with it."

A long, protracted silence followed when not even the captives spoke. At length, Larch nodded.

"All right. Monroe lives. For now," the director said emphatically. "You have authorization to dispose of the others."

A woman who was with the Truth

Seekers shouted in fury and fear and tried to lunge at Joe Levine. A pair of BBD operatives held her back. One of them jammed a rifle butt into her kidneys, and she went down on her knees in front of Poisson, who helped her up and let her lean on him as he glared at Larch and Remington.

"If only America could really see what goes on when it's not looking," Poisson said.

Monroe did not even spare them a glance. His eyes blazed as he stared at Carl Bennett. "My mother *trusted* you. You were like part of the family. Just tell me this: Were you always this much of a coward?"

"Dr. Bennett isn't a coward, Shane," General Remington sneered. "He's a patriot. Just like the rest of us."

Iris Green said nothing, merely stared at the ground as though she had surrendered her life already. Tarker frowned when the thought crossed his mind. That wasn't like Iris. It made him wonder if she had something up her sleeve.

But Iris wasn't his concern at the moment.

*Ames is a loose cannon now. When a dog goes rabid, there's only one way to deal with it.*

The words echoed in his mind and had frozen him for just a moment. Now Tarker sneered and reached inside his jacket for his weapon. As his fingers brushed the grip, he glanced down at the body beside him. The sentry's rifle was still clutched in his hands. A slow smile spread across Tarker's face and he slipped it quietly out of the dead man's grasp.

*Thanks, Hank,* Tarker thought. *You're a pal.*

He stood up, took aim through the scope, and shot General Remington through the back of his head. Hair and brain and bone fragments sprayed the tile floor, and Carl Bennett screamed like a little girl. The director immediately turned and hurried toward the front door, a pair of operatives flanking him, weapons aimed at the balcony.

Tarker let Larch go. He'd get another shot at the old man, and he had too many other scores to settle here today. He shot Joe Levine twice in the chest. You couldn't trust a two-faced mole like that.

Monroe, Iris, and the rest of the Truth Seekers who had broken into the base reacted immediately. The second that Remington's skull had exploded, they had attacked the nearest Department agents. There were shouts of rage and pain as fists flew, and Monroe's people tried to disarm the BBD operatives. If they had attempted it at any other time, they would have been shot down in seconds, so badly were they outnumbered.

But the rest of the BBD agents, the ones who weren't busy trying to keep hold of their guns and their consciousness, were otherwise occupied. With Remington dead and Larch fleeing, some of them dove for cover and others simply stood there, but they all began to return fire. Bullets punching the balustrade and the wall behind him, Tarker dropped the rifle and dove for the floor, then scrambled along the balcony toward the cover of the hallway, where he could disappear into the warren of corridors and stairwells in the office building.

Down in the foyer, shouts and gunshots echoed all through the rotunda.

Now the fun could really start.

By dawn, Tarker Ames planned to be the only person in the building still alive.

# CHAPTER SIXTEEN

*"For the first time in man's history, he has the knowledge with which he may interfere in cosmic processes."*
—Nikola Tesla

Shane couldn't breathe.

The shots that came from the upper level of the rotunda could only have been fired by one person.

"Ames," Iris hissed.

But now that the BBD agents had started to return fire, there was no sign of anyone up on that balcony.

Remington was dead in a pool of his own blood on the tile floor, and all hell was breaking loose. The traitor, Joe Levine or whoever he was, was dead. All around Shane, the Truth Seekers were fighting back, trying to wrest weapons away from the BBD agents. Shane did the same. A dark-skinned BBD agent with the lights gleaming off his shaved pate turned his weapon on Shane the second the shooting started, but there was no hesitation.

Shane was already in motion. Instead of trying to stop the man from taking aim, he turned sideways and shot out his hand, grabbed the man's wrist, and turned the barrel of the gun away. Then he shot a hard kick up under the man's arm just as Poisson had taught him, his foot striking the tender, vulnerable armpit.

The agent grunted and twisted up his features in pain. Shane yanked the gun out of his grasp and backed off. He had been lucky. The BBD agent had not expected his move, but the man had a great deal more hand-to-hand training than he did, and Shane knew better than to try to follow through physically.

"Take off!" Shane snapped at the agent.

The man glared at him, jaws clenched together, very unhappy that he had lost his weapon. He reached for something, maybe a knife or an explosive or another gun. Shane could not afford to have him get it. He squeezed the trigger and shot the man twice in the chest. The agent wore body armor, and Shane aimed carefully to avoid killing him, but the impact threw the agent back, sprawling to the floor.

Frantic, he glanced around for the other Truth Seekers and for Iris. Poisson was not far off, slamming a BBD agent against the wall. Iris was only a few feet away.

"Let's get out of here!" Shane called.

In the din, Iris did not hear him. Shane

started toward her. He saw a Black Box operative go down with a single gunshot wound in the throat. The guy grasped at his neck and tried to scream, but no sound would come out. Renata Cortes, a Truth Seeker Shane had met only once, lost the struggle for a weapon, and a blond-haired BBD agent shot her first in the lower abdomen and then in the head. When the BBD man stood up, weapon firmly in his grip, David Poisson stepped up behind him and ended his life in a spray of blood and bone.

Shane had reached Iris. He grabbed her arm from behind and she spun, weapon at the ready. When she saw that it was him, all the breath went out of her. She might have muttered some kind of reprimand, but Shane didn't hear her. Across the rotunda, he saw Carl Bennett disappear back into the corridor where they had been brought in.

"David!" Shane shouted, turning to spot Poisson not far away, the Truth Seekers grouping around him. "You want to do this fast? We need Bennett!"

With that, Poisson began barking orders. The BBD agents and the Truth Seekers were still exchanging fire, taking cover on the stairs. Some of the Black Box operatives had gone up the stairs after Tarker Ames, and the Truth Seekers had let them go. Now, though, the remaining combatants on both sides began to polarize. The BBD agents were pinned on and behind the stairs and near the glass doors at the front of the building. Glass shattered and sprayed the concrete and grass outside as bullets missed their targets. The Truth Seekers withdrew to the other side, leaving the tile scattered with corpses and the wounded.

Shane didn't want to shoot anyone else. The last thing he wanted was to kill someone. But when he saw Hayley take a bullet to the left shoulder, his stomach lurched and then tightened painfully, as if it had somehow begun to shrink. He lifted the gun he had taken from the BBD agent and began to fire at them.

Iris was at his side, and she twisted abruptly and fired across in front of him. If Shane had taken a step forward, he would have been dead. The gunshot was too loud, and his eardrums buzzed. But not so loud that he could not hear the cry of pain from the BBD agent off to his right who had been about to shoot him. Once again, Iris had saved his life.

"Bennett's getting away," he snapped to her.

"Poisson!" Iris called.

As they all slipped back into the corridor and began to take cover on either side of the entrance into the rotunda, David at last glanced around, expression desperate. With a frown, he turned back to the others. Hayley had a bullet in her shoulder but she was still standing, still fighting back.

"Cover our asses," he told her. "Keep these guys here."

Hayley nodded, and Shane silently wished her luck. It might work. The BBD agents didn't have nearly as good cover as the Truth Seekers. But if the Black Box operatives who had gone up the stairs after Ames decided to come down around the back, Shane's comrades could be in trouble.

"Watch your back!" he told Hayley.

"Go!" she called.

Poisson pointed to two Truth Seekers whose names Shane thought were Yvonne and Jonesy, though both were grim and silent and he didn't think he'd exchanged two words with either of them. Still, Poisson chose them, so he'd have to trust that David knew what they needed for backup.

Then Iris was standing in front of Shane.

"Which way?"

It took him a heartbeat to realize they were prepared to follow him. For a second, he hesitated. Never in his life had he expected to have this sort of responsibility thrust upon him. But he had built the Force Majeure project, after all, and he had been agonizing over the blame he felt for his friends' murders. This was his chance to make up for it, to do something about it. To stop these bastards before they killed anyone else.

*Bennett*, Shane thought.

Then he turned and started down the

corridor. "This way!" Carl Bennett couldn't have more than twenty seconds on them.

Despite the gunshots still resounding in his head, their footfalls on the tile sounded too loud echoing off the walls of the corridor. Shane was in the lead, with Iris at his side. Poisson followed up with Yvonne and Jonesy. There was nothing in the hall ahead of them. They passed the elevator bank, but the digital numbers beside each one were static. No one on the elevators. Which made sense. Bennett wouldn't have stood there and waited for an elevator. He hadn't had time to slip into one of the offices they were passing, either, not without risking being seen.

Shane's mind whirled and he ran faster, sprinting to the double doors at the end of the hall. He reached them, tried to shove them open, and they wouldn't budge. He slammed his shoulder against them, shouting in frustration. It was all happening right now; there was not a second to spare. Lives hung in the balance, and not only his own and those of his friends, but so many others'. He had put extraordinary power in the hands of these people, and now he was going to take it away.

"Here!" Iris said. She slapped a panel on the wall, and the doors sprang open automatically.

Another day, Shane might have felt foolish for not noticing the door controls. Tonight he was just grateful. He raced down the hall,

gun held firmly in his hand. The corridor
deadened ahead. He stopped, soles actually
sliding along the floor. At the junction he
glanced around, thinking they were going to
have to split up. There was no sign of Bennett
in either direction.

Then, in the back of his mind, he had an
image of the building from outside. The way
it had been designed, the front of the building,
where the rotunda was located, was several
stories shorter than the back. The climate
control chamber at the Foundation had
required five stories to effectively create the
atmospheric conditions for a hurricane. There
was no way the equipment could be at the
front of the building.

"This way," Shane snapped.

"How do you know?" Poisson demanded.

Shane did not bother to reply. He took off
down the hall, running full tilt toward the
place where the corridor jagged left. The others followed as well. They passed an interior
stairwell on the left, and the sounds of gunfire
echoed down to them from above.

"Ames?" Shane asked.

Iris nodded. "Gotta be."

"Let's hope they keep him occupied long
enough for us to get out of here."

Iris said nothing to that, and Shane felt his
throat go dry. The former BBD operative obviously did not think they had a prayer of getting out of there without running into her

former partner. Shane shook off the tremor of fear that swept through him then. He was afraid of Tarker Ames, no question. But he couldn't let that get in the way of what they had to do here.

At the end of the corridor, they turned left.

A door was closing halfway down the hall.

"Bennett!" Shane yelled.

They ran to the door and he hauled it open, crouched low. Above and behind him, Iris and Poisson leveled their weapons, just in case Dr. Bennett got the idea he ought to defend himself. Only another hallway awaited them beyond, but this one was barely twenty feet long and ended in another pair of double doors. Through the rectangular sections of glass set into the door, they could see the laboratory beyond.

"It's in there, somewhere," Shane said, though the words were mostly for himself.

The doors were locked.

Shane stepped aside and gestured to Poisson. "Open it."

"Back behind those doors," the man instructed them.

As Shane and the others all obeyed, Poisson pulled a pair of small, egg-sized concussion grenades from a satchel he had been wearing all along inside the rear waistband of his pants. The BBD would have discovered it eventually, but Shane was glad they had not.

Poisson threw the tiny grenades onto the floor and took refuge with them behind the first set of doors.

The explosion blew the outer doors open, throwing them backward. But the interior laboratory doors were torn from their hinges with a screech of metal and a crashing noise as they fell to the floor, striking equipment.

Iris and Poisson went through first, weapons sweeping in arcs across the air in the room, waiting for an attack. But Shane knew there wasn't going to be an attack. He glanced around the room, saw a variety of metal cases and one enormous box made of thick black plastic. It looked almost like a portable toilet. In his head he had worked out the details a hundred times, what it would take to spark a real tornado. To generate the kind of magnetic field and atmospheric charge necessary to replicate his Force Majeure project in the open would require a super Tesla coil almost exactly like the one he had built in the lab— only much, much larger.

About the size of the black plastic crate he was staring at.

Instinct took over.

"Bennett!" he roared, gaze darting about the lab. "We don't have time to fool around with you! The Truth Seekers are your best, maybe your only, chance of getting home alive tonight. Hundreds of people, probably thousands, have died because of you! My life has fallen apart. You ruined it forever. Maybe you were even involved with the death of my father. I'd like to shoot you myself, Carl, you son of a bitch. But get your ass out here right now and maybe you'll walk away from this!"

Deeper inside the lab, among the many cubicles where computers sat on unremarkable desks where people could have done research to help save lives instead of take them, someone moved. With a bump and a whimper, Carl Bennett gave away his location.

But he did not stand up. The man must have been frozen under there, holding his breath.

"Get up!" Shane yelled.

He took aim and shot the computer monitor above the desk where he thought Bennett was hiding. The man let out a little shriek as the glass tinkled to the desktop and the shattered computer was thrust back and tumbled over to crash to the floor.

"Shane," Bennett whispered. "Just don't shoot me, all right? I'm your friend. It was me who convinced the director not to have you killed. Jesus, weren't you paying attention?"

Iris stepped up beside Shane. Poisson and the others were faced toward the other directions, guarding their flank.

"Get up," Shane said again.

Shaking, Bennett rose up within the cubicle, his hands in the air. "It wasn't meant to be like this, Shane. I never wanted it to—"

"Shut your mouth and listen. You've used Force Majeure several times that I know of. Probably more. You're getting more accurate every time. To do that, you'd need air support, planes that could seed the atmosphere to create cloud cover, to start a rainstorm. It'd have to be damp weather already, humid. Even better if it was already cloudy, but you could do it even if the sun was shining if you got high enough. You'd have to have a massive temperature difference between the upper and lower atmospheres to do it with the sun out.

"Then you'd have to start the damn thing in a box, just like we did in the lab, and set it loose into the altered atmosphere you've just tinkered with. To do that, you'd need a Tesla super coil ten times the size of the one I built, and you'd need a portable version that you could build and then take apart for transport. That's why they used this base, isn't it? So they could fly the equipment and the seed-planes in and out of the area without being noticed. I'm guessing most of that equipment is on board planes or trucks here at the base already."

Dr. Bennett said nothing. He just swallowed, eyes wide with terror, and stared at Shane.

Iris Green took a step closer to him, raised her weapon, and pointed the barrel at his head.

"Yes. That's right," Bennett rasped. "That's one of the reasons the neighbors have been so on edge. When they saw some of the planes coming and going, they asked, and the BBD had to craft a story about a study of possible uses for the base."

"But the meteorological instruments are still here, aren't they? In those metal cases. And the super coil is right *there*." Shane pointed at the huge black plastic crate.

Bennett nodded.

"Fine," Shane said. "Take me to the environmental control chamber. The one that you and I built at the Foundation. I know you resettled it here with my original Tesla coil to keep doing research, to perfect Force Majeure. Where is it?"

There was no argument left in the man. "This way," he said, and carefully began to edge toward the back of the lab, where another corridor ran off to the left.

Shane glanced at Iris. "Let's go. Follow him." But as he turned back to Poisson, he heard shouts in the hall and the sound of weapons being cocked. A single shot echoed in that outer corridor, the same one they had come down, and a chunk of plaster was torn like a divot out of the wall not far from where Jonesy stood.

Poisson and the others had cover, and they could return fire and then slip into that short outer lab hall again to shield themselves, but eventually they would run out of ammunition.

"Hurry up, Shane!" Poisson snapped back at him. "Destroy it and let's get out of here. Find a way out back there and give us a shout when you're set!"

Shane nodded, but he glanced at the black plastic crate that held the giant Tesla coil, and he knew it wasn't going to be that simple. With Iris beside him, Shane ushered Bennett down the hall at the back of the lab and they followed the man to an open door. When Shane glanced inside, he was struck by the familiarity of the room. It was almost identical to the space in which he had labored so long to create Force Majeure, to bring this monster to life. At the back of that room was the thick glass of the environmental control chamber. The panels and computer setups were the same. All the same instruments. Including the original Tesla coil he had created.

*This is it. This is the thing Spud and Geoff and so many others died for. This is the thing they ruined my life over.* In all the ways that mattered, it was his creation. But he hated it.

"Iris," he said, glancing at the grim-faced woman. "Cover him."

Her hair was pulled back, out of her face, but tendrils of it had come loose. She looked anxious and exhausted, but when he hesitated, waiting for a response, Iris managed a tight smile. "Do it."

He went to the instrument panels, laid his gun on the desk, and began to boot up the operating system for the environmental control chamber.

"What are you doing?" Bennett asked, instantly alarmed.

Shane picked up the gun and aimed it at him again. "Did you change the codes?"

Bennett blanched, his face going deathly white. "You don't need the codes to destroy the equipment, Shane," he said slowly, eyes wide. Then he turned to Iris. "Talk to him, Agent. He's going to get us all killed."

Iris raised an eyebrow and stared at him.

"Maybe," Shane replied. "But we're never going to get out of here alive otherwise. We're seriously outnumbered, and that doesn't even factor in that Tarker Ames is running around loose in here somewhere. If I'm going to die, I'm taking all this tech with me. With all this destroyed along with the Tesla coil in the other room, the equipment you've got on those planes out there is useless. So I'll ask again. Did you change the codes?"

"Shane . . . ," Iris said cautiously.

He stared at her. "We could still get out. Heck, the odds might be better if everyone was running for their lives, don't you think?"

Iris slapped Bennett in the back of the head. "Answer the man's question."

Bennett shook his head. "The codes are the same."

Shane punched in the numerical sequences on the instrument panel, and then he was in. He had committed the voltage and angles for his original Tesla super coil to memory, and now he gauged the relative size of this new, much larger version, and calculated the alterations that would need to be made. The math had been done before, of course, but he was more comfortable relying upon his own estimates than upon numbers others had programmed. There was a hiss as the chamber sealed, and the glass—and the walls around them—shuddered.

Computer readouts flashed by on the screens. Temperature gauges and moisture levels were right on target. Seconds ticked by and they seemed to last forever, the echoes of gunshots drifting to them from back along the hall in the main laboratory.

He glanced back at Iris one last time. Despite the gravity of the moment, she nodded her encouragement, a tiny, crazy smile at the corners of her mouth.

Shane turned on the fans. The room began to vibrate around them. The thick glass partition was spattered with condensation. The readouts fluctuated a moment, then stabilized, and Shane activated the Tesla coil. Electricity shot through the atmosphere in the environmental containment unit, lighting up the glass.

Inside the chamber, it began to rain.

Having only one eye had taken some getting used to. Tarker's depth perception had been slightly altered. But given that he had taken Remington and Levine out without a problem, he figured his marksmanship was back to about 90 percent. It might never be 100 percent, but he would just have to live with that.

Killing Shane Monroe would help him adjust.

Out in the lobby rotunda, the standoff continued, a handful of BBD operatives against an even smaller handful of Truth Seekers. The few Black Box agents who had come upstairs after Tarker were no longer an issue. Though they had been former allies, he wasn't about to let sentiment get in the way of getting the job done. Any one of those guys would have put a bullet in his head on Remington's order. Not that Tarker needed to rationalize. He rarely needed an excuse to kill.

Now he crouched in the stairwell that went down to the first floor and wiped his hunting knife clean on his pants leg. Lindsey Kellogg, the last of the BBD agents who'd been stupid enough to pursue him into the stairwell, had bled a lot, and the grip of the knife was tacky with her drying blood.

Tarker sheathed the knife and then dragged his bloody hands along the walls to clean them.

He was on his own now, and maybe that was for the best. Fix Monroe's little red wagon, gut Iris Green just for giggles—and maybe a little spite—and then hit the road, Jack, and don'tcha come back no more. He'd head to Europe, hook up with some of the covert ops people he knew there, go freelance maybe. Tarker Ames had the kind of skills that were sought out the world over. He wouldn't remain unemployed for long.

With a grin, the rhythm of his heartbeat starting to sound like a crashing drum solo in his head, Tarker slipped out into the hallway and started toward the back of the installation. At this distance he could no longer hear the dull thud and pop of gunfire up at the front anymore, but he figured the foyer battle had quieted down some by now. As they kept killing one another, the BBD and Truth Seekers were likely to slow down, take their time, pick their shots. Some of the damn fools probably thought they were going to live till morning.

It was almost funny.

'Cause that was not going to happen. When Tarker was done back here in the lab area, he was going out the front door and he wasn't going to leave a single living soul behind him.

He ran now, assault rifle in his hands. Quickly and quietly, he reached the end of the hall and slid up against the wall, peering around the left corner. A quartet of BBD operatives stood twenty feet away, their weapons trained on the double doors that led into the main laboratory area. One of the doors was propped open, its surface scorched and buckled as if from a fire or an explosion. Tarker could not see what they were aiming at, but he didn't have to see to know.

The lab. The rest of the Truth Seekers were pinned down in there. Monroe and Green had to be in there too. It was perfect. Tarker smiled as he stepped out into the hall behind his former comrades-in-arms. He had never gotten very chummy with any of the simple grunts who played soldier for the BBD, so though he might have known some of them, he did not recognize them from behind. Several shots were fired from beyond that blasted door, the Truth Seekers firing back at their attackers.

Tarker steadied himself, raised the assault rifle, and strafed the corridor ahead of him. All four BBD agents were wearing body armor, but he shot them in the legs and arms, in the backs of their heads, in the places where the Kevlar vests ended, just above the pelvis, shattering the lower vertebrae. It wasn't easy to control a weapon with that kind of kick, but he had practice. And at this range, as long as he kept shooting, he was going to kill someone.

All four someones, in fact.

The assault rifle felt warm in his hands. The echo of rapid-fire gunshots played off the walls as he stepped past the dead men, trying to avoid slipping in the blood that pooled rapidly around them. He moved up against the wall, just outside that short hall that led into the main lab. The Truth Seekers would have pulled back into the lab by now, waiting beyond that second set of doors to shoot anyone who dared set foot into the narrow, twenty-foot hall that led into the lab. It was a killing corridor now. The second he tried to go around that corner to rush them, they'd shoot him down.

Tarker grabbed the nearest corpse, hoisted the dead BBD agent up to dangle him like a puppet, Tarker's big hands working him like some macabre marionette. With his left arm, Tarker clutched the body against him, even as he raised the assault rifle in his right, steadying its barrel against the corpse's hip.

Then he rushed into the corridor and began to fire. His bullets tore up the walls and ripped through the lab beyond. The Truth Seekers at the other end of that killing corridor kept most of their cover, leaning in just enough to get the barrels of their weapons around the corner and to take aim. They fired, and bullets punched the corpse Tarker was holding. The force of the impact was tremendous, but his own momentum carried him forward, using the dead man as a shield.

He aimed at the corner at the end of the corridor and fired. At least one of the bullets punched right through, because the female Truth Seeker there shouted in pain and stumbled backward, gut shot. Her hands went to the blood on her abdomen as she went down in a sprawl on the floor.

Then Tarker was nearly at the end of the hall. The Truth Seeker to his left was still firing, and one of the bullets passed through the dead man and caught him in the shoulder blade. The bone cracked, and the bullet tore through him and then Tarker had no control over his left arm and he had to let his cadaverous shield drop to the floor.

Tarker roared as he raised the assault rifle and shot the Truth Seeker half a dozen times. Even as the corpse hit the ground he scanned the lab, looking for Monroe and Iris Green and the others. *These can't be the only two. Where's the leader, Poisson?*

"Come on, Shane!" Tarker shouted into the lab, his voice echoing. "Where are you, partner? Time to face the music."

The music, thudding in his head, was not just a drumbeat now but a kind of low rumble underneath it all, like thunder, with all the drama that entailed.

Tarker frowned. The rumble wasn't in his head. It was in the lab. The whole room had begun to shake, and he could feel the floor trembling beneath the soles of his shoes. "What is this, now?" he asked.

Movement in his peripheral vision caught his attention, and Tarker looked up to see David Poisson sprinting from an office cubicle to the cover of a hallway at the far end of the laboratory. *He must have scrambled back there just before I shot my way in*, Tarker thought.

Tarker raised his assault rifle with his right hand—*one eye, one hand*, he thought— and let off a stream of gunfire that shattered glass and chewed up plaster. But there was no shout of pain. Poisson had eluded him for the moment.

But not for long.

Carefully he picked his way toward that hallway at the back of the lab. The floor continued to rumble so much that shards of broken glass danced and sifted on the tile floor. Things began to jitter on top of desks and slide off, first pencil holders and paperwork, and then a computer crashed to the ground.

Tarker felt the hairs on the back of his neck stand up, static electricity filling the air. The room felt too close, suddenly, too moist, and he wondered exactly what Monroe was up to. Then there was another loud rumble, like thunder.

*No*, he realized. *Not* like *thunder*.

*It* is *thunder*.

* * *

A crack appeared in the thick glass of the environmental control chamber, long and thin at first but then spiderwebbing out with frightening speed. Within, the Tesla super coil continued to spark, tendrils of electricity reaching up from Shane's creation into the atmospheric stew enclosed in that space. The glass seemed to breathe, heaving and shuddering. Beyond it, the air churned.

"Jesus," Iris Green whispered.

Shane nodded grimly and stared through the glass at the tornado he had created. "Force majeure," he whispered. Then he turned to Iris and Carl Bennett. "Let's get out of here."

"Where to?" Bennett whined. "You've killed us, Shane. Shut it down. That's the only way."

With a burst of rage that stunned even him, Shane rushed across the room and cracked Bennett across the temple with a savage backhand. "I killed us? None of this would have happened if you hadn't been in bed with the BBD, Carl."

Bennett only glared at him, a sullen child.

The walls shuddered, and the cracks in the glass spread even further. The beast was caged, but only for a moment. The storm was about to break loose. He had told Poisson what he planned. He could only hope that the man would see what was happening and order his people to evacuate, and that they would get down to the bomb shelter or out to a safe distance in time. The biggest problem with a tornado, though, is there's no way to know what a safe distance is. It might tear up the entire building and all of Benson AFB at the same time, or be far more selective—this bit of fence, this side of the building, snatching up one truck while leaving another just beside it completely untouched.

That was the most terrifying thing about tornadoes, in the end; they were completely unpredictable, moving around at their own devastating whim and then running out of energy and simply disappearing, leaving wreckage and death behind as the only evidence they had ever been there at all. And that had been why the BBD wanted to be able to create them in the first place: no evidence. What they had never understood—or perhaps simply had never been concerned with—was the fact that though they could control where the tornado began, and so take out much of their target area, they could never control where it went afterward or how long it would last.

The collateral damage could be terrible.

Even now, with the storm Shane had just begun, innocents might die. But how many more would die if he had done nothing? Shane only prayed the tornado would burn out before it reached the houses around the air base. Given the size of the base, it was quite possible. But he could not be certain. That was the nature of force majeure. There was nothing to do now but pray.

"Shane," Iris ventured. "Time to go?"

"You read the schematics," he reminded her. "Off the basement there's a bomb shelter."

Bennett's eyes went wide. "Stairs," he said quickly. "There are stairs this way."

Shane already knew that. They had studied the layout of the place very carefully. This was not the outcome they had hoped for, but it was something he had prepared for—as much as anyone could ever prepare for a tornado.

"Come on."

Gun gripped in his fist, he rushed out of the lab just as the control panel on the environmental chamber creaked. The wall buckled slightly, and the computer panels sparked. They had waited too long. Shane swore loudly. The whole building seemed to pulse and heave. Any second might be the last one.

They raced into the corridor, Bennett in the lead and Iris right after him. Shane followed, about to turn right and head for the emergency stairs, away from the gunplay out in the main laboratory. But Shane nearly collided with David Poisson.

The leader of the Truth Seekers had terror in his eyes as he glanced around at the trembling walls, but he said nothing. He only fell in beside them, and then all four of them were sprinting down the corridor toward the emergency stairs.

Shane raised his voice to be heard over the thunder and roar of the storm. "What happened to the others?" A terrible dread welled up within him. He had remained calm in the face of what he was doing with Force Majeure, but seeing Poisson alone spooked him.

"Hayley's squad may still be all right, back where we left them. But Jonesy and Yvonne are dead," Poisson called back.

Just ahead, Bennett and Iris had reached a thick metal door with a bar across it. The bar had words printed bright red upon it: WARNING: EMERGENCY EXIT ONLY. ALARM WILL SOUND.

"What happened?" Shane asked, glancing over at Poisson as he ran side by side with the man.

Poisson opened his mouth to utter a reply that never came. Bullets burst through his forehead and chest with a spray of blood, and then he was falling, flailing, already dead. The corpse struck the floor and slid. Shane's legs became tangled, and then he was falling . . . falling . . .

He struck the floor, clothes and hands smeared with David's blood, and as he did, bullets tore up the walls above him. Shane glanced back along the corridor the way they

had come and saw the towering form of
Tarker Ames blocking out the other end of
the hall. The grotesquely scarred figure stood
just outside the Force Majeure project door,
assault rifle in his hands, strafing the corridor.
The noise of the gunfire in the enclosed area
did not drown out the thunder of the growing
storm and the rumble of the architecture
around them. Instead, they joined together,
the sounds of chaos.

*Iris*, Shane thought. He glanced up at her
just as she pulled Carl Bennett in front of her,
using the screaming man as a shield. Iris
raised her leg and kicked the bar on the emergency door and it swung open, the alarm bells
adding to the din.

Tarker's bullets tore through Bennett's
chest and his protests died with him, the last
of their echoes swallowed by the cacophony
around them. Then Iris slipped through the
open basement door, screaming for Shane to
follow. She ducked back into the hall from
the safety of the stairwell and fired several
times at Ames, but the monstrous BBD operative just began walking down the hall.

David Poisson's corpse jumped as a bullet
struck it.

Shane flipped onto his stomach, propped
his gun on the dead man's leg, held it in both
hands, and fired three times. Two of the bullets struck Ames in the chest and the man
staggered backward. Shane swore aloud as he

remembered the body armor all the agents wore.

"Shane, now!" Iris shouted over the clamorous noise in the corridor.

She stuck her head out into the hall and fired again. Shane saw Ames grunt as Iris's shot tore off his ear. The man roared in agony and clapped a hand to the side of his face. In that moment it seemed that all trace of sanity and humanity went out of Tarker Ames. He was still just a man, but Shane thought maybe he had forgotten that, for in his gaze was only animal rage.

David Poisson was dead. Carl Bennett was dead. Both of them men who had been mentor to him at one time, for better or worse. Two more lives stolen by nothing more than the lust for power.

Firing wildly, Shane stood up and ran backward toward the open stairwell door. His eyes were wide with horror as he saw Ames raise the assault rifle again. Then he felt Iris's hand on his jacket and Shane was hauled out of the corridor . . . out of the line of fire.

Over the clang of the alarm it was hard to make out what Ames screamed at them then. Some sort of threat, of course. In a way, Shane thought it did not matter what the words were. Their meaning was clear enough.

"Move!" Iris screamed, and she put a hand on his back and propelled him along beside her as they started down the stairs. "He'll be on us any second."

"I'm moving!" he shouted back. "But it isn't Ames I'm running from!"

For just a moment, the sound of the alarm rang more clearly. The walls stopped shuddering. They rounded the landing halfway to the basement and started toward the bottom. Ames shouted again as he appeared at the top of the steps.

"An eye for an eye, Monroe!"

Then a blast of gale force wind burst into the stairwell with as much power as a flood. Tarker Ames was blown off the top landing and thrown out over the stairwell where he struck the wall and then tumbled down to the steps below. Shane and Iris were thrown from their feet as well, and they were swept end over end and slammed against the door that led out of the stairs and into the basement.

Shane rose to his feet and grabbed the handle, but the wind blew so hard that he could not pull open the door. Frantic, he hauled at it as best he could but he was nearly pinned to the wall himself. He glanced down at Iris, and he saw in her eyes that she understood.

They were trapped.

The tornado was loose. This was nothing but the precursor, the windstorm surrounding the twister itself. Up on the landing midway between floors, Tarker Ames sat up, blood spilling freely down his face from a gash on his head where he had struck the wall.

The entire stairwell began to quake as though the earth itself were about to split open. Granite and concrete groaned and metal shrieked, and it felt as though the building had been picked up by a giant and was being shaken, a dollhouse being shattered to pieces.

At the very top of the stairs the emergency door through which they had come was torn from its hinges, and the flimsy plaster and wooden walls began to rip away. The sound of the tornado was deafening now, and Shane could see the gray air above them, a voracious cyclone that was destroying everything in its path, consuming the building from within like some virulent parasite.

The wind died and reversed. As the tornado grew in size and intensity, still fed and nurtured by the Tesla coil, the air began to tug on them. Shane snagged the door handle again, and this time when he turned it, the door was sucked open and slammed against the wall with a bang.

Iris reached out to grab hold of him and Shane helped her through the open door. In the basement, the power of the tornado was not as strong, but as Shane glanced back into the stairs, he saw Ames holding on to the metal railing and hauling himself down toward the door. Shane wanted to close the door against him, but it was too late for that.

"Come on!" he cried to Iris.

Then they were running full tilt down the hall, no thought of Tarker Ames on their mind. Shane felt the wind tug his gun out of his hand and he let it go. The ceiling was ripped away, beams and plaster ripped up, and the corridor behind them seemed almost to explode as though someone had planted kegs of dynamite under the floor.

The bomb shelter was really a subbasement. The door loomed ahead of them at the end of the corridor, and Shane felt a tugging at his clothes and his skin as he raced for it. So hard was he struggling against the pull of the wind that he slammed into the door full force.

This was the oldest part of the building. No key card necessary here. There was a keyhole instead, and he said a silent prayer to a God who had been far too uninvolved of late, and then he hauled open the door.

It wasn't locked.

The door swung open. Shane reached back without looking and took Iris's hand. With his other hand he grabbed the door frame and hauled himself inside. Even as he turned, Iris was pulled out of his grip, and he shouted as he tried to grab at her again.

But it wasn't the tornado that had her.

It was Tarker Ames.

The wind sucked at them as the two agents struck each other. Ames slammed her up against the wall and then he and Iris went down hard on the floor. Shane screamed her name twice, then a third time, for Iris could not see what he could see.

The basement was disappearing behind her. The corridor was being torn up, churned, and eaten by the cyclone that progressed toward them, growing, ripping the building apart. The tiles of the floor were pulled up, the walls ripped open as if they were tissue paper. Girders squealed and snapped.

"Iris!" he screamed again.

But Ames had Iris down, and he was beating her. His right fist fell again and again, striking her face and chest and abdomen. He used his body to hold her down, for his left shoulder was wounded. The assault rifle hung from a strap around his neck, forgotten completely in his primal urge to savage her with his hands. The weapon wavered, tugged back by the wind, straining on its strap to be free, to be sucked into the vortex. Blood still dripped from Tarker's forehead, but the wind leeched it away as if fed by it.

Shane was deaf now and wondered if he would ever hear again. The roar of the tornado drowned out everything else. Shane was frozen, there in the doorway of the shelter. If he closed the door now, he might live, but he would be leaving Iris to die.

Ames and Iris slid a few inches away from the shelter, the power of the tornado dragging them. Something snapped in Shane's head then, and all his hesitation disappeared. Knowing that at any second he could be hauled off his feet, he dove across the floor at Tarker Ames. He reached up and grabbed the man's assault rifle and turned it around so that its muzzle was only inches from Ames's side.

Shane felt the wind tug at him inexorably, and all three of them slid several inches along the floor.

The tornado ripped up the corridor twenty feet from where they lay.

He pulled the trigger.

Ames was wearing body armor, but at that proximity it did not matter. Some of the bullets tore right through the man's torso. Others were stopped by the Kevlar, but the impact shattered bone beneath the skin. Tarker Ames slammed into the wall and then began to slide backward, sucked toward the vortex.

"Iris!" Shane screamed.

He could not even hear his own voice, but it did not matter. Iris's face was a mess of bloody bruises, but she was alive. Together they fought the wind for the few feet toward the door to the shelter. It had slammed closed, but Shane hauled himself up by the knob and forced it open again, just a couple of inches at first. Then Iris grabbed hold of him and together they fought the wind and slipped through the door.

As it slammed shut, they both glanced

back into the corridor one final time, just as
Tarker Ames was torn from the floor and
pulled into the vortex along with timber and
plaster and torn and twisted metal. The man's
one good eye was open wide, and his limbs
were flailing. Despite the bullets and broken
bones, Tarker Ames was alive when the
storm swallowed him whole.

The vortex sucked at the door and it
slammed shut. Shane threw the massive steel
bolt across it, and he helped Iris down another
long set of metal steps to the deep granite
shelter.

The shriek and wail of the storm's
destruction was only somewhat dulled there
in that stone chamber. But it was not long
before the roar of the winds began to subside.

Shane sat against the cold granite wall,
Iris leaning her head upon his chest. He
stroked her hair gently, careful not to touch
her battered face. For a long time, neither of
them said a word, not even when the world
above them had fallen silent.

# EPILOGUE

*"The present is theirs, the future for which
I really worked, is mine."*
—Nikola Tesla

*It's like a whole new world.*

That was the thought foremost in Shane Monroe's mind two weeks later as he drove through the busy streets of Santa Monica, California. The windows were down, and the morning drive chat hosts were dishing the latest celebrity gossip. He did not know if he had ever seen a sky so blue. If he kept on driving along Santa Monica Boulevard, he would eventually hit the Pacific Ocean.

*No, not a new world. Just the other side of the old one.*

He had come through the other side and managed to live to tell the tale. Shane thought that was something to celebrate, but the specter of all the people who had died to get him here still hung over him like storm clouds. Too near. Too soon.

Still, on a day like today, with the ocean

breeze and the crystal sky, he was almost willing to believe that something good might come of all this. Shane had to move on. His life had been changed forever, but in the process he had also found a purpose, the kind of ambition that made every breath more precious, every passing moment more electric. Shane Monroe had become the last thing in the world he had ever expected to be: a soldier.

The light turned red just ahead of him, and Shane pulled to a stop beside a convertible black Mercedes with the top down. The woman behind the wheel had a mane of long blond hair and a perfect face, stylish black sunglasses concealing her eyes. She caught Shane looking and smiled flirtatiously. He smiled in spite of himself and turned away, one hand coming up to stroke his goatee. The glasses he wore were almost identical. It was the uniform here in L.A. His hair was still dyed, but instead of the brown he had tried before, it was his old blond streaked with orange highlights.

Voices chattered on his radio, which seemed louder now that the car was stopped. Holly and Jeff were the hosts. Jeff was going on about something or other and mentioned the president.

"Let's not go there," Holly cut in, exasperated. "Seriously, Jeff, with the week they're having in Washington, I'm just completely disgusted. Can't we talk about death or taxes instead?"

"Don't bury your head in the sand, Holly!" Jeff chided her. "We're part of the media circus, aren't we? It's our responsibility to help our brethren rake the prez and Congress over the coals on this one. I mean, come on! We've got some black ops group funded by the government that's so covert, it doesn't even have a name. Not even, y'know, initials like all the others."

"Please!" Holly replied. "No more! The FBI's own investigation hasn't come up with a shred of evidence that anyone in Congress or the White House had a clue these guys existed. So a bunch of mooks in the Pentagon go down for diverting funds into a black budget, so what? How much time do you think they'll spend in jail? I'm willing to take bets. We should start an office pool."

"Oh, they knew, all right. They knew."

Jeff sounded very sure.

Shane smiled. Of course the man was right, but what more could he say? According to Iris's former colleagues at the FBI, the Black Box Department had been dismantled and there was no sign of its director, Theodore Larch. Iris had suggested that he might have been assassinated for what he knew, but Shane doubted that. He suspected that for the same reasons Larch had been salvaged by whatever shadowy individuals had dreamed up the BBD to begin with. No way had the FBI gotten the real people behind it, just a few figureheads thrown to the wolves so that Congress and the people would think justice had been done.

*Justice*, Shane thought, shaking his head.

The light ahead of him turned green, and he accelerated. The blonde in the Mercedes took off, much faster, as if daring him to give chase. He let her go. One of the rules of the Truth Seekers was that you never drew attention to yourself.

On the radio, Holly and Jeff had found other topics to argue over. Shane cruised past brightly painted stucco buildings and row upon row of hotels and restaurants and theaters. Eventually he turned left on a side street and kept his eye on the rearview mirror in case of a tail as he weaved in and out of narrow, short back roads.

The radio hosts had other things on their minds today, but he did not have that luxury. The Force Majeure project was done. At least, as far as he knew, all of the vital tech and data had been destroyed, and with the obvious exception of himself, anyone who could recreate it from whatever remained was dead.

Tarker Ames . . .

*He's dead*, Shane insisted, gaze locked on the road ahead of him, looking for the opening in the stockade wall on his right that would take him into the lot. *Ames is dead.*

According to the FBI, they had never found Agent Ames's body. It might have been tossed into some farmer's field or hung up in a tree by the tornado. It could still be buried somewhere under the rubble at Benson Air Force Base. They would find it eventually. They had to. Because Tarker Ames was dead.

Shane pulled the car into the walled-in parking lot behind the office and warehouse complex that was home now. Up until the previous spring it had been the set for a television series about cops who hunted monsters, but when the show was canceled it had remained vacant. He imagined that there were a lot of properties like that scattered around the Greater Los Angeles area.

He climbed out of the car and slammed the door, then clicked the key chain so that the alarm chirped. The heat rose up in waves off the blacktop as he marched passed the many other cars parked there in the lot, but he did not mind the heat. Not with that breeze off the ocean.

As he approached the door, Shane removed his sunglasses, folded them, and slipped them into the pocket of his shirt. He reached for the bell, but even before he reached it, the door buzzed. When he pulled the door open, Iris Green was waiting for him in the comparative darkness within. The bruises on her face had either disappeared completely or lingered only as patches of yellow discoloration.

"You're late," she said, the twitch of a smile on her face.

"California does that to me," Shane replied.

They shared a moment of pleasant warmth and she reached out to squeeze his hand, just for a moment. Shane squeezed back. They had lived through a lot together in a short time and it had changed them both, and bonded them.

"They're waiting," she said.

Iris turned and led him down a long hallway. They passed armed guards on the way, each of whom nodded silently to Shane but did not stray from his post. When they moved through a large office space filled with cubicles, Hayley Booth was waiting for them. As she fell into step beside them, only the occasional wince gave away the fact that she had taken a bullet a couple of weeks before. Hayley, three other Truth Seekers, and four BBD agents had been the other survivors of that horrible night, the night of the storm.

When the storm had started tearing the building up, they had managed to get out of there before it all came down. There might have been others who got out of the building in time, but the tornado had swept across the base before it spun itself out, and chances were that there had been some people unlucky enough to be snatched up off the ground even after they had thought they were safe.

The surviving BBD operatives had disappeared after the tornado had ripped through the base. Hayley and her squad had not bothered to try to stop them. They were too busy staying alive at first, and later trying to locate other Truth Seekers who had survived. It had been Hayley who first spotted Shane and Iris crawling from the wreckage above the bomb shelter. It had also been Hayley who had gotten them back to the empty theater in downtown Boston, and then out of the city completely.

They had stayed underground, moving from one cell of Truth Seekers to another, making their way across the country until at last they reached Los Angeles. Most of the major players in the organization, including some of the people who secretly financed the group, were gathered here now. Once they realized that Joe Levine had been a mole, the Truth Seekers had given Shane's mother yet another new identity and moved her to another secret location in Canada. Nothing Levine had known could be relied upon as secure information. Shane still hoped that his mother might eventually be brought back to the States with her new identity, but he had no idea how long that would take.

Hayley led Shane and Iris down a set of stairs on the other side of the building, and then out into a courtyard framed by a sixteen-foot-high stone wall, the office building, and the warehouse where some small portions of the canceled television series' set still stood. The courtyard was abandoned, but that was to be expected. This sort of thing couldn't be done out in the open.

They entered the warehouse by a small door set into the metal wall. This part of the set had been gutted and now only wooden frames remained. There were perhaps one hundred people waiting for them inside, maybe more. For a moment Shane froze, staring at all those expectant faces. Then Iris nudged him, and he moved forward with Hayley.

A white-haired woman with ebony skin stood up and strode across the concrete floor toward him. The woman smiled and stuck out her hand; on reflex, Shane shook.

"Call me Pandora," she said.

"Your name is Pandora?" Shane asked, surprised.

The woman laughed, a light, warm sound that put Shane instantly at ease.

"No, Shane. It isn't my name. It's just what you can call me. We're all very interested in hearing what you have to say."

Pandora turned to the others, some of whom murmured assent but most of whom just waited. Some of them stood, others sat in metal folding chairs. Hayley nodded her encouragement and stepped back to lean against the wall, arms crossed. Shane felt as though someone ought to announce him, but then he realized how stupid that was. Obviously, everyone in that warehouse knew who he was. He glanced over at Iris, and now her expression was very grave. She stared at him, just as expectant, just as urgent as the others.

Shane cleared his throat. "Good morning. I'm sorry I'm a little late." Dead silence. "As many of you probably know I've spent the last few days working with Bryan Cole deciphering the rest of the files we, uh, appropriated from the BBD offices in Cambridge a few weeks ago.

"As we expected, the project I . . . the Force Majeure project, that is, was far from the only thing the BBD had in the works. Fortunately, most of their research was incomplete. But we have to assume that that research is in the hands of whatever organization is going to come after the BBD, whatever covert agency rises up in their place. And there's no way to know how much they've done since then. Some of those files might not even have been current."

Pandora had retreated to a chair near the front of the group, but she lifted her chin now and spoke up. "What sort of projects are we talking about, Shane?"

He paused, the burden of the volumes of data they'd decoded in the last few days heavy upon him. At length he shrugged. "Where to start? They're trying to bioengineer better assassins. They want to manufacture other natural phenomena, the way they did with Force Majeure. Earthquakes, floods—never mind the viruses they're toying with creating. I guess the one that disturbs me the most is a thing they're calling Total Gravity. It's an effort to create an artificial, controllable black hole. You could obliterate a city—hell, an entire small country—without any radiation, without any fallout, and without sending in a single soldier, tank, or plane."

A rumble of horrified gasps and mutterings went through the place.

"I know," Shane said quickly. "But you have to understand, there's no reason to think they're ever going to achieve any of this. It's only the tip of the iceberg as far as some of the insane crap that's been tried over the years and didn't work out."

"But what if they do?" asked a deep, rasping voice from the back of the assembly.

Iris Green stepped up beside Shane. "If they do, we'll be ready. That's why Shane is here."

Shane nodded. "I'm going to study all their existing research and re-create it. Then, with all of your support, I'm going to try to perfect the experiments they've only attempted."

"You're going to do their work for them? Are you out of your mind?" demanded a lawyerly looking man who stood just behind Pandora.

"In order to combat them, to figure out how to stop them if they do figure these things out, we have to beat them to the punch. Scientifically, we have to get there before they do, know more about their own projects than they do themselves. In the case of a virus, we have to have the antidote before they ever get a chance to make anyone sick. With their other research, we have to understand it if we're going to come up with ways to combat it. This is the only way we can protect the world from dangerous men like Theodore Larch."

"The hell with Larch," Pandora said appreciatively. "As of this moment, Mr. Monroe, you are officially the most dangerous man in the world."

"And the most endangered," Iris added.

Shane shuddered as he glanced back at her. "Thanks a lot."

A ripple of awkward laughter went through the gathering, and people began to approach him, offering encouragement and promises of support and security. He would have whatever he needed to accomplish the job he had set out to do.

Iris moved in beside him, even closer now, and he was comforted by her presence. Her eyes roved the faces around them, always on guard, always suspicious. When she caught him looking at her, she leaned in close and whispered in his ear. "Don't worry," she said, the scent of her breath sweet and warm. "I've got your back."

Shane nodded. He believed her. It was true that he would be in constant danger now, for as long as he lived. But what Pandora had said was true as well. As far as people like Larch were concerned, the research he was about to embark upon would make him the most dangerous man in the world. Whatever science they could throw at him, Shane was determined to turn against them.

Science was meant to advance human society, not to destroy it from within. Yet there were always going to be people who wanted to use science for their own cruel, selfish ends; people who would spill as much blood and take as many lives as they deemed necessary to achieve their goals. His father's blood. His friends' lives.

Someone had to keep an eye on those people, to watch their every move.

*Someone like me.*

Shane looked around at the people gathered there on that empty soundstage, people with secret lives and secret names, fighting to unveil even darker secrets, seeking to reveal the truth to the world. He wondered what it would have been like if none of this had ever happened, if he were still back on campus, cruising through his classes, hanging out with his friends, blissfully ignorant of the dark machinations that went on under their noses every day.

There was a lot to be said for ignorance. A lot he wished he had never learned. But there was no going back. This was his life now, and he would work and fight so that he could save others from having that blissful ignorance— their innocence—taken away from them. He had seen a lot of people die in a very short time, but he suspected he had also saved countless lives in the process.

He hoped to save many, many more. Thousands. Perhaps even millions.

And the world would never know.

## ABOUT THE AUTHORS:

**CHRISTOPHER GOLDEN** is the award-winning, *L.A. Times* best-selling author of such novels as *The Ferryman*, *Strangewood*, and *Of Saints and Shadows*, as well as the Prowlers and Body of Evidence series of teen thrillers, the first of which was honored with an award from the American Library Association as one of its Best Books for Young Readers.

Golden has also written or co-written a great many books and comic books related to the TV series *Buffy the Vampire Slayer* and *Angel*, as well as the script for the *Buffy the Vampire Slayer* video game for Microsoft Xbox, which he co-wrote with frequent collaborator Tom Sniegoski. His other comic book work includes stories featuring such characters as Batman, Wolverine, Spider-Man, The Crow, and Hellboy, among many others.

As a pop culture journalist, he was the editor of the Bram Stoker Award-winning book of criticism, *CUT!: Horror Writers on Horror Film*, and co-author of both *Buffy the Vampire Slayer: The Watcher's Guide* and *The Stephen King Universe*.

Golden was born and raised in Massachusetts, where he still lives with his family. He graduated from Tufts University. There are more than six million copies of his books in print. Please visit him at www.christophergolden.com

**THOMAS E. SNIEGOSKI** is best known as a comic-book writer who has worked for every major company in the comics industry, including DC, Marvel, Image, and Dark Horse. Some of his more recent works include *Batman: Realwords* for DC, and the Hellboy spin-off miniseries for Dark Horse Comics *B.P.R.D: The Hollow Earth*. Sniegoski has recently expanded into other areas that showcase his interests and talents. He was one of the co-writers on Pocket Books' *Buffy the Vampire Slayer: The Monster Book* and co-scripted the Buffy the Vampire Slayer video game for Xbox with frequent collaborator Christopher Golden. His first Angel novel, *Soul Trade*, was released last spring. Sniegoski is currently working on a new series for Simon Pulse called *The Fallen*. The first book will be published in the summer of 2003. He lives in Stoughton, Massachusetts, with his wife, LeeAnne, and their five-year-old Labrador retriever, Mulder.

Aaron Corbet isn't a bad kid—he's just a little different.

On the eve of his eighteenth birthday, Aaron is dreaming of a darkly violent and landscape. He can hear the sounds of weapons clanging, the screams of the stricken, and another sound that he cannot quite decipher. But as he gazes upward to the sky, he suddenly understands. It is the sound of great wings beating the air unmercifully as hundreds of armored warriors descend on the battlefield.

The flapping of angels' wings.

Orphaned since birth, Aaron is suddenly discovering newfound—and sometimes supernatural—talents. But not until he is approached by two men does he learn the truth about his destiny—and his own role as a liason between angels, mortals, and Powers both good and evil—some of whom are bent on his own destruction....

the
**fallen**

a new series by Thomas E. Snigoski

Book One available March 2003

From Simon Pulse

Published by Simon & Schuster